THE
GONE

THE GONE

"The Convergence of Prophecy and Current Events"

James L. Larson

The Gone

Copyright © 2019 by James L. Larson. All rights reserved.

No part of this publication may be reproduced, stored in a retrieval system or transmitted in any way by any means, electronic, mechanical, photocopy, recording or otherwise without the prior permission of the author except as provided by USA copyright law.

This novel is a work of fiction. Names, descriptions, entities, and incidents included in the story are products of the author's imagination. Any resemblance to actual persons, events, and entities is entirely coincidental.

The opinions expressed by the author are not necessarily those of URLink Print and Media.

1603 Capitol Ave., Suite 310 Cheyenne, Wyoming USA 82001
1-888-980-6523 | admin@urlinkpublishing.com

URLink Print and Media is committed to excellence in the publishing industry.

Book design copyright © 2018 by URLink Print and Media. All rights reserved.

Published in the United States of America
ISBN 978-1-64367-740-8 (Paperback)
ISBN 978-1-64367-741-5 (Digital)

09.08.19

Thank you Bob Danner for all of your help
Thank you Faye, for all of your support

FORWARD

The GONE is written with the authors understanding of the convergence of Biblical prophecy and current events and how we are rapidly moving to the end of time. The novel is written in the timeframe shown in the book of Revelation from just before the rapture of the church to the taking away of the tribulations saints. It ends before the seven bowls of God's wrath are poured out upon the world in Revelation 16.

It is this author's opinion that the United States is going to be taken out of the role as world leader through an event or events, which have yet to take place. There are several events which could effectively weaken the United States current leadership role. A large earthquake, a nuclear event, or even a political movement within the United States to become an isolationist nation, will effectively minimize the United States in the coming conflicts. A twenty-trillion-dollar plus deficit (at the time of this writing) and an out-of-control government are but two additional factors leading to the future weakening of the United States as we know it.

The author has not tried to present this time as a time of only doom and gloom, but rather as one of hope and encouragement to people who have to go through it. God is love and he would have us all come to the point of salvation through acceptance of his son, Jesus.

The following chart shows the Chapters in the book of Revelation and the corresponding chapters of *The GONE* as it fits within that timeline.

	Book of Revelation	Book Timeline of "The Gone"	
Revelation 6	Start of 1/4 killed by Four Horseman - (Pre-Tribulation)	Prologue	
Revelation 7	Start of Tribulation - Multitudes before throne – 144,000 sealed	Chapter 1,2,3	
Revelation 8	Scene in Heaven – The opening of the seventh seal	Chapter 4,5	
Revelation 9	Start of 1/3 killed by fire, smoke, sulfur 200 million troops	Chapter 6,7,8,9,	
Revelation 10	Scene in Heaven – Seven thunders	Chapter 10,11,12,13	
Revelation 11	**Two Witnesses on Earth**, Seventh trumpet, judging the dead	Chapter 14,15	
Revelation 12	**Mid Tribulation** -- Israel in Desert -- War against Christians --Saint over comers	Chapter 16,17	
Revelation 13	Beast out of the sea - Beast out of the Earth - Mark of the Beast 42 Months	Chapter 18,19	
Revelation 14	Angel proclaiming FEAR GOD over all the earth, 144,000 in Heaven	Chapter 20	
Revelation 15	Over comers of the beast system in heaven - Jewish and Christians	Notes from the Author	**Timeline of the Beast**
Revelation 16	Seven Bowls of God's Wrath - Armageddon		
Revelation 17	Prostitute On Many Waters Wrath of God	End of Book "The GONE"	
Revelation 18	**Two Witnesses Taken to Heaven** -- The Fall Of Babylon Wrath of God		
Revelation 19	The Beast and False Prophet are Captured		
Revelation 20	The Thousand Years		
Revelation 21	The New Jerusalem		
Revelation 22	The River Of Life		

The GONE is written in a novel format and the people in this book are fictional.

PROLOGUE

Four Horsemen released
Events in the time of Revelation 6

Sweat streaked the heavy gray dust covering Yostock Jeshanah's face as he shoveled volcanic ash into his bucket in the cramped tunnel. He was beginning to feel uneasy because the light dust falling from overhead made the space feel even smaller than it was. Earlier as he was digging, he had felt a brief panic of claustrophobia but he managed to shake it off. The closeness of the cramped quarters and the constant falling dirt from above was very hard for him. He hated being in such tight quarters and briefly wondered why anyone would deliberately choose working in mines.

The secret hidden for over twenty-five centuries would soon be revealed to the outside world. He sensed that each bucket he filled was covered with the lives and martyred blood of his predecessors. The barren gray mountain overlooking the Dead Sea never revealed its secret through the passage of time, but a heavy price was paid to remain silent.

From each generation, seven rabbis from the tribe of Levi were selected to keep the secret of the ages, and some had kept it with the spilling of their blood. Each rabbi had taken a solemn oath to die before disclosing the location. Throughout history there were many who had come seeking what lay just before him, but the covenant of the ages was never broken and the location was never revealed.

Yostock had been raised in the synagogue and at fifty-two years old he was the oldest of his family. When he was seven years old his mother and father brought him to the synagogue, dedicated him to God, and left him to be raised by the rabbinical priests. He grew up being taught and prepared for this moment in time.

Two weeks prior, when the rabbis were praying together, an angel appeared before them and told them, "The time is now. Open the chamber and prepare to reveal to the world what has been hidden."

As quickly as the angel appeared, he was gone.

The thought of what lay ahead both scared and fascinated each one of them. Centuries had passed but until now it was not the time to open the chamber. None of the generations before them ever saw what they were guarding and what some of them died defending.

To be alive in this time, the time of all ages, was a great honor. The world would soon know, beyond any doubt, this was the time spoken of through the prophets of old and that the end of time, as determined only by God, was near.

From the accounts passed down through the centuries, they estimated the burial chamber would be eighty to ninety feet into the mountain. There was concern among them because the excavation was already nearing one hundred feet in depth and they still had not broken through.

A rope had been laid down on the floor of the tunnel as it was filled, but time had disintegrated much of the rope and only traces of it could be found as they moved forward.

The passageway had been deliberately filled with rubble and then blocked with a landslide to protect and hide the entrance. The rabbis were concerned they might have deviated from the original tunnel because of a reported earthquake that took place several hundred years earlier causing a massive landslide that covered over the entire Eastern slope. There was no way they could tell how much additional rubble had covered the original site. There was also the possibility that the earthquake might have changed the angle of the slope in a way that they might have started the digging at the wrong angle to hit the inner chamber.

THE GONE

Now was the time Israel and the outside world would see the Messiah, the King of Kings, who is to come in great power and who will rule the world.

The events that would lead to the rebuilding of the Temple of Solomon in Jerusalem were coming about in ways they knew could only be orchestrated by God. Few people even suspected the most significant event in all of history was about to take place.

When the Prime Minister of Israel was assassinated a number of years ago, many people throughout the world mourned his death. The outside world and many of the non-traditional Jews thought he was a great peacemaker because of his efforts to bring peace to the Middle East region. He was awarded the *Noble Peace Prize* and was recognized worldwide for his effort to bring stability to the Middle East region.

Many of the Orthodox Jews, however, held fast to the promises God gave Abraham; the land of Israel was to be the inheritance of the people of Israel for all time. For the Prime Minister to give any land away, even for peace, was considered by them to openly defy God. Indeed, many felt he signed his own death warrant with the agreements he had put in place with the Palestinians.

After his death, the Orthodox Jewish Likud Party was elected into power. They quickly began to dismantle the peace accords he put into place. They would not betray God by giving land to the Palestinians.

What followed was a back and forth battle in Israel for control over whether a land for peace effort would or should go forward. Many world leaders tried to bring Israel and Palestine into a peace agreement that would be lasting. The United States Secretary of State and others tried several times to bring a peace accord to fruition but had little lasting success. Every agreement put in place was broken shortly after it was initiated. The Muslim brotherhood in Gaza launched rockets into Israel destroying any headway on agreements with only short periods of cease fire marking the way.

Since the events of 9/11 and the destruction of the Trade Towers in New York City, the acts of terrorism throughout the world had greatly increased in number. Suicide bombers began a reign of terror throughout the world and made it dangerous in many countries to go anywhere crowds were gathered.

After the angel appeared to them, they privately reported to the Jewish leaders what the angel told them. It was quickly decided by the Jewish leaders to prepare to rebuild the Temple as soon as events made it possible. For many centuries, the resurrection of the Temple was what the Orthodox Jews had been praying for. It would fulfill the prophecy required for the return of the Messiah, and for the ultimate redemption of Israel.

The time frame to complete the rebuilding of the Temple was estimated by the rabbis to be ninety to one hundred twenty days from the time the corner stone was laid. Every piece of the temple had already been fabricated and numbered, and would be brought out at the proper time from where it had been hidden. Every stone was cut and numbered. Every piece of wood was cut and numbered, and every piece of gold and all of the utensils needed in the temple, were fabricated to duplicate the originals. The world would be shocked at the speed the temple would be built. Indeed, few outside of the Orthodox Jewish community would realize the significance of the unfolding events.

Yostock was sure he was getting close to reaching the entrance to the chamber. During his four-hour shift he had to move several large rocks, and the process was going very slowly. He was greatly encouraged because he had just found fragments of the rope in the dirt. He passed word back to the others, and excitement spread among them because they knew that they were still digging in the right direction.

Yostock was tired from the cramped quarters and from being on his hands and knees for so long without being able to sit upright, but finding the rope fragment renewed his strength.

They all agreed before they started digging that the high priest would be the first to look into the chamber once they broke through. They could only speculate what would happen to them when they looked upon what lay buried in the chamber. Only the most high priest would enter until they were sure of what would happen because the high priest might be the only one who could enter the chamber and live.

It would take at least two to three additional months; with the few they had digging, to enlarge the opening of the tunnel enough to bring it out. It was decided they would first dig the crawl space large enough to get into the chamber and do repairs if necessary while the remaining digging and shoring up of the tunnel was completed.

Yostock's shovel broke through into what appeared to be a large opening beyond. As anxious as he was to look into the darkness, he yelled and quickly crawled backwards away from the opening. Immediately, the excitement of the breakthrough spread to the others. They rejoiced as the high priest put on his priestly garments and they helped prepare him to crawl through the tunnel to the chamber opening. He had been fasting and praying for days for sanctification in preparation for this moment, and the final preparations would not take long.

After completing a time of intense prayer with the ritual cleansing and donning of the ephod, the high priest slowly crawled toward the opening, reciting ancient rituals long forgotten by the outside world. When he reached the opening he cautiously enlarged it, so he could enter into the chamber. As his eyes slowly adjusted to the darkness, he brought his flashlight to the opening.

The brilliance of what he saw overwhelmed him, and his mouth instinctively dropped in awe as he gazed at what no man had seen in over 2,500 years.

A heavy layer of dust covered everything. Beneath the dust, he could see gold cloth filling the room and woven gold tapestry covered the floor. In the middle of the chamber sat a box draped with embroidered gold cloth. He could make out the shape of gold cherubs facing each other. From under each end of the cloth, he could see two gold-covered wood poles protruding out on each side. It was readily apparent that nothing had penetrated the chamber through the centuries and it was undisturbed from when it had been sealed. The hand of God protected it all these years. It remained as magnificent as it was when it was hidden and was everything they had imagined it would be.

The high priest smiled knowing the Ark of the Covenant from the time of Moses was undamaged. They would begin expanding the tunnel to safely remove it, and make the final preparations needed to bring it into the Temple.

On the other side of the world Pastor Jim Franklin dipped the coffee from the familiar blue can, and put four scoops into the coffee maker. It was the first rite of his morning awakening. The smell of fresh brewing coffee was something he never seemed to grow tired of, and he especially enjoyed his first cup before breakfast.

He looked at the brilliant sunrise streaming through the kitchen window and he was sure it would be a good day for some serious fishing. After he finished his coffee, he would walk the half-mile to Hampton Lake and hopefully catch a few pan fish. Even as a young boy growing up, bluegills and sunfish were always his favorite. Fish and homemade chips with melted blue cheese crumbles on top would be a welcomed change tonight.

He liked Indiana this time of year, and he especially enjoyed this area of the state where he lived. The summers up until the last few years were generally not too hot, and the fields were always so green in the summertime. Jim had traveled extensively across the United States and he felt that Ft. Wayne and the Midwest had a lot to offer, especially in the summer and autumn with its vivid splashes of color.

Jim always enjoyed the freedom of driving through the country and wandering about the side roads. He liked to call it "two-tracking" on the dirt roads that are so plentiful in the area. He never knew what he might see in the back roads: deer, fox, raccoon, and even occasionally, he would get a glimpse of an eagle flying over.

Jim felt he could not get lost because of his built in sense of direction. He could always find his way home. He missed just driving around now because his back had a tendency to flare up if he was in the car for an extended period of time. *Just getting old*, he thought.

One thing that had changed for the better though, was that the attendance at Liberty Church, where he was pastor the last four years, was up dramatically even though the offerings were not. Even though he did not believe in global warming, he could see that the farmers were getting fewer yields around Ft. Wayne at least largely because of the three-year drought. The drought made the summer seem hotter than he remembered it being in years past.

He guessed the rise in attendance was because everyone needed to feel there was hope, and being part of the church was what helped them make sense of their lives. The truth is that it made him feel better to have more people attending on Sundays.

Lost deep in thought, he put the wheat bread into the toaster and pushed down the lever. He had a couple of magazine articles he needed to look at. The articles were the cover articles in some of the magazines the church received on a monthly basis, but lately he seldom took time to read. The articles were on the end times and the rapture of the church.

Breakfast would be a good time to read the articles.

He assured his oldest parishioner Andria Parzinski he would read the articles because of her concerns.

The cover story title was: "Ministers and Prophets are Declaring the Time of the Second Coming of Christ Is at Hand."

He told Andria that throughout history many people tried to predict when Christ would return. He reminded her that just before the year 2000 when the Y2-K panic was approaching, many people said the same thing, and nothing happened. In 1988, some pastors said they were expecting Christ to return that year because it was forty-years after the time Israel became a nation. Jesus said that the generation who sees Israel become a nation would see everything come to pass. The pastors felt a generation was forty-years. Again, when the tragedy of 9/11 occurred, many people felt that it was the time of the end, and the second coming of Christ was near.

Everyone wants to believe they are special and set aside from the beginning of time to be part of the finality of Gods' plan. Jim was sure that some of the preachers were creating a lot of commotion for only that reason.

Jim heard that some who were considered to be of the more right-wing radical church groups had prophets declaring; "Store up food and provisions for the coming time of revival for many will need help." They were declaring the food would help those left in the tribulation time.

Grace, one of his long-time advocates, was very concerned about what she was seeing on television and was reading in some of the Christian publications. He tried to calm her fears, but the unrest was spreading, and it especially upset old Mrs. Parzinski. She was saying Pastor Jim was wrong in what he preached about the second coming of Christ not being a reality. She told the others that if they did not repent and prepare to meet Jesus, they would not be part of the rapture of the church.

Jim realized he would have to address the second coming of Christ, and explain the views some denominations hold on the rapture to his church. Jim had always been taught there was no such thing as the rapture of the church, and he felt the rapture teaching was not true. He would preach on it next Sunday.

Jim personally felt, when God decided to come, there would be no rapture like many were preaching. God would just come, and each person would be given a chance, at that time, to repent. He felt as though everyone would go to heaven but some would have more rewards when they got there than others would have. After all, he knew God was all loving, and an all-loving God would not destroy his own creation. God would give each of them every chance to repent.

Jim believed all people make mistakes and are sinners but those who improve the most would receive the largest rewards in heaven. All of us have an after-life, and all roads lead to to the same place. Those who help others in society the most will receive the biggest rewards. He made sure his church did much to help the homeless and the destitute. He preached they should be accepting of all religions and all sexual orientations because God made them that way. Even in his own life, he felt his sins and discretions were forgiven because he was made that way, and it was the human side of his life.

He would address the fears of the people in his church in the next week's service. He would especially be sure to address the fears of those who did not understand what was taking place and how many preachers were going overboard preaching about end-time doctrines.

Pastor Jim was nearly fifty-eight and carried proudly his salt-and-pepper hair. Within a few years, if things went well, he would retire and leave the ministry to the younger crowd. He was having a lot of breathing problems, and although he didn't want to publicly admit it he knew it was from smoking for so many years. He quit smoking cigarettes several years ago, but the heavy breathing and wheezing, especially when he climbed stairs, still remained. He thought when he retired that he might move to Arizona where the climate was dryer and it would not be as hard for him to breathe.

The toast popped up, and Jim took it out to butter. He remembered the orange marmalade in the refrigerator and treated himself with a generous covering over both pieces. As he poured out his coffee he began to skim through a couple of the articles brought to his attention.

"Ministers and prophets are declaring the time of the second coming of Christ is at hand."

All of the prophetic preparations needed for the second coming of Jesus have now been fulfilled and the stage is now being set for what is commonly referred to as the rapture of the church.

The world has degenerated and come to the point where if God delays any longer He will have to apologize to the cities of Sodom and Gomorra. God destroyed them by fire for no more than what the world has turned into now. Every abomination of mankind has run rampant, and the world as a whole is rapidly getting worse.

The events after the rapture will affect each remaining person differently. Each person will be affected in different ways according to the area of the country and world they live in, their life styles, and even their age at the time the rapture takes place. A person who is retired will be affected differently than a person who works for a living. A person who does not work will be affected much differently than a person who works on Wall Street, but one thing is certain, *all* will feel the change. The economy, famine, government controls, blood in the streets, and the world unrest that has taken place over the last several years is but a glimpse of what is to come.

One thing remains, and that is everyone will have to make his own decision for their eternity. If a person makes no decision then they have made it, for what is required is to make a commitment, and non-commitment is a decision.

There are many varied reasons people will remain after the rapture. The tragedy is though, that there are many good people who will spend a Christ-less eternity regretting their lack of decision to seek those things of God, and not taking the time to know God through His written Word: ... through His Son Jesus. "

Everything is set and ready now for the final end of time to begin. Even the Antichrist system has been established using the fears of the people and the demonic influence over the one-world government system. While most politicians and leaders claim to have only the best interests in mind for their constituencies, they have clearly fallen into a path leading to the destruction of the world.

There are only three things needed for the reign of the Antichrist:

- A one-world government —now being established into ten regions
- A one-world religion – under a "Universal Earth" covering
- A one-world monetary system – already being put in place

Jim read the first few paragraphs of the article, and pushed the other magazines aside. They were all the same. He saw no difference between what was being said now and what preachers had been saying for as long as he had been going to church. Even as far back as the first-century church, people thought Jesus would return at any time, and now was no different. He would address the issue Sunday and put his congregation's fears at ease.

Jeremie Abrahamson was beginning to get dressed for his walk to church. For most of his life he was considered different than most kids his age because of his strong convictions about right and wrong. To Jeremie there was no gray area-only black and white, right and wrong. At the age of nineteen he was still a virgin. He never changed his views on why he wanted to remain that way. *There was too much emphasis put on sex and drugs,* he thought.

From a very young age, he read the Bible and would read it even into the late night hours after the family went to bed. He was born Jewish and for most of his life, was raised in the Jewish Synagogues. He often studied there as a child.

Eight years ago, his father died and his mother, who was not a real strong Jew, married a Christian preacher. He proved to Jeremie that Jesus was the Messiah the Jewish people, and indeed the entire world was waiting for.

A tall boy, at nearly six-feet-one inch, and with a powerful build, he looked very much like a long-distance runner. Jeremie was naturally good at sports. He had a look about him the girls loved, but he never found a girl with the strength of convictions he had. With his sharply chiseled facial features, and quiet demur, he was considered to be the prize catch of Washington High School.

Jeremie was always concerned about where the world was time-wise in Biblical prophecy and eschatology and where the world stood in God's end-time plan of events.

Churches were being affected at least partly because of progressive liberal policies, and a school system that no longer allowed God in the schools. As a result many people were moving away from churches, and there was a growing apathy to the things of God, because the children were no longer being raised up in the way they should go.

There seemed to be a division in many of the church denominations as well, and as a result people left the churches in mass. It was being reported that some underground Christian groups were experiencing explosive growth as they embraced "A New Sound of Heaven," evangelistic explosion led by teens.

"A New Sound of Heaven" originated across the Skyway Bridge from St. Petersburg, Florida, in Bradenton, and was spreading explosively through *LINKFORCE E* – an apostolic evangelistic group at an old mall of all places that was using all of the means necessary to spread the Gospel of Christ throughout the world.

Jeremie felt that *LINKFORCE E* was a prophetic voice preparing those who would listen, to know what was coming before the events took place. They were teaching the people what to do to prepare for coming events.

CHAPTER ONE

5:10 A.M. EST DAY ONE
Beginning of Tribulation
Events in the time of Revelation 7

The cold night mist silently closed around Chinney as he walked down the dark alleyway. The only sound he heard was his rain-muffled footsteps echoing off the red clay warehouse bricks. The light rain that fell earlier in the evening left the street and the brick walls shimmering from the streetlight. The mist penetrated Chinney's coat and chilled him deeper than most of the late night summer rains so common in Michigan.

Most people would never walk alone in this area of Detroit so late at night, but it is where he lived, and he had no other choice. The still sound of the night was unusual, the cold mist and the late hour emptied the streets of many of the familiar people.

There were still two prostitutes standing in a doorway as he passed by, trying to keep themselves dry. They hooted at Chinney in a familiar teasing way and Chinney knew they were hoping to catch the night's last john. They would give up before long and leave before the daylight caught them. The streets were too empty for them to continue to wait much longer. There were just too few night people left.

Chinney would be happy to get to bed. He had been up nearly twenty hours and was at the point of being sleep-sick. He knew when that sick feeling came the only cure was to sleep. He had been up much too long without sleep.

He was streetwise, and he was a good businessman who was always looking for a way to make money. He wanted to set aside enough money to get out of Detroit. He was sure Detroit was one the armpits of hell. He hadn't counted it yet, but he knew he had a good night.

The bad economy in Detroit was actually increasing his sales. Go figure. People were coming up with money for drugs but couldn't pay the mortgage. In Detroit, he wondered if there was any other business but drugs that were even making a profit.

Chinney was nearly sixteen. At five foot ten and with a fairly stocky build, he did not look his age. When you were hustling on the street, your image was everything. For a black boy from the city, the way he carried himself helped him to survive. If people felt you could hurt them, then you were in control, and they would let you be.

For as long as he had sold crack, he still didn't understand why anyone used it. One man, Joe, a squirrelly looking guy, would come every night after he got out of work and buy from him. Chinney thought he looked like an accountant type, and he thought probably a banker by the look of his suit. In the short six months he had known him, Chinney could see the change in him, and Joe needed more and more to keep him high. Chinney would continue to supply what he wanted, though, because the money he made was the only thing that would buy him a way out.

What someone else did was none of his concern. He could never allow himself to be concerned with anyone else because it was too dangerous. He decided a long time ago he would do anything he had to do and get out of Detroit. A couple more years and he would have enough money to leave.

"I just want to leave this stinking rat hole," he thought as he turned the corner to the street he lived on.

Growing up here was different than most kids growing up in the suburbs could even comprehend. Many of his friends wouldn't make it, and the ones that do, don't have much of a life to look forward to. Unemployment in Detroit was so high, even in good times, and most people never found their way out. He was told it was over 40 percent unemployment for black men. Only stealing, drugs, or death ever bought anyone a way out. Only death was the sure way out.

Some of his friends were dead already. Rags from the DOGS gang killed his friend Hooper two years ago in a knife fight. As far as Chinney knew, the police never did get close to catching Rags. Chinney wasn't there, but he heard Rags slit Hooper from ear to ear on a bet. Hooper was small and was always frail and never caused anyone any trouble. Hooper was killed as a way for Rags to prove himself. The chances of Rags ever being caught in this neighborhood were small, because most crimes go unnoticed by the cops in this part of the city. The police remain much healthier by staying away from downtown and the politicians get reelected when the rich side of town stays safe.

Street justice has its own code and was dealt in its own way. The people of the neighborhood understood the code and were not surprised when Rags was shot by Hooper's' brother in revenge.

If anybody ever knew Chinney was afraid to die he would be showing his weakness, and on the street that could be death to him.

A year ago, Chinney was walking with his girlfriend Ginna, on Emlenton Street when she was shot. The bullet was meant for him, but they missed him, and she was hit instead. Chinney saw Andy's car rounding the corner and wildly swerve over to their side of the road moments before they started shooting. Ginna was shot in the upper leg. The doctor said the bullet hit her artery. Ginna died in his arms before the ambulance ever got there. Chinney never saw so much blood. Sometimes in the still of the night, he would wake up and would see and smell her blood and hear her cry through his anguish.

As Chinney began to think about Ginna, he felt that familiar hurt inside which never seemed to go away. He never loved anyone before, and Ginna became everything that meant anything to him. He was sure she was the most beautiful woman God ever created. She filled his every waking thought. She asked him once if he loved her or was he "in love" with her. At the time Chinney couldn't comprehend the difference and didn't understand what she was trying to say to him.

"You can love a cat. You can love a car. You can love money, but you can only be 'in love' with one person at a time," she said. "Chinney are you in love with me? Do you think about me all the time? Do you miss me all the time?"

All Chinney could do was agree he did, but he never really understood until she was gone what she meant. Now all that ever seemed to be on his mind was the constant hurt inside which never gave him rest. It was the kind of hurt beyond his understanding, the kind that sometimes would hurt so much it felt like his chest would explode. He didn't ever think he wanted to be "in love" again. He didn't think he ever could survive so much hurt again.

Just over a whisper, and with tears of hurt, Chinney said. "I am still in love with you Ginna." His voice seemed to shout it in the brisk night air, and the hurt busted from his insides. Through his tears, he cried out in pain. *"Damn, I wish this hurt would go away*, he thought. *Why won't it just go away?"*

He only needed to save a little more money and he would leave Detroit and go north. Maybe he would even go as far as Upper Michigan. *Yeah, that's what I want to do*, thought Chinney. *I got to get out of here."*

The only vacation he ever went on was with his dad. He remembered the place they went to in the Upper Peninsula as the most beautiful place in the whole world.

Chinney was only seven or eight when they went across the Straights of Mackinaw to the Upper Peninsula, but he still remembered it so vividly. He remembered how crispy-cool the nights were and how alive he felt when he went outside with just a light shirt on.

The colors of the trees were so bright, especially along the river with the twin waterfalls. The beautiful trees lining the river were painted with brilliant reds, yellows, and silver colors. He tried, but he could not remember the name of the river. He made a mental note to look it up when he found a map.

They stayed the week in an old cabin about forty miles northwest of the Mackinaw Bridge. The cabin was within a five-minute walking distance of Lake Superior. It was the first time and first place Chinney ever remembered being really alone. When he walked down the shore away from the cabin to look for rocks, he remembered looking up and realized he could not see or hear a car, plane, or a person anywhere. He remembered the peace of being totally by himself for the first time in his life, and he liked it.

It hurt Chinney deeper than he ever let anyone know when his father left. Chinney tried to hate his dad for leaving but as he grew older and some of the hurt left, he just missed him. He often wondered if he was the reason his dad left. His dad was a big man, over six feet five and close to two hundred forty pounds, but he still had a lot of kid in him. That's what Mama always said. Dad still had a lot of kid left in him.

He used to tell Chinney, "You only live once and you have to make the most of it. Even if others think your way is stupid, you must follow what is true to you or you'll never be happy."

After he got over the anger of his father leaving, he remembered what his father said. He was sure his father, even now, was living out what he felt was being true to himself. The only thing he ever remembered his dad failing at was not being able to accept the loss of the only work he knew how to do.

Chinney really enjoyed that trip and had his best time ever there. It was the last time the family ever did anything together. It seemed when all the bad things were taking place around him, he would run back to that time in his mind.

"How I you miss Dad," he thought.

"How I miss you Ginna," he whispered.

A lot was going through his mind as he walked along the street. Yeah, it was a good night for him. Pretty soon, he would be able to get out. *"It really sucks here man, this place......sucks,"* he thought.

It was late, but he would sleep late this morning. As he stepped into the house, he turned on his cell phone and looked at the time. It was just a little after 5 a.m.

Chinney pulled the blankets back on the bed and laid his head down on the pillow. He was almost asleep, when what he would remember later, was a slight warmth that came over him. It felt almost like gentle electricity surrounding him.

That was when the clouds in the sky lit up like a giant flash bulb that almost hurt his eyes. Chinney ran to the window to see what it was and saw what he thought looked like someone in the cloud, and then the light was gone.

It was just before the sirens started their nonstop death wail across the city.

Ann Trippen arrived at the office early as usual. Her new job as morning editor for the *St. Petersburg Sun* gave her enough income to have the freedom she needed. She reveled in the power and responsibility of the job. Ann did well at making the decisions affecting the day-to-day operations and pulling the pieces together to make it all work. Having the ability to pull things together gave her not only the feeling of making the *Sun* work but also let her feel as though she was in charge of her own life.

There was nothing that made Ann feel more fulfilled than her job. Everything she did in life revolved around her work and getting ahead. Important as the money and power was, more important to Ann was being recognized for the job she had done. An "at-a-boy" was more important to her than what she ever wanted anyone else to realize. If she had any weakness, that was it. She was a real patsy for a compliment.

For a number of years the newspaper industry had been on a downward spiral and there were many newspapers that had gone under over the last few years. The Internet, iPhones, and cable news stations gave instant access to the news, and the papers were having difficulty competing because as one of her friends said, "They were a day late and a dollar short."

The *Sun* was no different than other papers, and after sixty-eight years of continuous operation, they were struggling to survive. Because of the drop-off in circulation the add revenue also decreased, making it increasingly difficult to survive as a business. Ann had a strong sales background and the governing board felt she would help to increase the sales and viability of the paper. The board clearly let her know her job was to bring in additional add sales to take the paper past survival and make it profitable again.

Something she could not explain to anyone was the excitement she got from her work. She sometimes felt she was a little like a fossil hunter turning over a rock no one ever saw before. News was like that, and when a story came into the office, it was like she was the first to turn it over. The news stories others read were only what she felt were the most worthwhile. Somehow, having the control over what so many other people could read gave her the feeling of power that she needed so much in her life. The governing board of the paper were very left-wing, and she had to make sure the general storyline reflected their views, especially that of Mr. Franklow. She enjoyed the challenges that writing to their expressed views presented.

It seemed as though the entire world of news was moving at a much faster pace than she ever remembered before. Every day, and sometimes every hour, they had to sift through the news for what would make the best headlines.

Ann was thirty-six now, and many men told her how beautiful she was. With her lightly colored blond hair and soft complexion, she never seemed to age the way other women did. She always took care to treat her skin and body with the respect it deserved.

Ann had a beautiful thirteen-year-old daughter. Patty was a gift from God, and Ann cherished the time they were together. If there was anything in any area of her life Ann was especially happy with it was Patty. She really missed Patty in the summer months when she stayed with her ex-husband Mike and his wife.

The summers were always the loneliest for her. It was during that time she always had the roughest time in her personal life. When Patty was around she filled in those times of loneliness that always seemed to hurt Ann so much, especially at the holiday times. When Patty was with her Ann seemed to have more self-respect, and she related to others in a much healthier way, especially men.

She almost remarried, but it just never quite worked out. She finally got to the point where she gave up on finding anyone who could fill all those needs inside her. She had given up on finding that special someone and had already decided she would marry the next man who asked her, if he was good in bed and wanted sex as much as she did.

She desperately needed someone who wanted to know and take the time to know the Ann inside. Ann was sure finding those qualities in someone was the impossible dream. She told many of her boyfriends, "Ignore me and I'll go away." And indeed she did.

"I hope I find someone soon. I'm not sure if I can take another summer alone like this," she thought.

The job was going well and with the raise she got as editor, she was able to afford to buy a foreclosed condo, at a good price. She began to decorate it and fill it with the furniture she always wanted. The condo was in Largo by the jogging trail they made using an old railway train right-of-way. The county paved the trail from one side of the county to the other. The trail was under construction for several years and was finally completed two years ago. Ann enjoyed skating on it with the new roller blades she bought.

She was proud of how well she could skate now, and every time she went out, she was gaining confidence and stability. She improved to the point where she actually could stop and turn well enough to not be a hazard to herself or anyone else. It was good for her, and she was very happy that she was a fast learner. It was one of those things, while small, the accomplishment of doing it better than many of the other people she saw, was a real ego boost for her.

After moving from Ohio she especially enjoyed being able to enjoy more of the outdoors. There was much about up north she still missed, but being able to get out in more enjoyable weather seemed to make up for it.

It wasn't the weather and snow that Ann moved from, it was the lack of sunshine. It was always overcast in Ohio, at least that's what she remembered most about it. When the sun finally would shine, she saw it as a cause for celebration. Just before she moved, she remembered distinctly the news said it had been overcast for forty-five days straight. The news report was enough to convince her it was time to move south.

The trail she skated on ran by several lakes and one of them had an alligator that Ann would often see. He seemed to have staked out his claim to the bank next to the trail. She would stop and watch him sometimes. He almost acted as though he knew her, and when she stopped, she could see him quietly move in her direction. Ann called him Al, and Al seemed to always be watching for her. *"Probably wants to invite me to dinner,"* she thought with a smile.

She enjoyed her new condo. It needed some work, but over time she would fix it the way she wanted it to be. Homer, her cat, seemed to like it too. Patty wanted a kitten a couple years ago, and Ann finally relented and got one for her. Ann never realized how much company a cat could be. Now with Patty gone for the summer, she really appreciated the company and not being alone. It seemed pretty silly to talk to a cat, but maybe that was one step better than talking to yourself. Someone told her Homer was a Russian-Blue breed. As far as Ann was concerned, Homer was an alley cat of the highest order. In fact, she remembered Homer's mother's name was Alley. Anyway, Homer was good company, and even though he had a mind of his own, he wasn't any bother.

As Ann was thinking about Homer, she remembered a sign she saw on the way home from work the day before, and she began to laugh out loud. It said, "Cats rule and dogs drool."

Ann's thoughts continued to wander over the recent events in her life until Jerry, from the print room stuck his head in. Jerry was slim, a good-looking man, and Ann thought probably in his early thirties. He walked with a slight limp from a car accident three years ago, but it never seemed to slow him down at all.

"Morning, Ann. How's it going? You're in here particularly early this morning, even for you."

"Yeah, I just can't seem to stay away, or I should say I just can't find anybody to stay away for. What can I say, I love my work."

"Me too," said Jerry. "But I don't make a habit of staying here all the time."

"You mean your wife won't let you stay, don't you? She won't let go of you long enough for you to stay here. I saw you two hanging all over each other at the picnic last week. How long have you been married anyway? We've been taking bets around here. You guys are too grabassy to be married very long. How long have you been together?"

"We've been married six years now," said Jerry.

"I'd like to know your secret and so would everybody else. What's your secret anyway? You two ought to bottle it. You're a trip," Ann quipped.

"She just can't keep her hands off me." He laughed.

As Jerry laughed, an electric feeling covered them. Both of them began looking at each other in amazement, and Jerry was the first to talk.

"What's going on Ann?" he said in amazement. "Are we going to be hit by lighting or wh---?"

Before Jerry finished his sentence, a blinding, brilliant flash of light filled the building. Even before they could again see clearly, they heard a distant explosion, and the never-ending sirens began.

Janice Alton slid her feet from under the covers to get herself out of bed. She had never been an early morning riser, but with John's night job, she forced herself to get out of bed to be up and waiting for him when he got home. She knew he would be home soon, so she headed to the kitchen to start the early morning coffee. John always seemed to enjoy the morning coffee time together even though he was tired and ready for bed.

Janice hated his being on night shift even though it did pay pretty well. They definitely needed the money, but with the ten-hour days and not being able to sleep well during the day, John was always tired and out of sorts with her.

She couldn't understand why John didn't realize how she needed to make love more often. She never had an affair, but she had her chances, and she was thinking lately of what it would be like to be with another man. She thought about it because she needed to ease the tension building inside her and the problems it was causing her at night when she tried to sleep. She got to the point she wasn't even sure John would even notice if she had an affair. He was always so physically tired from the long hours he was working. Would she smell different or act different or be different enough that he would even notice? John kept telling her he would only be on the graveyard shift a little while longer and, soon, he would be transferred to first shift. Janice knew if he didn't get on first shift, their marriage would soon end. It would mean a cut in pay, but they needed to be together more.

Her psychic, Everia, told her John would not accept the spiritual awakening Janice was beginning to receive. She was really excited about the things she was beginning to learn from Everia. Everia showed her things from the spirit world and how she could learn through the spirit guide in her crystal.

It absolutely fascinated her when the crystal would move from her angel in the spirit world. Everia explained to Janice how, when she called on the spirit world, she could tell whether it was a good or evil spirit that wanted to come over. The spirits always told the truth, and when she asked them to reveal themselves, only good spirits could move the crystal to the right. It amazed Janice every time the crystal would dance when she would ask it questions. Janice never messed with the evil spirits even though Everia said she was protected.

What she was learning and what she was being shown fascinated her. She liked having a spirit guide to talk to. Even though she didn't see him, the crystal would answer questions by the way it danced for her, and she was sure sometimes she could hear the voice of the crystal speak. Funny, she thought of her spirit guide as a person. *Yeah, it must be they are like people only spirit*. She thought. She would have to ask Everia if they were like people when she saw her Saturday. Everia knew more about spiritual things than anyone she had ever met. Janice had much she wanted to learn from her.

Janice finished getting the coffee started. Four scoops, that's the way John liked it. She always made the coffee to please him even though it was too strong for her taste. When she finished putting the water in the coffee brewer, she turned and walked to the shower. Janice never was much of a morning person for lovemaking, but she hoped maybe John could be persuaded this morning. *He might be raped if he is not careful,* she thought.

She started the water and began to feel the water gingerly to make sure it got up to temperature before she got in. A long time ago, she learned to respect the hot water in this house. Once when she climbed in the shower before it fully got as hot as it was going to get, she was nearly scalded. She and John went a few rounds over the water temperature, and its one fight she ended up losing. John felt the water needed to be kept super-hot for sanitary reasons and wouldn't back away from that position and change the setting.

Everia told Janice her life was going to change dramatically over the next two months. Janice began to fantasize about meeting someone who would meet all her sexual desires. Everia was right about so many things, and Janice was beginning to already look forward to what was going to take place in her life. She didn't understand why, but it seemed the farther she felt from John, the more her fantasies seemed to mean to her. She almost looked forward to her daydream time more than reality. Sometimes, she felt she lived two lives and wasn't sure which she enjoyed more. Her dreamtime was so strong, and so real.

Janice knew if things didn't change soon between John and her, she would ask him for a divorce. She probably would have long ago if it weren't for their daughter, Jennifer. Somehow it seemed better for Jennifer if they stayed together, at least until she was out of school. Jennifer was only ten, though, and Janice was beginning to feel so unfulfilled she didn't think she could wait much longer. John treated her well, but she needed so much more from her life. They would definitely have to sit down and talk about what was bothering them so much if there was going to be any chance to save their marriage. Janice began to have many doubts as to whether they could save their marriage, and she wasn't sure she even wanted to.

Janice was nearing forty, and if she waited much longer, she was afraid she would not find a great deal of pickings in the dating field. She was well proportioned, but she was becoming concerned with the gray hair she was coloring to cover up. Only her hairdresser knows for sure she chuckled. Where was that saying from anyway?

Convinced the water was as hot as it was going to get, Janice stepped gingerly into the shower. The water felt so good beating on her chest it was almost erotic to her. As she began to rinse the shampoo into her hair, she never noticed the brilliant flash of light filling every part of the house.

John Alton was on his way home after working the graveyard shift at the paper mill. He hated working third-shift, but they needed the extra money to help cover the house payment and some other things they thought they had to have. Janice never seemed to lack for things to spend money on, and like many of their friends, they were way overextended buying their first house.

Janice wanted to be in "just the right neighborhood," and he needed to placate her. It was a great house though, and John enjoyed having a house he felt proud of, and he was anxious to fix it up just the way he wanted it. Even though the house stretched them financially, it was nice having something to work on, and John was beginning to be known as a regular Mr. Fixit.

He decided to do some light remodeling and started a new project in the family room. He always wanted a bar but never had a place for one. He knew exactly where he would put it. It was almost as though he could see it sitting there before he started. He picked the wood up for the framing from Handyman Hardware a couple of days ago. As he traveled along, he began to design the details of the bar in his mind. John again became lost in the half-sleep world between reality and dreams.

The extra ten percent he made working nights helped pay the bills and get the things they needed to get established. Janice wanted the new house and the car, but she seemed to think they could get them and he could stay home besides. She always seemed to complain lately about how little energy he had when they made love. It seemed as though she was always complaining about something.

Hell, these long hours and overtime just never seem to end. What does she expect from me anyway? The seven-day weeks and ten-hour days are not compatible with having a lot of energy, he thought.

Hopefully, he would get the foreman job once Goff retired in two months. The extra money would really help, and in a couple of years, he might get into the front office or as foreman of the boiler room. The foreman's job would mean he could get on days all the time, and that would make it worthwhile.

John did not have a good feeling about Janice for the last few months. Something was bothering her, and he wasn't sure what it was. Like a lot of couples he knew they didn't communicate well anymore, at least not on anything more complicated than the weather. *I'm so sick of weather reports and whether or not it's going to rain or be sunny or whatever it's going to do. What happened to sweet nothings in my ear that mean something to me? I want to be with someone who takes the time to know me. I wonder if maybe she's having an affair or she's mad at me for some reason,* he thought. *Maybe we need to get away on vacation and take some time to be alone. I really hope she works through this soon.*

As he turned the corner onto Fourth Street he began to get a funny feeling and he wasn't sure what it was. It felt as though he was being hit by electricity or something. He read an article on the Internet that said sometimes people get a feeling like their hair is going to stand on end just before lightning hits them. He wondered if maybe lightning was about to hit close by and if it was could it hit his car?

A blinding flash of light filled the car and brought John back to reality in time to see the early morning city bus veering across the median and into his lane.

The last thing John saw was the bus did not have a driver.....

As he prepared his notes, Jeremie reflected back on what took place when the Lord came for his people. Just before the flash of light when Jesus came for the church, an angel came to his bedside and woke him. The angel began to speak, and he told Jeremie he was chosen, and set-aside since the beginning of creation. He was to bring the message to the Jewish people of salvation through Jesus Christ. The veil that had been placed over their understanding would be lifted at the middle of the tribulation time. They would all soon understand Jesus is the Messiah they have been waiting for. Many would believe and be saved. God's wrath would soon be poured out upon mankind.

The time remaining for Satan was short.

God set aside 144,000 who had not been defiled, who would go forth to teach and preach. Jeremie was one of the chosen. Many of the non-Jewish would be saved as well. Jeremie was sent to bring the message to the Jewish people in the Tampa Bay area of Florida. Any who would come and accept would be saved. He was to turn none away, regardless of who they were. He was to go to a large church across town, which would be empty because most of the congregation was gone. Everything would be prepared for him there.

Jeremie was told that even if no one came, he must preach. He must begin to preach, and they will come. The angel told him even if there was no one in the pews, he must preach.... *He must!* As long as he spoke the word, some would come to hear. He told Jeremie words spoken, even when no one was present, have great power in the spirit realm. The words spoken in truth are substance, and life, to a dying world.

The angel told him. "Begin now for the time is short and many must hear."

The angel walked over to Jeremie's bedside and took a hot, smoldering coal from what appeared to be a gold basket filled with light. The angel told Jeremie as he touched Jeremie's lips with the hot coal, "When you speak, the Spirit of God will speak through your lips."

When the coal touched his lips, Jeremie began to speak in a language completely foreign to him. It was beautiful! The last thing the angel told him was, "No matter what language the people speak, and understand, they will hear you in their own native tongue. They will all hear in their native language, even all at the same time. This is the time for the final harvest of souls, and those who continue to harden their hearts now will be lost for eternity."

That was it. The angel disappeared. Jeremie got up and paced the floor. He went to his Bible and began to read with great anticipation what the Lord had shown John in the book of Revelation. He read it many times before, but now the reality of what was written was upon him.

When dawn came, Jeremie began his walk to the church the angel told him he was to speak at. As he stepped out the door, he could hear the sirens across the city. The sounds seemed to echo even louder off the silence of the early morning dew.

When he arrived at the church, the door was open, and the light was on. He walked to the podium and looked around. Someone had been there earlier and placed a glass of water on the podium. The water was still cold to the touch. *I wonder if he knew I was to come, and was obedient to his inner witness to leave the water for me,* he thought.

Jeremie took a deep breath and began to speak.

The first day he arrived at the church he preached to empty pews for several hours as the angel had told him to. By the end of the day two people came. The next day, the same two people returned, and no more came. Jeremie continued speaking out about what God was doing, and telling them Jesus is the Messiah the Jewish community was waiting for. By the end of the week there were twenty-two people. Each one repented, and gave their lives to the Lord Jesus. God's work for this time would be a quick work, and he could see the work was beginning to take root.

What Jeremie found out shortly after he arrived, was that the pastor of the church wore the same size shoes, and the same size clothes. Suits, shirts, ties, and every article of clothing he needed, were neatly pressed and laid out. Everything seemed to be put in order so he would not have any distractions for what needed to be accomplished.

Near the end of the first week, two rabbi came saying they were told in a dream that Jeremie was sent by God, to bring a message to the Jewish people-to show them Jesus is the Messiah they have waited for.

The rabbi worked with Jeremie in shifts to keep the doors open continuously for the people coming. The Jewish community was amazed in the clarity of the proclamations of the end times, and some understood that Jesus was the Messiah they were waiting for.

CHAPTER TWO

DAY ONE
Events in the time of Revelation 7

Ambulances were screaming incessantly across the city. Ann was at her desk, and every phone seemed to be ringing at once.

As the staff began to piece together the incoming stories, it soon became apparent what happened was a whole-world event that took place at the same time. Mass bedlam existed everywhere. Reports of plane crashes, explosions, and people disappearing were filling every corner of the airways. Both local hospitals were already becoming overloaded. It was impossible for any of the office staff to understand or comprehend the scope of what was taking place.

"Ann, what do you want us to do first? said Jerry, the print-room supervisor. "Most of the staff still aren't in, and I can't keep up with the phones! What's going on Ann? Everything's falling apart!" Jerry was clearly rattled.

"Calm down!" said Ann. "I need you to concentrate on what you can find on the international reports and see if you can find anything that would verify if what is happening here happened in other places as well. Find Sid in the pressroom, and let him know I need to see him right now.

"Ann, did you hear the explosion we heard was at Tampa International?"

"Yeah, I did Jerry. I just was told they think there's maybe as many as six hundred dead. Get Sid for me will you? I need to talk to him now!"

"Sure thing. Ann!" Jerry said as he left the office.

Ann began to try to put together some of the pieces in her mind. *So much happened so fast*, she thought. *How could this all be happening at once?*

First reports were saying a 767 on approach for landing at Tampa International crashed into the main terminal building, and they are estimating at least five to six hundred people were killed. The plane gave no warning, but it just veered off course and hit the building, causing a huge explosion and fires. If it had happened any other time of the day, the death toll would have been much higher.

Flight 592 was an international flight and was fully loaded with people. Thankfully, the terminal was nearly empty and there were only a few people boarding the red-eye flights. The large numbers of people who were usually in the terminal hadn't arrived yet. At nearly the same time it was reported, an F-18 in Chicago on a routine training flight crashed near the Sears tower. From nearly every incoming line were reports of plane crashes, car crashes, and even a report of a large cruise ship running aground and apparently sinking near New Jersey.

Ann kept muttering to herself, "It just doesn't make sense. Thousands killed in one night; it makes no sense at all."

Interspersed among the reports of the many accidents were eye-witness accounts of people disappearing. In some reports multiple witnesses verified the people didn't leave, they just vanished. They simply disappeared from in front of their eyes, and all that was left was a pile of clothes. Unconfirmed reports indicated the same thing might have happened all over the world at the same time.

Jerry burst in and nearly shouted to Ann, "Hundreds have died in England from an explosion at a petrol plant! Apparently, a man doing a coupling hook up of some kind disappeared right in front of two people, and fuel spilled to the ground. Before they could get to the coupling, it caused an explosion. The fire, which followed, is still burning out of control and has already covered ten city blocks.

The firefighters think there may be as many as a thousand or more people killed. One high rise, which was engulfed in flames and is still burning, has over three hundred families, living in it. There also seems to be a lot more plane crashes in Europe and Asia than here. Apparently, what happened here happened throughout the rest of the world at the same time. What do you want me to do?"

Ann, almost in a daze, ignored Jerry's question and posed one of her own. "Dear God, what is happening?" she said. "Jerry did you find Sid?

"I haven't been able to find him anywhere," said Jerry. "I had the crew stop the press and let them know to have Sid come up as soon as they see him. I'll try the john and see if he's there."

"Do that," said Ann. "I want to get this changed. Even if we get it out three hours late, we need the front-story changes put in. This is bigger than 9/11 or anything else ever in our lives, maybe even all of history."

"Yes, boss! Right away. I'll find him. I know he's here somewhere. He's got to be here somewhere."

Ann began to piece together what she felt the front-page story had to be, and what she wanted to say of the news filling the airways. As she began to read through the Internet reports, one of the common stories took her by surprise and brought out of her a gasp that she did not realize was left in her news-hardened heart. It was only preliminary, but reports from three separate hospitals said all the babies disappeared! Sun City Hospital said a woman began delivery of a baby, and just as it was crowning, the baby vanished with no trace!

Jerry stuck his head back in and told Ann he couldn't find Sid anywhere and would continue to look for him.

Many of the office staff were beginning to come in, each with their own horror stories about what took place throughout the city. It was very clear much of the city was in shambles. Everywhere was chaos. Several large fires were burning out of control near the downtown section, on the north side. One of the clerks who came in late said he belonged to the National Guard and he was called to active duty. Rioting and looting was already taking place in many parts of the city.

The noise of the phones was incessant. Many of the office staff put the phones on silent so they could get to the business of putting the paper out. There was no doubt in anyone's mind the story of what had taken place was the story of the century, and maybe the story of all time. Ann knew the story of what was taking place would fill the headlines for a long time to come.

Throughout all the stories was one thing, one common thread that bonded them all together. It was indisputable that most of the accidents throughout the world happened at the same time. Many of the reported accidents told of people who disappeared, seemingly vanishing from the face of the earth.

One of the reporters stopped at a car-bus accident on the way to work. He was told by an eye witness who was on the bus, that as he began to walk forward to get off at his upcoming stop, the driver disappeared from in front of his eyes. The passenger tried but he couldn't grab the wheel in time to keep the bus from hitting the car on the other side of the road. He said the driver of the car had no chance to keep from getting hit and was killed instantly.

"Ann, we're getting ready to shoot the front page, but we still don't have a good handle for what's going on. We need to shoot it and begin the run if we're going to have any chance of hitting the streets at a good time today," said Jerry, as he stepped through the door. "Should we go with what we have?"

"Let me see it first," said Ann.

"Sure," said Jerry. "I think we pretty well covered it for today. I think you'll be happy, but I'll bring it right in."

"Jerry, I know it's late for you, but would you stay and help me with getting the run finished? I could really use every hand right now. I'm in a bind, and I can use all the help I can get. Did you find Sid yet? I need him!" said Ann.

"No, Sid has disappeared. No one has been able to find him anywhere, and yes, I'll stay, but I can't stay for very long. I haven't been able reach Sandy, and with what's going on I'm really worried about her. The phone lines are either cut to the house or maybe down somewhere, but I still haven't been able to even talk to her. Once I know she's safe I'll stay as long as you need me. If I have to I'll even sleep in John's office. "

"I'm sorry," said Ann. "I didn't even think about Sandy. If you can't get hold of her you should go now. I know how worried you must be. Bring me the copy, and we'll go over it right now, and then get your butt out of here. If you can, I do want you to plan on staying late tomorrow, and until this resolves itself, I know we'll need all the time you can give us. Let everyone know, though, I need Sid to come to my office when he's found."

"Okay Ann, and thanks. I'll plan on staying here late tomorrow."

Pastor James Franklin slept later than normal. He was disturbed by the commotion outside the rectory of his small Fort Wayne, Indiana, church. The constant noise of the ambulances going by distressed him greatly.

He turned on his phone to get the local traffic watch, but the phone was out of service. He went into the living room, and turned on his television, to see if the local news station had anything about what was happening downtown. He felt his heart sink as the news anchor was reporting the stories. It appeared that millions of people had vanished, leaving in their wake accidents and destruction. *CNN* said it appeared all the people who vanished throughout the world disappeared at the same time! All had vanished about 5:10 a.m. eastern standard time. Every corner of the globe reported massive death and destruction. Riots broke out and had become violent in many metropolitan areas.

There was still no official statement of what happened or what the government was doing to help. Jim got a sickening feeling in his stomach, and slowly got up and walked to the kitchen.

All of his life, he heard the fundamentalists talk about the rapture of the church, and they said it would be happening soon. Those reports just a week ago that Andria Parzinski wanted him to read and he blew off, could they have been true? Could it be possible it happened? Surely not! God is all love and all understanding, and he would not possibly condemn his own creation, to the prophecy written in the Book of Revelation.

Jim knew God loves everyone. The idea of the rapture of the church was preached by many of his contemporaries. His contemporaries also preached against sexual preference and homosexuality. Jim felt God created all people as individuals. Each individual was God's creation and God would forgive them because it was God who made them different. Even the Catholic Pope had basically been saying the same thing over the last few years, and had been pushing the Catholic Church to a more tolerant view point.

He was very strong in his beliefs that God, his loving God, would not condemn to hell those who were different. California and a number of other states legalized same-sex marriage after a long court battle. He had many homosexuals and lesbians in his church, and Jim felt they needed a church as much as anyone else. Many other churches rejected them by the very words they preached. They constantly preached against homosexuality and said God would not accept homosexuals unless they would repent of it and change their ways.

There was a scientific report that came out just recently that proved the brains of homosexual men had formed differently than those of heterosexuals.

He recently read an article published a short time ago, about the Catholic Church having marriage rights for two members of the same sex from early church times. His feeling was if God made them different, then God would not condemn them for that difference. The people in his congregation needed to hear what he said, and it comforted them to know it wasn't by choice they were homosexuals.

If there was a rapture of the church, then why wasn't he in it, and wouldn't all those in his church go as well? No, there had to be another explanation. Something else would explain it. Those in his congregation would be gone because they helped many in the community in so many ways. They helped the homeless and often took collections and donations for those in the inner city areas who were less fortunate.

He knew the self-proclaimed prophets of "the church" must be wrong. Still, he could get no relief in his stomach from the nervousness he was feeling.

Chinney was back on the street. He only got two hours of restless sleep, and he was extremely tired. His friend Jinx came over to get Chinney and woke him a short time after he lay down. Jinx had a wild sense of urgency about what was going on outside. He told Chinney all hell was breaking loose on the street. "Man, we got to get what we can, man," he told Chinney.

Jinx told Chinney people from all over came out after the fireball, or whatever it was, went by. Jinx was sleeping when it happened, and he didn't see it, but everyone was talking about how bright it was. With all the noise of the ambulances and people shouting and screaming all over, he couldn't believe Chinney could have fallen asleep. Chinney left with him quickly before his mama would wake up. He knew better than to let his mama know what he was doing.

Chinney never before felt anything like what he felt just before the light lit the sky. If he had not been up for so long, there was no way he could have slept at all. He kept going over and over in his mind the feeling of gentle electricity or something that was in the air, and he couldn't get over what looked to him, like a man in the cloud. He never felt anything like it before. He felt a peacefulness, which covered him and was within him at the same time. It was such a strong feeling he nearly cried. The feeling passed so quickly by him he became angry and didn't understand why. The only thing that seemed to even be close to the feeling was how good it felt to step into a hot shower when you were real cold, and had been out in the snow too long. It was a kind of tingly feeling of something warmer than your skin bringing you back to life.

There was a life feeling he felt, it was life itself he felt, and it passed by him, and over him.

As they walked the street, everywhere they looked, they could see the people stepping out from their hiding places. There was a craziness going down all over. It was a scene of uncontrolled bedlam every place he looked. Some people were screaming and running about in pitiful agony, yelling their children were gone. There was a man who looked to be dead, and he was lying in the street not far from the apartment house.

A man was throwing bricks and smashing windows in a brownstone apartment house. Two shots came from inside it, and he ran off. They saw several fires off in the distance. Loud crashing noises were coming from a group of buildings at the end of the block.

Everywhere it seemed his world had turned to a free-for-all. Chinney could see some of the shops near the end of the street were smashed open. If they wanted to get anything, it was for the taking, but they would have to hurry. Both of them knew it would only be a matter of time before the police would be moving in. Whatever they were going to do, they would have to do it quickly.

A man ran by them, carrying a flat-screen television. Never before had Chinney seen anyone with that kind of look in his eyes. The man had a wild look that scared Chinney because it seemed to be the crazed look of a rabid animal. There were gunshots coming from the next block over, and Jinx reminded Chinney he brought his .38 and he would do anyone who even looked at them funny. They would have to hurry to get what they wanted, but they would have to be careful as well.

"Let's go to Abraham's and get the television set. You know, the big one," said Jinx.

"No, that's stupid," said Chinney. "Let's see if we can get to one of the gold shops on Woodward. We can't get away very fast with no damn television! I don't want to be shot carrying no television."

"Yeah, you're right," said Jinx. And they hurried toward Woodward Avenue.

When they were within two blocks from Woodward, they saw an old pickup crashed through the Army Surplus front window. Two guys stepped out the store with several rifles and boxes of ammunition, and ran towards the alleyway.

"Let's go in," said Jinx. "We need another gun and ammo."

They stepped through what was the glass window front into the store. The noise of the broken glass crunching beneath his feet disturbed Chinney, but he wasn't sure why. He really hated that broken sound.

Chinney wasn't comfortable being there with Jinx. Jinx always had a habit of "going wild" when he was excited. If he were ever going to be caught doing something, it would be when he was with Jinx because he had no sense at all. Jinx even looked the part, his hair was always sticking straight out, and never combed. Chinney often kidded Jinx about looking like he just stuck his finger into an electric plug.

His mama warned Chinney about Jinx. Of all the people he knew mama would always single Jinx out as being a bad seed. Mama called him "a bad seed."

Shots went off not two feet behind where Chinney was standing. He turned to see Jinx laughing and pointing in his direction.

"Jinx, you idiot, you scared the hell out of me!" he said. "Let's get what we can and get out of here, man. You stupid, don't you ever do that to me again!" Chinney said, half scared, half mad.

Jinx didn't say anything; he just continued to laugh at his own joke. Shots rang out from two stores down, and they both scrambled to grab what they could as they stepped over boxes laying on the floor on their way out of the store.

Brenda Morsen hurried to get ready. The call she received was greatly troubling to her. The hospital called a disaster "code one alert," and all personnel was needed immediately.

As director of emergency services, Brenda knew it meant everything that she spent all the time preparing for; all the disaster planning and training they did would be put to the test. A code one alert had never before been called in their hospital. As she stepped out from a quick shower, she thought she best take an extra set of scrubs with her. There was no way for her to know when she would be getting home. She also thought it best to put her toothbrush and a few personal things in a bag just in case it should stretch out a few days.

Brenda had been director of emergency services at Westside Hospital in St. Petersburg for nearly six years. She started working at Westside shortly after her husband of twenty-two years died of a heart attack. She lost herself in her work, and it was a blessing to her. Her work was her biggest enjoyment in life. She was beginning to feel it, though; her age at forty-seven was beginning to show. The emergency room was a very stressful part of the hospital, and she was older than most of the other people who worked in critical-care. She never was one to take care of herself physically, and being out of shape along with her age she tired easily. She must do something about working out, she thought, as she rushed to finish getting ready.

The night supervisor was sketchy about what was going on. She just told Brenda she was needed asap. All hell had broken loose, and Brenda knew she needed to expect the worst.

Janice was worried. John should have been home over an hour ago. The ride from where John worked in East Tampa was not over an hour to the house. Usually, it took only forty-five minutes in the early mornings when the traffic was light. John was not the type to go drinking after work or stop with the guys. All the sirens she heard in town were making her nervous.

The not knowing what was going on was always the worst for her. She could deal with anything as long as she knew what it was. She dialed John's cell phone, but she did not get any response. It was not like John to not have his phone with him and turned on. The constant noise from town and the sound of explosions in the distance worried and bothered her.

It was almost time to wake Jennifer for breakfast. She consented to send Jennifer to Bible camp for the summer. Janice didn't think much of the church camp. It wouldn't hurt Jennifer to go though, and it would give Janice some time to be alone for a while.

Jennifer told Janice she accepted Jesus into her heart and he lived there now, and he was her friend. *Well, whatever,* Janice thought. She remembered when she was a kid they tried to feed her that too, and it didn't hurt her any. Besides Jennifer really wanted to go to the camp, and a couple of her new friends were going too. Janice wondered if the friends were boys or girls. She tried to think back when it was she began to take a serious look at boys. She smiled a smile of relief when she remembered, at ten years old, Jennifer would probably not be interested in boys for at least a year or two yet.

Damn it! Where's John? she thought. *Damn John, I'm going to be horny all day now because he's decided not to come home on time. Not only that, but I could have slept another hour or more if he would have let me know he was going to be late.*

Janice turned the television on to see if the news would tell her what was happening downtown, and her cable was out! John was not home, she didn't have a car, and now the cable was out! "What's next? It looks like it's going to be one of those days. I can't believe with the price of cable, they can't keep the damn thing working all the time. I'm going to ask for a day's refund when I send the payment in next time. "Damn, John, where are you anyway?" she mumbled.

Janice tried to get the thoughts of John having problems pushed to the back of her mind. Even with all the problems they were having lately, she didn't want anything to happen to him. She would definitely give him hell when he got home for what she was going through.

Next to herself, Jennifer was the hardest person to get ready. As Janice walked toward the stairs to go up to Jennifer's room, she realized she was really worried about John. For all the bad things going through her mind, she was concerned.

She had tried calling the mill, and the lines must be down because she could not get through and could only get a busy signal.

"Damn it! Damn it! Damn it!" she said as she opened the door to Jennifer's room, and looked in. It was at that moment she knew Jennifer was gone!

The news they were getting into the newsroom grew increasingly worse. Ann began the impossible task of sorting out the stories, which seemed most important for tomorrow's edition. There was so much to print that it boggled her mind. Patterson Street and all the way to Windward was a war zone. The guard and homeland security were called in, but they were not yet successful in quelling the riots. The Governor declared every city of over ten thousand people in the State of Florida to be under marshal law. The state was woefully unable to handle the situation on such a large scale.

As more reports continued to filter in, it verified what she had been finding. The common thread holding all the stories together was the bright light and the feeling like electricity, and some people even thought they saw someone in the cloud. *It was kind of like a flash bulb*, she thought. *That light caused people to disappear, and then the accidents followed.*

Many of the people said just before the light, what they felt was an electric feeling in the air. They didn't, or couldn't describe it much different. Throughout every story ran the same thread. The government still was not able to determine what took place. The only announcement the government made was that something of immense proportion's worldwide caused people to disappear.

The phone and electric service became intermittent, and getting the updated news was extremely difficult. At first, the people in the office took their phones off the hook because of the constant ringing, but now when they tried to call out they were rarely getting through, and even the cell phones were not working any more.

The phone system was really screwed up. Ann wondered if the phone companies were damaged when some of the buildings were burned from the rioting downtown. The telephone company was not far from Patterson Street. Of all the times to lose their communications, it couldn't get any worse. One bright spot was that the Internet was still seemingly working well. She was grateful that they had a direct cable access installed, but she thought that the phones were on the same cable. She would have to ask Jerry when she saw him.

Ann sat at her desk trying to put enough pieces together for the front page of tomorrow's news. Only two o'clock, and she was worn out. So much had taken place so fast she was already feeling overwhelmed with what work she knew was ahead. Ann had only a few fragments of the world news from the Internet, but the pattern of the disappearances of the people was clear. She needed to get out of the office. How many times could she continue to go over the same things anyway? She needed a cup of coffee and a break.

The break room was small. There was just barely enough room for the coffee machine, candy machine, and the small break table. The candy machine was in the opposite corner from the table, and it was habitually empty of what she liked. She was in luck this morning though, there was a Butterfinger in the machine, and they were her favorite.

I wonder who designed this room anyway, she thought. *Must have been five-foot-two, weighed one hundred pounds and wore size-twenty pants. There's no way any normal sized person could ever fit in here. The place was a pigsty. Papers on the floor and table… Damn what a mess.* She wondered where the janitor was, and she realized she hadn't seen him all day.

A man had stopped at the office a short time ago. He was ranting and raving like a lunatic. He said the rapture took place and Jesus came and took his church out. The wrath of God was coming upon the world, and God was pouring out his wrath upon the world because they rejected his Son, Jesus. He said the Antichrist was loosened upon the world, and for the next seven years, the world will be ravaged by disaster. He said mankind rejected the one living God and the tribulation time was upon us.

Why not? Hell, that story is as good as any, she thought. She hadn't heard anything about the rapture since she was a kid. Her mother always made her go to church with her grandfather. He would drop her off for Sunday school. He raped her more than once. He didn't rape her as people usually thought about rape, but he sexually abused her. He would sneak into her room at night. He told her she couldn't tell anyone about it or he would tell them how bad she was, and how she was leading him on. He hurt her so much, and so deep with what he did. She could never understand her mom insisting she spend her summers at her grandfather's cottage in southern Florida.

Every time she tried to tell her grandmother or her mother about what her grandfather was doing, she was cut off. They wouldn't hear of it. It was like they knew what her grandfather was doing to her, but they wouldn't even allow her to say it. Her mom's refusal to listen was almost as painful as what her grandfather did. After years of therapy, the only thing that seemed to come out of it was the realization of why, in some Freudian way she preferred older men.

The coffee seemed to go down surprisingly well for as rotten as it was.

Ann began to think about her date for the weekend. *I really hope he's as good as he looks,* she thought. *He's damn cute, really cute butt too. It's been so long since I've been with someone who's really good. I sure hope he's not the slow methodical type who wants to get to know me and spend months talking before getting it on. You're bad Ann. You're really bad! I sure hope my date this weekend is ready for this girl.*

Just then Sue, one of the new office clerks, came into the break room and interrupted Ann's thoughts. Sue was short. She looked to be five-one or two and she dressed well, not like she had a lot of money, but rather just very tastefully with what she had.

"Hi Sue, how are you doing?" said Ann.

"OK, at least I guess so," said Sue. "We've been losing power and the Internet is out now, it's really getting frustrating to try to work. I know it seems petty with all that is happening. I, well I'm just frustrated about all the problems we're having. I just get started on my computer, and the power goes down, and it must be my battery backup needs to be replaced because it cuts out. Do you know if Florida Power said anything? I can't get anything done without having some steady power. Is there an extra laptop around not being used?"

"Ann, I'm sorry. I'm talking like it's a regular day. I'm just so nervous and frustrated not knowing what's going on. Four people didn't show up today. Do you know Tina Parsely? I heard one of the guys downstairs say she was in a car accident on the way to work. They thought she might be hurt pretty bad."

"Yeah," said Ann. "Christen from downstairs told me Tina was in bad shape. I hope she's all right. It looks like the whole world just went down the tube. Have you heard if any more has come in about the crash at Tampa International? The last report we got was probably four to five hundred or more were killed. The plane just slammed into the terminal with apparently no call to the tower or anything. If it took place at any other time of the day, who knows how much worse it would be. Jerry and I heard the explosion from here right after the light flash. Did you see it, Sue?"

"No I didn't, I was still sleeping. I heard about it though, everybody's talking about it. I wonder what it was. I got to tell you the truth though, I'm more worried about what's happening now. I don't even know if I can get home tonight. The way they're talking about the riots downtown, I'm not even sure if I have a home. The riots have got everybody spooked."

"Some of the people I heard talking in the hall a little while ago said some of the people just disappeared. Jon Pierce, the new marketing guy, said what happened is God got rid of all the people who could not accept their God consciousness, or something like that, and he killed them all. Jon's really big into metaphysics, and he studies spiritual things a lot. Anyway he said the people who are gone couldn't accept their God consciousness, and couldn't accept the God within them, so God got rid of all of them at once. He said this is the Age of Aquarius, the dawn of the new age of man."

"Did you hear all the babies are gone too Sue? Even the babies in the mother's womb disappeared? You can't tell me if this is the new age of man, God is getting rid of all the babies because they wouldn't believe in their God consciousness. I think Jon Pierce is full of crap."

"Well maybe so," said Sue." But I haven't heard of anything that makes more sense. This coffee sucks! How do you stand it anyway?"

"It is pretty bad isn't it? I need to get back to my desk," said Ann. "I'll see you later."

As Ann walked toward her desk, she wondered if maybe there was something to what Jon Pierce was saying. After all, the man who stopped earlier said it was God too. The only difference is the man who stopped earlier said God took the good people out. *I guess one explanation is as good as the other,* she thought. *We'll know who is right when we find out whether or not there are any politicians and lawyers left. If the politicians and lawyers are all left, we'll know God took the good people out and left the crooks behind.*

CHAPTER THREE

DAY TWO
Events in the time of Revelation 7

Janice was hysterical. She still had not heard from John, and after searching all day yesterday, she couldn't find Jennifer. She started a door-to-door search to find Jennifer, but no one remembered seeing her. Mrs. Greive, who lived in the green colonial house at the end of the street, told Janice her husband left to search for her eighty-five year old mother-in-law, Marianne, who left the house. She couldn't imagine her mother-in-law just leaving like she did. Marianne left the shower running and her clothes in a pile on the floor, and she just took off. Mrs. Greive hoped her husband would return soon. He was gone such a long time. She couldn't understand what would cause her mother-in-law to leave that way. Mrs. Greive asked Janice if she thought her mother-in-law might be getting Alzheimer's disease. Her husband, Fred said he didn't know how she got out of the house because she would have had to walk right past the two of them to get out.

Most of the people Janice tried to talk to when she was searching for Jennifer, were either not home or were locked inside. Old Mr. Drem, the hermit who lived three doors down from the end of the block actually pointed a gun at her! A gun, like she was some kind of dangerous criminal or something!

Her iPhone was not working, and the Internet service was out. It was the same for everyone she had a chance to talk to. The phone service being out added to her panic and she found herself booting the phone up every five minutes to see if it would work.

After she had searched several frantic hours throughout the neighborhood for Jennifer, Janice turned to go back home and check to see if anyone had left word for her. She was hoping John would be there or would have at least called and left a message. There was also the chance the police might have called with some word of Jennifer.

There were a few people wandering the streets, most of them seemed in a daze and unable to comprehend what was happening to their world.

Janice stopped to talk to one man who said his wife disappeared from before his eyes! Just disappeared! He said it must be space aliens. He asked Janice if she saw the light when his wife disappeared. He said it was real bright. The man's eyes were glazed, and he looked as though he was on the verge of totally going off the deep end. Janice could see in his eyes the fear she felt inside. She had never before felt as much fear as she did at that moment. *Helpless is a hideous companion,* she thought, but she could do nothing but wait.

There seemed to be numbness about everyone she met. All the people seemed to be looking for loved ones or crying out for the police who never came. Janice finally went back into the house, locked the door, and began to cry, overwhelmed from the frustration and fear inside.

Janice tried to hide from everyone. For some reason, she seemed to think their grief would add to hers, and make her feel worse. *"Where is John?"* she thought. *"Where is John?"*

Jennifer was gone, and she kept going back into her room hoping she would show up, but she never did. Janice never felt so much pain! She never felt as alone as she did that time in the dark. It was the dark of the house she used to love so much.

Over twenty-four hours had passed since Jennifer disappeared, but nothing had changed. She kept reliving the same questions over and over. She was sure something horrible happened to both John and Jennifer.

The television cable and Internet finally came back on. What the news said did not give her any comfort and instead intensified her grief. What happened to both Jennifer and John was probably the thing with the light from the clouds. The news was saying millions of people disappeared at one time. She was sure it must be what happened to them both.

There still wasn't any official government response except something happened worldwide to cause millions of people to vanish. She had to face the fact she might not see either one of them again. She began to plan how she would get her focus back in a direction to insure her own survival.

There was a knock on the door. Janice pulled the curtain aside and saw a haggard-looking policeman standing on the front porch.

He told her John was in a car accident and she had seventy-two hours to make arrangements for his body. If she did not claim his body by then, it would be considered a ward of the court, and he would be cremated.

When she told him about Jennifer, he agreed to take Jennifer's description. He advised her she was not to bother calling the police station to inquire about Jennifer, though, because there were so many people missing. They would call Janice if they found her daughter. The phone lines were to be used for emergencies only and were not to be used for inquires. She was not to call. He told Janice he felt Jennifer would not be found. He was sorry but he had to go. Just like that, it was all he said. He was so unemotional Janice had a hard time thinking he was even human.

As he was leaving, Janice asked if she could get a ride to the morgue with him, and he told her, "No." He told her the police were severely understaffed, and he needed to stay on the street.

As he was driving away, Janice could see the dark smoke from burning buildings rising over the city. Fighting back the pain and tears, she thought of how right Everia, her psychic, was. Everia was more right than she could possibly know; Janice would never be the same again.

Reverend Jim Franklin was convinced the rapture took place and he missed it. "Why, God what did I do?" he said just under his breath.

He tried to get through to every one of the pastors in the church world he believed were men and women who sought after God's heart. He had very little success in reaching anyone. The phones and the electric were off and on for the last day and a half. He strained to remember how long it was since the nightmare started and realized it had only been a little less than thirty-six hours.

Smoke from the fires in town hung over Ft. Wayne in dark sheets. Jim always had breathing problems from asthma. Even though he quit smoking several years ago, he still had problems breathing whenever he exerted himself. The smoke in the air was causing him a lot of difficulty breathing. He closed the house windows tight and put wet towels along the door bottoms, hoping to keep out some of the smoke. It didn't seem to be helping his breathing much, but it was better than not trying at all.

He believed the news reports he heard between blackouts verified the rapture truly took place. The more he heard on the news, the more convinced he was the church was raptured. He was absolutely sure of it in his heart.

Jim already decided he would go north into Michigan, all the way to the Upper Peninsula to a cabin he knew. He would take everything he had on the end time studies and the most recent published prophecies.

"I may have missed what God wanted from me the first time, but I'll not miss it again," he vowed.

The rapture of the church seemingly took place, and he vaguely remembered from some of his studies there were some scholars who believed there was going to be another taking away within the next seven years after the Antichrist comes into power. He opened his Bible and found it in the book of Revelation 15:2-3. Jim found it was strange that as many times as he read it that he never saw before there would be saints that go through the tribulation time up to the time the wrath of God is poured out upon humanity.

> [2] And I saw what looked like a sea of glass glowing with fire and, standing beside the sea, those who had been victorious over the beast and its image and over the number of its name. They held harps given them by God [3] and sang the song of God's servant Moses and of the Lamb: (NIV)

He must try to survive until then, and find out what God's will is for him. He would try to lead as many into God's kingdom as he possibly could. First, though, he had to find out where and how he missed God. His whole eternity depended on his finding where he went wrong.

For the past thirty-six hours Jim studied some of the articles published recently proclaiming the rapture of the church was near and God was bringing his people home. Almost all of the articles said nearly all prophecy was fulfilled for the rapture to take place and it could occur at any time. He believed for a long time they were wrong, but now he was convinced he had been.

Not an easy thing to admit even to myself, he thought.

Jim, for many years, believed God was only love. He, for so long, believed God would never bring his wrath upon his own creation. How very, very wrong Jim felt now.

A knock on the door instantly seemed to lift the heaviness from his shoulders. Jim always enjoyed people, and to have some company now was a welcome relief. He looked through the window and saw one of his closest friends standing on the porch. It was Stu, one of the church deacons at the entranceway. Stu was one of Jim's staunchest supporters over the years.

Stu was a heavyset man, not really way out of proportion, but too heavy for his frame. He was nearing mid-thirties and already had a slight salt and pepper hair color. Although Jim knew Stu had many problems in his past, he really came a long way in improving his life in the last few years' time.

"Come on in, Stu," he said, as he pulled the wet towel from the bottom of the door.

"Jim, what's going on? Have you heard anything? The whole world seems to be falling apart in a hand basket. I just came from downtown by Martin Luther Drive, and all hell has broken loose down there! Martin Luther Drive is impassable at French Street and the National Guard, and police in riot trucks are stopping everyone coming near. I saw a man lying in a pool of blood, and a soldier glanced at him and continued walking by him like he didn't even care, like that dead guy didn't matter."

"I don't know for sure, Stu, what's going on, but I have a pretty good idea," said Jim. "Do you know of anybody missing?"

"No, I don't," said Stu. "I've heard a lot of people talking about a space ship or something vaporized a lot of people, and a lot of kids are gone, but I haven't been able to get the television to work since it happened. What do you mean by missing, you mean the space invasion thing?"

"Stu, the news has been full of people missing and disappearing, even disappearing from in front of witnesses. Before the electric went out again this afternoon they said on *CNN* that millions of people disappeared, all of them at about 5:10 eastern standard time yesterday morning and that scientists thought the cloud had something to do with it. I don't know anyone who is missing but most of the people I tried to call earlier today were not around. Stu, I think Jesus came for the church."

"What are you talking about he came for the church?" asked Stu. "We are the church, that's what you told us. We are the church."

"I mean the rapture. I mean the Lord took out his people. It's not aliens or space invaders. I truly believe it is the rapture. I went to every source I know of since this first started, trying to get more information, and I am absolutely convinced the rapture happened. We need to find out what to do to prepare ourselves for what's coming, and for the separation of the good from the evil that will happen sometime in the next few years. There will be a taking away just before the wrath of God is poured out upon the world. The Jewish people will have their eyes opened when the Antichrist desecrates the temple, and the Bible says in Revelations 15 the people harvested at that time will be singing the song of Moses, and the song of Jesus.

"Jim you said in church that anyone who was good and full of love for his fellow man is saved. In fact!" said Stu, his voice clearly rising. "I asked you what would happen if there was a rapture of the church, and you said the rapture was only the fundamentalist's interpretation of that part of the Bible, and you said there's no such thing!" Stu screamed it out. "I followed you and what you said. I believed what you said. I believed you!"

"I'm sorry Stu, now I know with all my heart I was wrong. I ask you to forgive me!"

Jim tried to calm him, but Stu would have nothing to do with him, and he left, slamming the door as he went out."

Stu was angrier than he could remember being in years!

"Man, what's he talking about? Rapture? Man, there ain't no such thing, it can't be true," he mumbled to himself.

Stu went to church all his life. He was married once but it didn't work out. His wife, Judy, literally turned out to be impossible to live with, but they did work out an amiable settlement a couple of years ago. She knew before they got married he was bi-sexual, but so was she. That was one of the attractions for both of them, and probably was the thing they had most in common. They both had their little affairs away from the house, but it was never a problem with them other than they both were concerned about getting a sexually transmitted disease. Anyway, it was over, and just as well, she was turning into a real dike.

Stu had been a member of Pastor Jim's church for almost two years now, and he liked the way Jim preached. God is love, an all-knowing God who made each man the way he is. Stu was sure God made him "bi." Stu began to think back over the last two years. *"Pastor Jim preached a good sermon, and he didn't come down hard on the way people are, and the way God made them different the way most preachers did. I'm sure I'm okay. In fact, I know I am. I've improved tremendously from where I was before. I went to church every week, and I was always helping with everything. I like people. I'm okay,"* he thought as he hurried along.

A whole lifetime seemingly went by in the last day and a half. Ann left the office only once in that time and only to run across the street to the Shell deli station for a sandwich. She was disappointed, the deli didn't get their shipment of bread in, and Ann had to settle for some oatmeal and juice. It was nice getting outside though. Just getting away from the intensity of the office was something she needed so very much.

She was hearing the police seemed to be getting some kind of order restored to the streets and the areas ravaged most by riots. Ann had lingering thoughts that maybe the rioting slowed down only because the people who were on the rampage wore themselves out. Riots took a huge toll on St. Petersburg, and most other large cities as well. It sounded as though Jacksonville was devastated. Many fires continued to burn out of control in the down town area by the I-10 and I-95 exchange west of the river.

Transportation in downtown St. Petersburg was at a standstill. Most of the roads were blocked and it became necessary to travel completely around the city in order to get where you needed to go.

Between the riots, the power outages, and the food shortages beginning to surface, talk of a major disaster unparalleled in history was on everyone's lips.

The police were stretched to the limit and the National Guard was being brought to St. Petersburg and Tampa to help maintain order in parts of the core areas of the city. Ann was told that United Nations troops were being brought into the larger cities throughout the world, to help bring the escalating rioting under control.

The Governor held a news conference earlier in the day. He reiterated that a state of emergency officially existed over the entire state of Florida, and it would remain under martial law for the foreseeable future. Anyone caught looting would be shot on sight, anyone caught shooting at any government official, would be shot on sight.

THERE WOULD BE NO TOLERANCE TO RIOTING AND LOOTING! Was posted, and being broadcast, throughout the city.

Many areas of the inner cities were still in complete anarchy. The governor declared it would most likely be a week, or more, before power was restored throughout much of the state, at least in part, because of the increased danger to the work crews. Armed security forces working in the inner cities will provide protection for the work crews as they restore power.

Ann respected the Governor for the way he spoke. The message was short and concise. She could tell from the sound of his voice the governor was clearly distraught, and at the point of exhaustion.

Governor Anderson imposed, earlier in the day, a mandate against all unnecessary travel. A state wide sundown curfew would be imposed throughout the state, until order was brought into the cities. Only persons deemed needed to restore order would have authorization to travel at night. This was being done to keep the most important basic services in operation for the people of the state.

Ann felt very fortunate the newspaper personal were counted among the people who could travel to work. She would be assured of work, because of the critical need for the people to be kept informed, especially on the local levels, to meet rapidly changing community emergency needs. People, whose jobs were in non-crucial categorized job areas, were unsure when they would be working again.

National news reports coming into the news room were saying the government still had not made any official declaration, as to why the people vanished Monday. Ann was sure it was because the government simply had no idea of what took place. From most estimates, at least twenty million people vanished from the United States, and some reports were saying it was much higher. Many millions more vanished worldwide. Ann doubted they would ever really know how many were gone. She personally knew of three people she could not find. Ann had no way of knowing if they disappeared from the light, or died because of it.

There were so many people injured, and hurt with the riots, the hospitals could not handle them all.

Local ambulance companies were ordered to take the youngest first, and then those with the best chance of survival, instead of those most critically injured. The hospitals already went to an emergency mode of operation throughout the city. No heroics were to be performed on anyone who was doubtful to recover, or had any history of terminal disease.

The government was clearly not in control enough to stabilize, the anarchy, and rising unrest moving across the United States. While they tried to seem as calm as possible, a total collapse of the country seemed near at hand. The President and Congress were trying to keep the panic, which was overwhelming the country, from becoming total anarchy.

"God knows that we are already close to it now," Ann thought.

It was not clear what would happen when they would try to reopen the stock market, but right now it looked very shaky indeed. *This surely could be the final downturn*, Ann thought.

A sharp knock on her door brought Ann back from the deep thoughts furrowing her face.

"Come in," she said.

Sue came walking in.

"Ann, did you hear that they are having difficulties at the markets bringing food in, and even getting the stores open?" asked Sue.

"Well I can understand why!" said Ann. "From what we're hearing around Patterson Street they're destroying everything, stores, cars, trucks, everything. That's bad enough, but they've also been shooting at everyone sent to help. I say let them starve down there until they get tired enough, and hungry enough, to be responsible for themselves."

"You're right, Ann, but we're having a lot of problems here too. We can't even get a sandwich because the bread man can't get to the stores. Frank said he walked to the Circle 'K' down by the bridge, and what little they had in there was ten times the price on the package. He complained to the guy. The guy said unless they got some shipments soon, what was there was all he was going to have. He told Frank to take it at ten times the price or leave it. In fact, he said, since Frank complained so much, it was fifteen times the price for him. Frank was hot! He walked out and didn't get anything. Now, I think he's sorry he didn't, and he's too embarrassed to go back and humble himself to that jerk for some stale sandwich!"

"Yeah, we're going to be in a world of hurt if they can't get food shipments in. Hopefully, the police will be able to get the riots under control so the warehousing can reopen, and they can get the trucks running again," said Ann.

"Sue, not to change the subject, but I'm going to leave for a little while. I need to get home and feed my cat, get a hot shower, and lay down in my own bed for a little while. If anybody asks, and is looking for me, let them know I'll probably be gone eight or nine hours, depending on when I wake up. My poor cat Homer is probably tearing the place into pieces by now. I'm afraid of what I might find with the freezer too. If the electric's been out since this whole thing started, I'm going to have a mess!"

"Do you want one of the guys to go with you Ann? With the riots and all, and everything going on, it might be a lot safer," said Sue.

"No," said Ann. "I'll be okay. I just live two miles from here, and I live away from down town. Besides, I need to be alone for just a bit and get my thoughts together. Homer needs me too. He doesn't like to share me with anyone. You should have seen him with the last date I had over. He went bananas and made sure he got between us. He's definitely my watch cat. I'll be fine. I'll only be gone a few hours. I sure hope I have some hot water, I really need a hot shower!"

"Not me!" Sue laughed. "It's been too long since I was with Alex. If I don't get some time with my boyfriend soon, I'm going to need a really cold shower."

"You're so right about that," said Ann, as she realized she hadn't thought about being with a man since Monday morning. "I guess there's more than one reason I want things to get back to the way they were." She laughed out loud.

In all her years of training, Brenda was woefully unprepared for what she saw when she got to the hospital. Every bed was filled when she arrived, and it steadily grew worse. The ambulance companies had no place to put the injured people. For a while, Brenda called for a divergence from the emergency room, but every other hospital in the city was under the same deluge of people. Every space available was filled with a body. Anyone who did not have an injury of a type that would prevent them from being on the floor was taken out of the beds and placed on the floors in the hallways.

Brenda hated having the responsibility of being the triage nurse, but she was the only one available with the training who could assume that responsibility. As the patients came in, she would quickly assess their injuries and have them moved to the most appropriate area for treatment. Often her decision would mean the difference between life and death because of how overloaded all the hospital services were. They could not save everyone. It seemed ironic to her how in one short event, they went from saving a life at any cost to saving those who could be saved without a lot of time involvement.

It rather resembled a MASH unit from the warfront. People who received a code-red tag were simply put aside to die. Code-yellow was anyone over sixty and those who were younger but whose prognosis was not good, and they were only to be made comfortable. Code-green was for people under thirty and those with the best chance for survival. Basically anyone who was not code-green was given only what he or she needed to keep comfortable but little else. There simply wasn't enough medical staff or resources to go around.

Brenda knew if they did not receive a shipment of vital drugs soon, even the basic drugs needed to ease suffering would only be given to those who had the best chance of surviving. She was concerned she would have to make drastic decisions very soon, and called an emergency meeting with the hospital administration to try to find some way of getting supplies delivered.

Many of the staff were having difficulty emotionally, dealing with what they were now required to do. It especially hurt them all when they could not save some of the younger people who came in, but equally hard on them was that they knew, under normal circumstances, they would have saved many who now were put aside to wait.

No children, at least not young ones, were admitted since Monday. She was told every baby in the hospital disappeared. One of the nurses was feeding a baby when the light filled the hospital, and the baby disappeared from her arms. Not only was everyone frantically trying to keep up with the patient load, but they were also stressed to the limit from not knowing what took place. Some of the staff still had not yet been able to contact members of their own families. It was non-stop pandemonium for the last day and a half, and there appeared to be no end in sight.

Brenda, as director of emergency services, had to give the order to the staff to begin alternating sleeping in the break room. Their dedication was rapidly beginning to take a toll. She had no choice but to order some of them to sleep before they collapsed. If they did not get to sleep in shifts, she would end up with all the nursing staff being too tired to function at the same time. She couldn't afford that happening. When she made the decision to sleep in shifts, it simply backed up the patient load even further.

The patients now were triaged and treated under the emergency room overhang outside. The only ones brought into the emergency room department itself were those felt to be most viable. Brenda was almost overwhelmed with what she saw when she let the numbness of the situation go for a minute. She looked out at the people waiting outside, and she knew many of them would not survive their injuries. Most though were still openly thankful to her, and for even the hope of being helped, and she began to cry for them.

Brenda decided to take a short walk. She had been inside the emergency room for the last thirty-six hours with only a few hours' sleep, and she needed to get away for a few minutes. She decided to quietly walk across the street to the tidal flat. The hospital was located directly across the street from the beautiful inter-coastal waterway. The water view was one of the main reasons she moved to the area to begin with. If she had investigated the area carefully before she moved, however, she might not have moved to Largo in such a hurry. The traffic was so overwhelming at times she felt she was locked into a moment of time she could not get out of, and she hated it.

The tidal flats were beautiful and very quiet today. She enjoyed the few moments alone with her thoughts. A slight smile crossed her face as she watched three pelicans circling the water and taking turns diving down to catch lunch. She needed to let her mind get to the point where she was free from thinking about the hospital. Just letting her thoughts wander over normal things was what she needed to relax and rest.

Chinney's world was falling apart. When he and Jinx stepped out of the Army Surplus store, they saw the National Guard two stores down. One of them yelled at Jinx to drop his gun, and when he didn't, they started shooting. Chinney went one way, and Jinx went the other. Chinney ran down an alleyway, and in the distance he saw six people with clubs and guns walking toward him. He did not want to risk trying to get by them, and quickly hid behind some dumpsters.

As evening approached, much of the noise had quieted down, and he crawled from behind the dumpster. He moved quietly, and tried to stay in the shadows to get to his mama's place.

What he saw when he reached the street was worse than any movie he had ever seen, or anything he could even imagine. There were fires burning throughout the city, and it looked like a war had been declared. Cars were overturned, and nearly every window on the lower floors of most of the buildings, were broken. The fruit stand of Henry Moeller's was burned to the ground, and the drug store across the street was ransacked.

Fires were burning in several of the buildings, and people were dead. Chinney saw two bodies lying on the street. One of them was a boy younger than he was. Throughout the day, he heard people screaming, and hollering between the gunshots and sirens. The people he saw outside their apartment house looked to be in a daze as they were trying to make sense, out of what made no sense.

He tried over and over, but his cell phone had no service. The service had been out since he and Jinx left his house.

He could hear constant cursing and shouts coming from a house two doors down, and an occasional gunshot in the distance. Scattered in the burned out debris, he saw several more bodies.

As he approached his street, he recognized the body of one of the boys who went to his school. He was covered in blood and lying in the gutter. Chinney didn't take time to see what he had died from but quickly ran to the shadows again. He kept in the shadows as much as he could until he got across the street from his mamas' house.

When the street looked clear, he ran to the old faded-green front door. Quickly, he unlocked the door and ran to his mama's apartment. As he opened the door, and stepped inside, he yelled out.

"Mama, I'm home! Mama! Mama!" he yelled.

He ran from room to room, and when he looked in his mama's bedroom, his stomach churned and spun around. He knew his mama was gone.

CHAPTER FOUR

DAY THREE
Events in the time of Revelation 7

Pastor Jim Franklin decided to leave Ft. Wayne because he was afraid of what would happen. After Stu left, three others from his congregation stopped at the parsonage. They were convinced that Pastor Jim had not told them what they needed to know about God's plan for the end times. The three began getting verbally confrontational and it escalated to the point where Jim was afraid he would be attacked. Jim finally told them that he would not talk any longer, that they had to leave. He locked the door and immediately began to plan his exit.

He was sure, as upset as they were, that they would come back, and he knew he had to get out of the parsonage before that happened. He decided he would go to a cottage he knew in Upper Michigan near Lake Superior. It was away from most people and away from the rest of the world.

He was fortunate that he had gas in his car. He had filled the tank the day before the rapture at the *Shell* gas station on Albert Street.

Jim began frantically going through the house to find everything that he thought he would possibly need in the wilderness of Upper Michigan. He made sure he would take all the magazines he had in the house that had articles on the end times and on prophecy that had been proclaimed by many pastors in the past few years. He needed a clear understanding of what he missed and what God was doing in his church for this final time.

He was sure that somewhere in the articles and his Bible, he would find the answers he was seeking. He knew he must, he knew that, according to the scriptures, he had less than seven years to find out what he had missed and where he went wrong. His eternity would depend on finding out where he missed God and asking his forgiveness. Jim did not want to go through what he knew would be coming upon the earth.

"Dear Jesus, please forgive me," he said softly as he rummaged through the kitchen drawers for things he needed to take.

Jim felt very fortunate as he loaded his car. He had bought an old Chevy Suburban a few years ago for a good price because the owner needed quick cash. He liked it because it had plenty of space to carry the many things needed for the church. The gas mileage on the highway was only around fourteen miles to the gallon, but it was a large tank and he would get a good way into Michigan before he had to get more gas. When they went on church trips, he had room for five people comfortably, and seven when they were in a pinch. Now, the size allowed him to load the car with all the food in the parsonage and the canned goods that had been set aside for the poor basket.

Jim loaded everything he thought could possibly be any help to him. He made it a point to grab the old twelve-gage shotgun and three boxes of shells he kept in the closet.

As he went through the cabinets in the back of the garage, he found an ax, some large knives, an old cast iron fry pan, and odds and ends utensils. He took everything that might even remotely be needed that he could fit into the car until there was only room left for him to sit.

Jim was sure that to remain in the city could be fatal to him. He really had never deeply studied the book of Revelation but he knew the tribulation time had begun and nearly one half of all the people on earth would die over the next seven years. "May God have mercy on our souls," he mumbled.

The Gone

The local news announcer said on the five-o'clock news that authorities were warning everyone to keep off the roads and do as little driving as possible. Many local gas stations had already closed, and the trip at best, would be difficult. He knew it would be dangerous to make the trip, but he could see no alternative which seemed better.

There was no way he could help anyone from the church because they would never again listen to him and allow him to help. Jim knew they had already rightfully blamed him for where they are.

"Father, I pray you have mercy on them, and forgive them Father for their sins and mine. With your righteous wrath, the wrath you are now releasing upon the earth, I can no longer help them, they will not hear me, but I ask your forgiveness, Father, for I know some of what is coming, and I do not want to be anywhere near the city," Jim prayed silently.

He pulled from the driveway just as it was turning dusk. Even with the failing light, he could see people gathering not far down the street, and he wondered if they were from his congregation. He couldn't recognize any of them because of the distance and decided he didn't want to know why they were there.

When Jim put the car into drive he looked for just a second at the empty cross on the steeple of the church, and he felt pain rising up inside because he had failed the people.

By the time that Jim turned the corner, he began to have doubts and wondered if he could even get through Michigan, because by now, the police had probably set up check points and they might not let him through. He was especially concerned about getting across the Mackinaw Bridge going into the Upper Peninsula.

He had enough gas to make it probably two hundred fifty to three hundred miles but to go beyond that, he would be at the mercy of the gas stations along the way. If he could even find one gas station for one fill up, it would be close to getting him to where he wanted to go. He put two five-gallon gas cans in the back and was thankful one of them was nearly full. The church had several hundred in cash in the safe. He had about six hundred in cash of his own and about one thousand dollars in silver dollars he had collected over the years. That was the extent of what cash Jim had with him.

The little news he got said that gas was already extremely scarce, because of delivery problems. There was a strong warning issued against traveling, and most states were already under marshal law with all unnecessary travel stopped. Indiana had not issued a decree yet, and he did not think Michigan had either. He would have to leave now if he was to have any chance at all to make it before everything shut down and got worse. He decided that he would stop every fifty miles or when he saw a station open and keep the tank as full as possible. With any luck at all he would find enough gas along the way to keep going.

Jim knew that nearly one-half of all the world population would die over the next seven years. All these things he knew would take place, but he also knew that he had failed, because even though he preached about Jesus, he never personally knew him.

Jim did not pay attention to the signs of the times and what was taking place. The Toronto Blessing, the Brownsville revival, the Lakeland Revival and the Bradenton Florida Sound from Heaven movement all were saying and pointing to the same thing-that Jesus was coming soon. Even global warming with huge weather swings, the many earthquakes, the economy, and the rise of terrorism all pointed to the return of Christ, but he refused to accept it.

Jim's mind felt more at ease as he crossed from the edge of town and toward the countryside. Jim felt that his best opportunity for getting gas would be along the expressways. He decided to stick with traveling I-69 unless he couldn't find any place open to get gas in the first hundred miles. The last thing he wanted to do was to run out of gas near a major city, he wanted to be as far away as possible from everyone.

Jim had a slight smile cross his face because he remembered to take his portable gas station, a six-foot-long piece of the garden hose to drain gas from abandoned cars.

So much had taken place in his world so fast. His mind seemed to dance from one thing to the next. There would be so many who would be lost, but Jim hoped that if God would allow him the time to live and read his word that he would find where he went wrong.

His thoughts bounced to the cabin he was heading to. He hoped that it was still what he remembered it being from several years ago when he went there with a couple of his friends for a week of fishing. The cabin had a hand pump for water, plenty of wood nearby, and the lake out in front of it that was full of walleye and pan fish.

He remembered cooking fish over the campfire they built outside by the shore one of the nights they were there. The fish tasted so good when they were done in tin foil with potatoes over the open fire. If the small aluminum boat was still there and the wood stove had not fallen apart he would be able to survive.

Jim had seen a movie not long ago about the Eskimos drying fish fillets on bushes and was sure that he could dry some of the fish and put them up for long-term food. He also remembered a cookbook from the sixties, was at the cabin, it was written by Gibbons, who taught about eating things from the wild and what was good, and what was not good to eat. He hoped that it was still there.

"Funny how my mind is going back to that, I do hope it's there," he thought.

An hour and half later, as Jim crossed the state line into Michigan, he realized how much at peace he felt. Four miles past the state line, he found an open truck stop that had gas. The price had risen to over twelve dollars a gallon and was cash-only, but Jim was thankful to get it.

The food at the restaurant was surprisingly good, but they were out of bread because the bakery had not made their delivery. They had a great bowl of chili, though, and he really enjoyed it even though it was hotter than he usually preferred.

It almost seemed normal at the truck stop, except for the army trucks, and soldiers in abundance. The old jukebox was loudly playing an old country song. He wasn't sure who was singing, but it really didn't matter. It was nice to just slip back a few days in time before the world came apart.

There was a nervousness that prevailed throughout the place, but being isolated, except by vehicle, almost seemed to set it apart from what was happening over the rest of the world. Jim found himself tarrying longer than he probably should have. Only three days removed from when the people were gone, it was already nice to pretend there was a normal place in life.

Jim thought it was strange because he did not hear anyone talking about the people who had disappeared but rather the economy and Washington mandates and laws and regulations changing so fast they were hard to sort out.

As he started the engine and began to pull away, he looked through the window to the people inside and could see the truckers and others trying to hold desperately on to what was left of their past life.

In three days, the world had changed and would never again be the same. How could he have been so blind? He was told by many of his colleagues that the time was near, but he had dismissed it as so much talk and had not seriously accepted what they were trying to tell him. Most of them were gone, taken away in glory to where he could not comprehend. The Bible says that there are streets of solid gold, and that no mind has ever seen or can comprehend what God has for those who love him. Jim tried to imagine what heaven was like as he drove along, and he knew that he had to find out where he went wrong.

"Please, Father, show me. Reveal to me what I have done wrong, that I am not with you right now," he prayed.

Jim thought that he could get to heaven even now, but it probably would cost him his life. Better to die with a bullet in the head as a martyr than to spend all of eternity in the lake of fire. He knew one thing he needed was to get away from the city and what was to come there, and to get away as fast as he could.

One of the books that he had found on the study of Revelation said that the mark of the beast would not be a factor until after mid-tribulation, as shown in Revelation 13:16-17, and he would have to study that in some depth. For years, all he had ever heard about the beast was that right after the rapture they would be trying to put the mark on everybody, but one of the end-time books that he had glanced through at the truck stop said that the mark of the beast would not be a factor until nearer the end of the tribulation time.

The Gone

He had grown up as a pastor's kid. "PK," they used to call him. Jim hated to be called that when he was growing up. He had been around religious people all his life, and he had taken the phrase *born again* as part of their belief system. After all, his dad had been a preacher all his life and his grandfather before him. They both made a living at it, and so did Jim. His dad had often told him that it was a lot of showmanship; if you make the people feel good about themselves, then God will bless you.

"We all need to just make it through as best we can, and we need to help others as well. Give them the show they need, and you'll be blessed too." And Jim had been a good preacher; the people loved his message and liked what he had to say.

Jim's mind was wondering all over as he made his way deeper into Michigan. *I'm going to take some of the back roads when I get closer to Lansing,* he thought, *in case they're stopping traffic.*

The radio had been announcing the government limiting travel. All Jim could find on the news was the government declaring they had everything under control, and that the President was going to address the nation in two hours on moving forward in unity.

At least they have a plan, he thought. *Maybe they will finally accomplish something with this government.*

As he approached Lansing, he came upon the familiar construction about ten miles south of the downtown expressway. He was sure that the road had been under construction for at least the last ten years.

"What's it been now? Two years? Three? Since I was here last, and I don't remember the road being any different than it is right now," he thought.

Jim soon came to an exit that would take him around the edge of the city and away from the government road blockades that he feared.

Chinney frantically searched the apartment house for his mama and his sister, knocking on every door in the complex. The only one who came to the door was Kyle Holman, who lived downstairs. Everyone else was too afraid to answer or was not home. Kyle, a long-time doper wanted some crack, but Chinney said he had to find his mother. Kile was in rough shape, and needed a fix. Chinney could see the telltale signs in him already. *How sad*, thought Chinney as he left his door to pound on the other doors down the hall.

No one was home; at least no one answered the door so he went back to the apartment. He remembered what his mama had told him that if she ever disappeared or was gone, that she had a letter with some important things in it for him. She told him to look by her bed stand in her Bible and that what she had was all the wisdom and help that she could leave him. As he went to the bedside, he started to go through some of the things on the nightstand. There, he found a letter addressed to him, and he opened it and began to read.

> My Dearest Chinney,
>
> By now if you are reading this then something terrible is happening to you. Chinney the Lord Jesus has come for his church and I praise God he has taken me with him! Chinney, many bad things are going to happen to the world. There are so many things you must do otherwise you are going to be damned to hells fire forever. The line is so thin and the penalty so great if you don't do what I'm telling you. I pray to God that there's still time for you.
>
> Take my Bible and keep it with you always. In it I've marked out all the things that you have to know and what you have to do to be saved. <u>Chinney, Jesus died for us when we were sinners. He died for you. No matter what you did, no matter how bad you think you are, it's not so bad that he won't forgive you when you ask him.</u>
>
> Chinney I know about those boys that killed Ginna, and what it did to you and what you did to them, even with that God forgives you of it right now if you ask him to. There is absolutely nothing that you ever did that God will not forgive

you of if you ask Him to. The Lord said to seek Him first and all these things will be given to us. He will never make you do anything. What He wants from any of us is to come to Him because we want to, you have to want to be with Him. The only thing is that we need to not refuse Him and deny Him. Jesus loves you and is waiting for you right now.

<u>I want you to say out loud:</u>

Lord, I ask your forgiveness for all the things that I did wrong, I ask your forgiveness for every sin that I have committed wrong. Lord, I believe that Jesus died on the cross for me and for every sin that I have done, I believe that Jesus came in the flesh to save me, and was raised from the dead. Lord Jesus, come into my heart to live in my heart and keep me. Thank You Jesus for saving me.

Now Chinney it is important that you read the Bible every day. The Bible is the word of God and the more you read it the more you will understand it, and it will become a part of you. Don't start with the Old Testament, but start with the New Testament because it teaches about Jesus and how much he loves you and it has his words in it. The words will teach you so much, and the words are life. I made a list of what I want you to read and I put them in the Bible. These are what I want you to read and read many times until you know, that you know, that you know, you are saved Chinney this bad time is going to last seven years. The Antichrist is on the earth and God is going to pour out his wrath, everything you will see will lead up to that and bring it to its final conclusion.

WHAT EVER YOU DO, DO NOT TAKE ANY KIND OF CHIP - LIKE WHAT THEY PUT INTO PETS TO IDENTIFY THEM, TATTOO OR

> ANYTHING ON YOUR HAND OR FOREHEAD FROM THE GOVERNMENT.
> If you do you will go to hell, don't do it honey, don't let anyone tell you got to do it because <u>you will go to hell if you do.</u> You belong to Jesus if you just say that prayer out loud now, because the Bible says you must confess with your mouth and believe in your heart and you will be saved. Jesus will guide you if you read your Bible every day. Make sure you pray to Him all the time and Jesus will help you.
>
> I love you son,
Mom

Chinney read the letter again. He tried to understand what mama was trying to tell him. He still couldn't understand how mama and Cappi could just disappear like that.

What did she mean that Jesus took her away? As he read the letter, he repeated out loud what his mama had written.

Chinney knew the time had come to leave. He had to get as far away as he could, and he knew that he had to go as fast as possible. He would go now to Upper Michigan. He had never gotten a driver's license, and for all the things he did know, driving a car wasn't one of them because they couldn't afford one and he always took the bus. He would have to get some way of going there, and he had to have it soon. Kyle Holman, in the apartment below, had a motorcycle he wanted to sell for some time. It was an older one and not very big, but he would buy it, and use it to go to the Upper Peninsula the way he planned.

As he knocked on Kyle's door, he began to make a checklist of what he would need and what he needed to take with him. He had a small amount of crack left that Kyle needed, and a little cash, so he was hoping to make a deal. He would take everything he could carry from the apartment, including mamas Bible. Chinney remembered his old knapsack from school and his sisters' sleeping bag, which he could tie to the side of the bike when he left. From what mama said, there was no doubt in his mind what he had to do.

Kyle was happy to get the crack, and they quickly came to an agreement for the motorcycle. He agreed to show Chinney how to drive it. Chinney was happy to get it and get on his way. It didn't take Chinney long to get things packed.

After taking one last look around the apartment, he opened the door and stepped out. He turned and looked back and said; "Thank you Jesus for my mama and my sister. Thank you for saving me, please help me learn how to pray, Amen".

Janice was finally calming down and beginning to think a little more clearly. She still hadn't gone to the morgue to claim John's body, but she had been able to think and clarify in her mind what she needed to do.

She did not find Jennifer, and John was dead. Everything seemed to boil down to those two facts. The only thing she needed to do right now was to continue to try to find Jennifer and try to put her own life back in order.

She didn't know what to do about the house. She had been trying to get hold of the bank and see what she had to do, but all she could get was a busy signal. The insurance from John's company would get her in good shape financially. With as much as she and John disagreed on, she was happy now that he had a fetish for being what she thought of as over insured. *Never any good until you need it,* she thought.

The paper said that the government was taking control, and they had most things to the point of functioning again. By the end of the week, the authorities said they hoped to have most services back to working normally. The President was saying it would take everyone working together but the country would get through it.

Yeah, thought Janice. *What was left of the country might get through it.*

It seemed as though everyone on *CNN* and in the government was trying to explain what took place, and theories had gotten to be like butts-everyone had one. One of the things everyone agreed on, though, was that what had taken place was the most profound thing in known history. The President's advisors said that many of the scientists felt that the earth went through a time warp in space and that it affected only some people and not others. The religious people said that God took the church out, but then why were some of them still left?

Janice really missed Jennifer, and not knowing was the worst part. With the insurance money John had she knew she would be okay, especially if things get under control the way the government said it would.

She was hoping that maybe Margaret could take her to the morgue to make arrangements for John. She hated thinking about doing that, but she knew that she had to ease her conscience about the coldness she felt over his death.

The government was starting a massive house-to-house search to try to determine how many people were missing.

Janice knew that Everia, her psychic, was right, that her life would change dramatically. Now, though, she knew that it would be at a huge personal cost.

Ann began to tally the number of dead in her mind. Yahoo was back up, and as far as they had been able to tell, an estimated figure of twenty to twenty-five million people had disappeared, or had died in accidents or known suicides. Those figures were in the United States alone, and some sources were saying the figures were much higher. It was hard for her to even comprehend the numbers beyond what she could see for herself. If Ann applied that same percentage from throughout the world there probably would be over five hundred fifty million to seven hundred million either gone or dead. The impact of those numbers was staggering to her. *How could it be, how could something like this happen?* she thought.

Some scientists were saying that they thought that the world got too close to a small black hole, or possibly a parallel dimension, or something else that as yet is unexplained. The "or something" is what they were saying because they had no idea what happened. At some point they would probably understand what had happened to the people but it looked as though it would never really be known.

Ann's mind began to drift, to think of good things that would begin to put some enjoyment of living life back in her. It had only been three days, but she already was feeling as though she had been through the proverbial ringer of a lifetime. She had not been able to get any relief at work. There were too many people missing from the office, and everyone that was there had to do double duty to get the job done. She had no one to fill in and replace the ones who were gone.

Jerry had been a godsend, and he had been at the paper day and night after he saw Sandy and he knew she was all right. Ann was thankful that Sandy was doing well. She was thankful that Sandy understood how much Jerry was needed at the office now, and Ann told Jerry that if he wanted, he could set up a cot in one of the offices for Sandy to stay. It would be safer for Sandy not to be left alone.

The world was a mess, plain and simple. Ann continued to sift through the mounds of information that had come in over the past three days to see what could be corroborated. What had happened didn't make any sense to any of the scientists and people who study such things. With all the people disappearing, there was nothing in the news that really seemed to make any sense or give a logical reason for their disappearance.

Ann found herself thinking about her daughter Patty. If she couldn't get hold of her ex husband, Mike, pretty soon to find out about her daughter, she would have to find some way to have someone check on her.

The rioting downtown had stopped, at least slowed down, and Ann was thankful for the brief feeling that it might be over. It seemed as though the police along with the National Guard and government forces had brought things back into order. It was a heavy price though, and they were told at least eight-hundred people were thought to be dead from the riots in just the south St. Petersburg area.

The police cordoned off nearly ten square miles of the downtown section of St. Petersburg, before it had been brought under control. As much as possible, the grocery stores and banks, were being protected but many of the grocery stores sustained a lot of damage in the first few hours after the riots started. It seemed to Ann, from the police reports that they had received, that at least part of the reason that the riots had stopped was because there was nothing left to steal or destroy.

So stupid, she thought, *so stupid. They destroyed everything they had in their own neighborhoods. Why couldn't they see that they were only hurting themselves?* After all this time, the people still had not learned from what happened in Ferguson, Watts, and Detroit, and other cities. People only hurt themselves by destroying the very places they live.

With all that was going on, Ann found she was thinking about her date for Friday and that he had not called her. When she tried to call him, she couldn't get hold of him. There was no answer.

With the world falling apart around her, she needed someone to take her fears and hurts away. She needed someone to be in love with, the wonderful kind of in love that is so new, so wonderful, and yet always in the past had hurt her so. Ann thought several times she had found that in a man, but relationships that started so good never seemed to last when the sparkle wore off. She needed so much to be in love, she needed someone in her life just to hold on to right now.

She would give anything to feel love again.

CHAPTER FIVE

Release of start of woes
Events in the time of Revelation 8

Ann thought she had become hardened to bad news over the past two months, but immediately felt nauseated as she read the incoming news. Israel attacked Iran in a massive offensive first-strike move. The Iranian defense systems, which seemed so formidable, could not respond in time to stop them. Within a ninety-minute time frame Israel hit over one hundred nuclear and strategic military sites throughout Iran.

First reports were saying that with the first wave of bombers, Israel destroyed eighty percent of the Iranian nuclear capabilities. It appeared as though Israel launched every plane in their arsenal at the same time in a brilliant military move. The bombing was still underway. Hundreds of non-nuclear military sites were being bombed as well as the nuclear sites in an attempt to disrupt strategic military communications and radar facilities. Initial reports were saying that civilian casualties were running very high. Muslim leaders called for all Muslims to wage a worldwide Jihad against Israel and her Western supporters.

Because of the effectiveness of the attack, it appeared as if Israel might have had stealth bombers lead the way. Israel signed an order to purchase twenty of the stealth Lockheed Martin's F35 Lightning II at a cost of $2.75 billion, but according to the latest reports Ann read, they had not yet been delivered. The first reports in of the attack indicated that Iran had not been able to launch their Russian-built defense blanket in time to stop the Israel bombers.

Air battles between the Iranian air force, and the Israelis fighters, were continuing to be waged over Tehran and near the power plant in Bushehr. It was reported the Iranian air force lost many of their planes in the bunkers, during the first few minutes of the strike.

Because of the riots and damages from the people disappearing, there was nothing the United States could do to effectively stop the war.

Iran had been saber rattling for years, and Ann remembered that in 2010 Iran showed the world a new fighting drone designed to kill the infidels, called the; "ambassador of death". Iran said they would eliminate Israel from the face of the earth. Iran continued to develop their nuclear capabilities, even under cover of the 2015 peace agreement, which backed Israel into a corner. They now were paying the consequences.

Ann began to think about other things as she sat at her desk. She had never really thought about how she took for granted order in her life. It never seemed to matter much; in fact, of all the people she knew, she was probably the most disorganized in her own organized way. When she set in her mind that she wanted to do something a certain way, she would not change it, and if anyone tried to do it differently, they best be careful. The men she had been with in the past couldn't stand to live with her because she was organized in her way, and that's all she would accept.

Her mom often told her that she had a Jezebel spirit and always wanted to be in control. She had torn everyone apart that ever got close to her. It would take someone much stronger than she was to be her husband and survive.

Why she was thinking about that now, she wasn't sure. I guess it's because I haven't been with a man for some time now. *What's it been? Five months now? Six maybe. I'm horny, that's what it is... that's all it is. I need to be with someone.*

Sue walked in to deliver a file to Ann. As Sue stood near the door, Ann thought of how pretty she looked silhouetted by the light from behind.

"Sue, how about coming over tonight? I could sure use the company. We have a hot tub at the complex, and if the electric is on, we could even do that. I just don't want to be alone," said Ann.

"That sounds great, Ann. I hate being alone too. I've got a couple of old DVD's that I haven't seen in a long time, and that I was going to watch tonight. Would you want me to bring those?"

"Great," said Ann. "I'll be leaving here in an hour or so, I desperately want something that resembles a real life, even if it is for only one night. I've still got some frozen fish if they haven't thawed out from the last brown out we had. Why don't we try to have a dinner as well. They have the electric working pretty steady now, so hopefully we'll be okay. Just come over."

"I've got some canned corn and some asparagus I could bring," said Sue. "Getting together sounds really good to me, Ann, I've got a few things to finish up before I can leave. I'll stop back before I go," Sue said as she walked out the door.

Ann was excited about Sue coming over and briefly thought about what she needed to do for the evening, before she returned to reading the news briefs for the morning paper.

Maybe there is something that happened that's good to print, thought Ann.

Ann began to skim through the news articles on her desk. *Here's a sad commentary on the too liberal California,* thought Ann. California defaulted on debts and all payouts. They gave out IOU's similar to what they did in 2009, but most stores refused to accept the IOU's for payment. The government SEIU workers and many other people who were depending on state-issued payments started rioting and storming the government buildings in an effort to get paid.

Now it seemed that most of the world leaders realized most events were happening beyond their control. World leaders were in agreement they would need to work together in unity with other nations to survive. The United Nations was quickly moving toward voting on a one-world government system to help stabilize countries. A common thread ran through the world leadership, that was indisputable - the world was going wide open into disaster, and no one country had any solutions that could stop it. There was no country in the world that had not been dramatically affected by the weather changes, pervasive heat, lack of food production, and the famines and starvation already taking place.

The one-world government system that was being discussed, had been brought up many times in the past, and rejected, but the desperation now made it appear possible to get it passed. The article stated that the UN was looking at creating ten regions throughout the world. It was determined that by grouping nations into the various regions, they could better meet the needs of each individual country in those regions. The United States would become part of the North America region, along with Canada and Mexico. Without collaborative international food distribution efforts, there would be no way to disperse food to many of the poorest, and hardest hit nations. It was a consensus that millions, or even billions, of people would perish. Many world leaders were saying the world might never recover.

Already the doom and gloom crowd was carrying a new age-dark age message.

As near as Ann could tell the agreements being discussed in the UN to create a one- world government could bring some balance back, and help restore normalcy. Each country would be treated much in the same way a country of Europe is now, and would maintain national independence. What would follow not only would allow the separation of nations to continue, but also create a unity throughout the world. The vote to the one world government system was scheduled to take place at the beginning of next week, and it appeared from first reports that it would pass by a solid majority.

Sue knocked and stepped in.

"Ann, did you hear that Washington is saying that the scientists theorized that we were nearly hit by a black hole made of antimatter or some-thing, and some people who had more of a positive charge than others were vaporized? It was on *CNN* last night, and what it said made a lot of sense to me. Jon pierce, the marketing guy is still convinced that God did it. He said that God took out the undesirables, the people who were so narrow-minded and who couldn't understand or accept that they were a god within themselves and were convinced that their way was the only way. Jon said that he could prove it because the highest concentration of people who were missing were in Bible-believing Christian areas. He's got charts and everything to prove it. They're having a big meeting at his friends' house tonight and I thought about going over there. We could probably go to the meeting tonight before we watch one of the movies if you want."

"No," said Ann. "I just need a break from everything. You go if you would rather."

"Well, I just thought I would bring it up. The movie sounds a lot more inviting. Hey, listen, what time is good tonight?"

"Any time after five-thirty is fine," said Ann. "I'm going to leave early tonight. Just come on over."

"Okay, it'll probably be closer to six by the time I get there. I'll see you then, thanks for the invite Ann."

As Sue was leaving she couldn't help but think that Sue was a talker. *She's going to wear me out with her constant talking,* she thought. *It's going to be nice though to hear the sound of someone else's voice in the house for a while. It seems like such a long time since I had anyone over.*

Ann was sure that even, Homer, her cat would be happy to have some company over too. *Homer was more company than most people and probably more demanding too,* thought Ann. *You know come to think of it, I'm really his pet, not the other way around. I'm the one who is always waiting on him. Something's wrong with that idea. I'm going to have to change that, and make him beg for attention.* An old saying came into her mind: "Tough, tough titti,' said the big fat kitty." She smiled.

Just as Ann was beginning to leave she read an emergency update report on the Internet. An 8.2 earthquake in Hawaii hit at 1:25 EST and the loss of life was reported to be very high. The report said that the epicenter was four miles southwest of Honolulu. As she read the report, she found that, as devastating as it was, it was almost anticlimactic after the events of the last few months. In fact she wasn't sure that it would even make the front page, the war with Iran and Israel would take that spot.

A secondary emergency update followed the Hawaii report that said a second smaller earthquake happened just off the coast of Japan and it was feared that the reactor number four cooler collapsed in

Fukushima, causing a huge explosion. First reports indicated that large amounts of radiation were spewing out in a great plum.

I haven't heard anything about Fukushima in some time, thought Ann. *I thought that it had been taken care of long ago.*

"It must be the hours I'm putting in. Damn. I need the night away from everything, and I hope Sue does too," she mumbled as she straightened her desk to leave.

Stu was trying to comprehend the events taking place around him. Everything, it seemed was beginning to go wrong or had gone wrong in the last two months. Even getting enough to eat was hard now.

Of everything that happened over the last two months he was still most disturbed about what Pastor Jim said. *Why would the pastor tell him that he thought the rapture had taken place when there was no proof? And then when he ran out on the congregation like that, leaving so many hurting people, how could he do that? Man, that really hurt,* he thought.

There were still a few of the parishioners who gathered at the church, trying to find answers, but almost everybody stopped coming or were not around. Stu still went, and he tried to lead the church through the services which were mostly a few songs and open discussions about what to do to survive. "Pastor Stu" had a strange ring to it.

He told the few people who came that he would continue to have service until a replacement could be found. Not many were coming anymore anyway, but those that came needed to have that feeling of something normal still in their lives. He couldn't see a lot of reason to continue going because all they talked about was how they were going to get their share of food allotments. Everyone's depression seemed to make him feel worse.

Stu wondered if the movie house was still open. He doubted that straight people had any idea what went on in there. It was so easy to meet men in there, in the quarter movies. Leave the door unlocked, and usually before the first quarter play was over, someone would join you for sex. Stu didn't go in there anymore.

It must be a bad spirit or something, he thought, *I haven't thought about that place in a long time.*

Janice was doing better. The deep longing hurt that had so overwhelmed her had lessened, and she could at least see more clearly the direction she had to go.

From Patterson Street in St. Petersburg to the southern part of the city, the rioting had slowed and overall things were not as tense. Parts of south St. Pete were still under martial law, but the rest of town from Howard Street to her house had been opened to limited daytime travel. *The government mandates and the disaster plan they put into effect actually seemed to be working,* thought Janice.

Janice's psychic, Everia said that startling revelations have come forth from the spirit realm, and she had invited Janice to a meeting at her house that evening. Everia said that many of her friends and clients were going to be there. Everia had made arrangements with Clarice Joplin to pick Janice up at her house if she wanted to come. Janice was looking forward to getting out of her house and be with other people.

Everia was a trip. When Janice first saw Everia, she thought that she fit the stereotypical psychic to a tea. Everia had bright red hair and grotesque heavy eyebrows that seemed out of place on a woman. After she began to get to know her, though, Janice really enjoyed the way that Everia had of just cutting through the bull and getting down to business. Janice had gotten to where she respected Everia more and more each time they met.

The government was talking about a plan of confiscating the properties of people who had died or who were gone and putting a program in place to help those who lost everything. The President said it was a "social justice" priority, to help the nation out of the worst major economic downturn in history, and re-create a nation of equality for all.

On the brighter side, was that with the bank shut down, she didn't have to make any house payments. On the other hand, she hadn't been able to get hold of the insurance company to get the death benefit payment for John, and she could not make the payments without it.

When she could get a car she would be mobile again and would take advantage of the rationed gas and food as best she could. The government was asking for volunteers to help implement the programs, which was something she felt she could do well, and she thought it might help her to get a paying job later.

Janice paced the floor somewhat impatiently, waiting for Susan Joplin to pick her up for the meeting at Everia's house tonight. Finally maybe she could get some answers about what was going on. Her mind began to drift to thoughts of her daughter and where she might be. She thought how strange it was that she thought of John so very little now, and she wondered how she could seemingly get over him this fast, but the thought of her daughter was still a crippling pain in her heart.

When she thought about the last few years, she knew that she hadn't been close to John for a long time. She could not remember the last time they made love and not just had sex. She remembered how, when they first were married they made love for hours at a time. She smiled when she remembered how once they began making love at sundown and were still in each other's arms when the sun came up. They couldn't seem to get close enough to each other and couldn't seem to be together enough to satisfy either one of them. Where did that go? What caused that to slip away? Now, it was only two months after John's death, and she hardly grieved for him. *Maybe if he had died before, she would have grieved more*, she thought. Now, though, she was too wrapped in thought about just saving herself and finding her daughter to spend much time grieving for John.

Just then there was a knock on the door. It was Clarice.

"Hi, come in! Boy, it sure is good to have someone walk through the door. Would you like anything? Can I get you a cup of coffee? That's about all I have right now I'm afraid," said Janice excitedly.

"Yeah, a cup of coffee sounds good. I'd like that. My cupboards are pretty bare too," said Clarice. "I hope they reopen *Publix* so that we'll have more choices. I didn't realize that I took everything so much for granted before, did you?"

Clarice was much bigger than her voice, maybe even 250, thought Janice. *If there's any place to find food this girl knows where it is.*

"No," said Janice. "It's even hard for me to remember what it was like before. I'm really glad that the school the government is using for food distribution until the stores open back up is only four blocks from here. I've been able to at least walk over there to get what I need to survive. You're right, it's hard to believe how much I took for granted even going to the grocery store. When John was killed, it wiped out our only car. I'm hoping that I can get one from surplus when they get things in order. I really need to get a car and a job."

"Everia told me about John and your daughter. I'm really sorry," said Susan.

"Thanks," said Janice. "But I'm doing better these last few weeks. I guess everyone has their own story now. What about you? What about the people in your life? Are you missing anyone?"

"No," said Clarice. "I knew a couple of people that are missing, at least I guess they are, they could have been out of town or something and couldn't get back. I hope Everia has some answers tonight. She said that some of those things she has been receiving from the spirit world are incredible, and we are in for some excitement tonight. Everia said that the revelation she has been getting from her spirit guide is nothing short of awesome."

"This is kind of new to me. Do you really believe in it? Clarice, I have this crystal someone gave me a couple years ago. I've started reading the book that they gave me after you asked me if I wanted to go tonight. I mean, the new age of man we have entered into now, and the new age movement and all. Everything I've been reading makes a lot of sense, but I still have so many questions.

From what you've said, it sounds like Everia is amazingly accurate in her predictions. How does she do it anyway?"

"It's a gift. She walks in the spirit world like we do here. She knows all about the spirits and how they operate, and what they do.

Do you know that each one of us has a spirit guide and all we need to do is learn to communicate with them and they will teach us to walk in the spirit world with them? Have you ever heard of Wicca?" said Clarice.

"Sure, but I don't know anything about it," said Janice.

"Wicca is a form of worship where you communicate with mother earth through the spirit guide that is within you. Very powerful. Everia knows all about it. In fact, I understand that she is a high priestess. She was given the gift of seeing so she could help others understand what's taking place. Tonight, there's going to be a man at her house, Jon Pierce, I think his name is. He's from the St. Pete *Sun*. I understand that he really has an insight as to what's going on. We're really going to learn a lot tonight. I'm looking forward to it. We'll meet some really incredible people. I want Everia to give me a reading tonight to let me know what I need to do, and what I have to do to better myself, and where to go that's safe for me. I don't know what to do now or where to go. With what's going on I don't even want to be alone."

"I know," said Janice. "I don't know what to do either. The last couple of months have been a nightmare. I don't even turn on the news because I don't want to hear what's going on anymore."

"I just want to know what the future is going to be so that I can prepare for it. Everia has always shown me the way. I do better if I know what I'm up against," said Clarice. "This is good coffee. Thanks, I really appreciate it."

"You're welcome, Clarice, I appreciate the company. I'm glad you're here."

"What do you think, Janice? Are you ready to go? I'm really excited about going tonight."

"Well, we can, but do you think that we might have time for another cup of coffee first? I'm really enjoying just talking," said Janice.

"Yeah, we've got time. I'm a coffee drinker from way back. My mother had coffee going all the time when I was growing up. Boy that was a long time ago."

"My mom died about sixteen years ago now, I guess. Mom died of cirrhosis of the liver, she drank herself to death. Drinking ran in our family. Both of my brothers, my dad, and me all had drinking problems. I've been fighting this for a long time, all my life I guess. I finally just had to stop drinking all together. I couldn't just handle a few, I always wanted to get drunk and party. I ended up in more than one bed and didn't know how I got there. Anyway, I finally gave it up totally, it was the hardest thing that I ever did. I don't know how I got to all that from a cup of coffee. Oh yeah, from my mom making coffee all the time. I could tell you some stories that you just wouldn't believe. What the hell, we got some time."

"We have more in common than you think," said Janice. "My Dad was an alcoholic too, and I hurt for a long time because of it, but I finally got over it.

Clarice went on to tell Janice about the car accidents and the many troubles that she was in before she quit drinking. *Unbelievable,* thought Janice. *Either Clarice was the biggest hell-raiser she had ever met or the biggest bull thrower she ever talked to. If any of the stories was true, Clarice sure lived an eventful life.*

Janice had all her second thoughts about Clarice taken away by the time they reached Everia's house. If she was full of bull, then at least it was fun. Janice found herself laughing out loud to what Clarice was saying. *It's fun to laugh, it's been a long time, and it almost seems a lifetime,* thought Janice. A warmth began to fill Janice that she hadn't felt in a long time. It was so good to laugh again.

Clarice had an old Volkswagen bus. Janice thought that it fit everything about Clarice to a T. She reminded Janice of everything she remembered hearing about the sixties, the only thing the bus was missing were the flowers painted on the outside. "Maybe when I get to know her better, I'll suggest it," chuckled Janice to herself.

As they walked up the brick walk to the door, they both were excited, thinking that maybe it was going to be a good night. Over twenty people were at the house already, and they were broken up into several small groups. Everia met them at the foyer and began to personally take them around for introductions. Janice began to feel right at home. How good it felt to be part of something, of something that was so big and exciting. She did not want to be alone. Everia began the meeting soon after a few more had arrived.

While Janice wasn't sure she agreed with everything that was said, she did agree with most of it. Everia began by telling some of the people about their past before she told them about their future. She was absolutely brilliantly accurate about what she told them.

When Everia came to Janice, she began by telling her about John and her daughter and how she still had a future that she could look forward to. Janice was in awe by the accuracy of what Everia said about her past, even the things that happened long ago. Everia even knew about the time her father molested her. It had been so long ago that Janice had almost forgotten about it. She also told her that she would soon get the car she wanted and would once again have the freedom she needed.

Then to everyone's surprise, Everia told Janice that she had been chosen to bring forth the wind of a new message. When she learned more, she would be in the forefront of the new world system that even now was being brought into existence, and many would come to hear her speak. According to Everia, she would not be alone for long but would find someone new, and they would live together and would do many things together.

Everia went on for some time before Jon Pierce was introduced as guest speaker.

Jon began, "The new age has dawned and we are indeed fortunate to be living in this time. The peace of the ages will soon to be upon us and after a short time of confusion, peace will forever rule. No more will the old ways do, it will be a fairer socially just world for everyone. No more will hunger and discrimination exist, there will be plenty for all. It truly will be the dawning of the New Age."

Jon took a sip of water and continued. "God took away the people who would never believe and left those of us who will walk in spiritual ways. There will be yet another purification process, but before it is over we will each be taught by our own spirit guides how to accept the god within. Each one of you is a god. The god within you only needs to be accepted and brought forth. By the year 2028, we will all be purified and brought to oneness. It will be a beautiful place to live, and all the hurtful things of the past will no longer be in the world. All war will be gone, and all the bad people will be as well. The god within you will use you to train and teach others how to live the way they should. Do not be afraid because before it is over, as many as one half of all mankind will die, but you who are chosen to stay will live in peace, prosperity, and love. Do not worry about your loved ones who died and are gone, they will be reborn, and reincarnated into another body. It is the responsibility of those of us who are left to teach and train the people who will be reborn."

Jon continued for the next forty-five minutes, and Janice was enthralled with the message and vowed to learn everything she could about the coming times.

After Jon finished speaking she was talking to him after the meeting and something amazing happened. She had such a terrible headache, and he noticed her grimacing. He asked her if she was okay, and when she told him that she had a terrible headache, he called a couple of people over. They did a couple of chants of some kind, and the headache went away, it just left! They said that when you are in tune with the spirit guides, that you can ask the spirit guide, and he will bring a good spirit to you.

She really liked Jon Pierce, and she began to wonder if he had a girlfriend. She began to fantasize that maybe he was the one that Everia was predicting for her to be with. She felt thankful she met these people. Maybe things in her life would be all right after all.

Clarice and Janice had a long talk after the meeting. There was so much to learn, and it was such a good break for her to just get away from the house and be with other people. Janice told Clarice she would really enjoy getting together to go over some of those things she wanted to learn so badly. They agreed to meet the following week and go to the next meeting.

Janice held tight to the six books Everia had loaned her to study from as she said goodnight to Clarice and walked to the door.

Finally she had some direction in her life and for the first time since everything in her world changed, she was encouraged. She would study to the best of her ability to be the best she could be.

Jim had been at the lake almost two months. The trip went much better than he had anticipated and pretty much was without incidence. When he arrived at the cabin, it was exactly as he had remembered it. It was nice to be alone to try to sort things out.

He had killed his first deer with the 12-gauge shotgun two days before. Years ago his grandmother had given him a recipe for caning meat, and he tried it for the first time. The old fruit cellar still had the Ball jars and pressure cooker that Jim suspected had been there since the fifties. Jim managed to put up forty-eight jars of grandma's venison. He put them in the old fruit cellar to keep for winter.

Between the jars of venison and the fish from the lake, he knew he would be okay and he would be able to survive the winter. He had already cut twelve cords of wood, and the heavy snow was still a few weeks away.

It seemed much warmer than Jim remembered it being this late in the season, and he worked up a sweat cutting the wood. He wondered if the daytime temperature was because of global warming and the severe weather fluctuations that had been experienced in many parts of the world.

He was thankful for the old Kalamazoo wood stove that was in the center of the small living room. It was large enough to roast him out even on the coldest of days. *How old was that old stove? Must be at least fifty or sixty years old anyway, it's been here since I've been coming here*, he thought.

Even though the days seemed warmer than usual, the nights had been getting cold enough that there was frost was on the ground when he awoke in the morning. The trees were being transformed into the most beautiful colors of reds and yellows. Jim had forgotten how colorful the fall colors were in the Northern Michigan woods. It was so incredibly beautiful.

Jim made up his mind to begin gathering the winter wood further away from the house and keep the standing trees closer to the house. By leaving the standing wood next to the house, it would be much easier to get to if the weather turned colder, and he needed more wood for heat.

It was so beautiful looking outside into the woods and so peaceful, it was hard to imagine that the entire world had changed such a short time ago. Life now at this cabin, in many ways, seemed so much easier than what he remembered it being at Ft. Wayne. Being this far away from the people and the traffic, he felt more at peace than he remembered being for a long time.

Jim had been working so intently that is seemed almost a revelation when he realized how physically tired he was. It was a good tired, as his body responded to the exercise that he was not used to. The work had been very exhausting, but he knew he had to get everything ready for winter. Jim was sure he had made the right choice, and surviving at the cabin would be easier than it would have been in Ft. Wayne.

As far as he knew there were no other people living within five miles of the cabin. The distance between people had a way of demanding self-reliance more than anything else could. He would live or die by what he did for himself. One thing he knew with some certainty, that he was much better off than those who remained in the large cities.

He was taking this time to study and read the Bible every day to try to understand where he missed God. He knew he had to get right with God, and nothing was more important than finding why he was not in the rapture of the church. Jim was constantly praying and reading the Bible, and he found that even with his life so changed, he was the happiest he could remember being in a long time.

The news he heard over the car radio was even more of a confirmation of what God was doing to bring the entire world to the end of time. Israel attacked Iran in a pre-emptive strike against the Iranian nuclear and military plants. According to the same reports, Syria was preparing to mount a retaliatory offensive against Israel and the reporter said that Israel was concerned Syria might use chemical weapons as they did against their own people in 2013.

He would re-read the Old Testament and study it because he was remembering it was stated there would be at least two coming major wars in the Middle East countries and he was pretty sure the Israel-Iran war was one of them.

The cottage was small, but the size was just right to keep heated. There were actually two bedrooms, and he had already decided that he would seal the smaller one off and keep smaller pieces of wood in it to keep dry to use for kindling. The old stone fireplace in the small living room had long ago been closed off. It had a nice homey-rustic feel to it, but Jim knew open fireplaces were extremely inefficient for heating. The inefficiencies of the fireplace would waste wood, and he could not afford that.

If a blind man follows a blind man both shall perish. I need to find out where I went wrong. When I know what I did wrong, I will preach to the people near here to let them know what they have to do. I must do that even if it means my death, thought Jim. He would continue to ask God for guidance and understanding.

One thing Jim realized was that in this moment of history all of the prophecy written in the Bible regarding the end-times was now being fulfilled.

As Jim began to read again in Revelation, he glanced out the window and saw that a very light and unusual mid-September snow began to fall. Even for the Upper Peninsula, it was early for snow he thought, especially as warm as it was earlier in the day.

Jim looked across the fresh falling snow, and smiled at how beautiful it was. He decided to start the first real fire of the year and felt relaxed for the first time in a long time. As the warmth of the fire filled the room, he began to read the Bible from the light dancing off the ceiling.

Jim would have to try to get to town some ten miles away to get more kerosene and some extra wicks if he could find them for the lamps. He knew the nights would be long, and he had much to learn.

"Dear Jesus, please teach me what I need to know, teach me where I missed you, and teach me what I need to know to teach others so they may not perish but have everlasting life with you. This I pray, amen."

The Gone

Ann began to go through the pantry shelves to see if she had anything to go with the fish. With what was left in the pantry and with her corner grocery store being open now, she would be okay.

One of the men in the National Guard that came into the paper told her that before long they would be eating steak. Before too long, if she were lucky, she would be back to a somewhat normal life.

Homer is purring so loud and being such a good boy today, Goofy little fur ball that he is. Ann thought, as she reached down to pet him.

It was hard for her to understand how she could be so taken with a cat of all things. Boy, did he have her wrapped around his little cat paws. He was more company than most people she knew, and at least twice the fun.

The cat hospital, what was it they had on their billboard a couple of months ago? "Have a PURRRRRFECT day." Today was the best day she had in a long time. She felt more relaxed inside than what she had been since this whole thing started.

Just then the doorbell rang. It was Susan smiling with the semi-frozen vegetables. It would be a good night, Ann was convinced, it would be a real good night.

CHAPTER SIX

Start of Woes
Events in the time of Revelation 9

The world as we know it has come to an end, Ann thought as she began blocking out the headlines for the day's paper. It seemed that there were so many things taking place the paper couldn't possibly print it all.

She quickly glanced through the recap sheets. She decided to call a quick meeting to get everyone who was available working on the layout to make sure they hit their deadline.

Ann pushed the intercom button to Sue. "Sue, could you get Jerry and the news crew together for a quick meeting in the conference room in five minutes? We have to make sure we block out the pages to get everything covered. I have to run to the restroom, and if you could grab me a coffee on the way in, I would appreciate it."

Ann walked back to the conference room, and Sue was already there.

"Everyone but Frank is on the way up," said Sue. "He said he had a scheduled meeting starting in five minutes, so he will come if his meeting gets done in time."

"Thanks Sue, and thanks for the coffee," said Ann as the others stepped into the conference room.

"Hi guys. I called this meeting because there is so much to cover. I felt we needed to make sure we are on the same track to get this out. Only so much can fit on the front page, so we will have to come in agreement on the best approach," said Ann.

"There are several stories that break my heart, and we must cover them, but let's do it in a way that is as soft as we can. We will start with the collapse of the Fukushima nuclear number four building. We have been following this for a number of years, and it has caused a lot of problems primarily on the West coast. A little over a week and a half ago, there was a small earthquake, and the primary building collapsed causing the cooling pool to drain. They believe the reactor lost all water from the pool, and they did not have all of the fuel rods removed. As many of you know, the fuel rod removal started in late 2015, I think it was, and over half of them were already removed when the collapse occurred. It has been difficult getting information on what happened, but it is now clear that a nuclear explosion took place sending massive radioactive clouds into the atmosphere," said Ann.

"Jerry, would you hook the computer to the screen for me please? I want to put this article up so we can briefly discuss it." Thanks, said Ann.

As the article came up on the newly installed large flat wall screen, there were several comments on how good it was to finally have some of the newer technologies in the conference room.

Ann started the meeting. "I will email this to you all so you have them after we finish. Let's go through these so we can get a better idea of what we have to get done," said Ann.

- The radioactive cloud from the collapsed number four reactor of the Fukushima nuclear facility is passing north of Hawaii and approaching the coast of Washington State and Northern California. The estimated time of land fall places its arrival at the first of the week, depending on wind currents and ground speed.
- The cloud is carrying a high level of radioactivity, and it is expected it will cause radiation sickness and cancer throughout much of the northern population. Many people who have heard about it are trying to escape the West Coast and are fleeing to the south and east, causing massive traffic backups, but it appears, at this time, that

depending on the upper wind currents, there may be no safe place in the northern hemisphere to escape. It is now feared the radioactivity, over time, will affect all of North America.

Ann gave them a few seconds to read and began to speak. "As we read through this, I want you to think about how much impact this can have in Florida, and especially the St. Petersburg area. It appears that this area is probably the safest place in the United States to be living right now. I shudder at the thought of what the people must be going through who lived in Canada and along the West Coast, and I don't think we can even imagine at this point how many people may permanently move into the area. The massive migration to the east and especially to Florida is not something I want to speculate on, but we need to keep in mind that it probably will happen. Let's read further."

- According to the National Weather Service, the air currents, which are carrying the radioactivity, is at a very high level in the jet stream at this time, and if the low-pressure system remains stable over New Mexico, most of the high concentration of radioactivity will be over the western coastal areas and the very most northern states. It is generally felt, western Canada and Alaska will be hardest hit and over time will probably be totally uninhabitable.
- The Implications of the radiation spread are so huge and on such a world-wide scale, they won't know for some time just what the end effects will be. Scientists are trying to study long-range jet-stream models to try to determine what will happen to people living in the affected areas over an extended period of time.
- A mass exodus is expected to take place from Canada and the northern states, but there is no way that the southern part of United States can handle the immigration. Many fights are already braking out along the border between the people fleeing to the south and east, and the people living

- there who are struggling to survive on their meager food supplies.
- Most scientists agreed with the initial reports stating that with the current information and wind currents, Alaska probably will never recover. It appears as though the radioactivity levels in Alaska will make it uninhabitable well into the next millennium.

Ann had tried to remember the date when the tsunami hit Japan. She was sure it had been at least ten or twelve years now. She had all but forgotten about it because there were so many things happening that were more pressing. She was under the impression that it had been repaired some time ago by the scientists in Japan, but now it was quickly becoming one of the most catastrophic events in history.

It was such a short time ago that she was so excited about her job and being able to see the news first, but now she dreaded the morning briefings. It would be nice to have something good to share for a change.

"We just got this in as well, and I know some of you might have already seen it, but we need to make sure it is covered. The radiation cloud coming from Japan has put the war, which just ended between Israel and Iran, as a secondary event," said Ann.

Ann continued. "We do have good news though, and let's make this tomorrow's front page lead in to page two. We want to emphasize that a peace agreement is being negotiated, and right now, although it's still extremely tense, both sides are on stand down. Hopefully the war will continue to de-escalate and an agreement can be reached. Finally, we have good news that we can print from the Middle East, we need something good for the people to read. As you know, the war from all accounts ceased after sixteen days. There continues to be a number of localized skirmishes, but now there is a feeling of optimism that the war is over. The word that we just got in is that a seven-year truce is being negotiated as we speak, through a number of world leaders."

"Again, emphasize the peace agreement being negotiated at this time guys. We need something good going out of here," said Ann.

"I know that all of us are concerned about gas prices and this is going to make it worse. The gasoline prices we are now seeing in the Tampa Bay area are expected to rise again by the end of the week, but will be much higher in some other parts of the country, if they can even get it. I will talk to the owners to try to get some relief for everyone who has to drive. It's a good idea if we all car pool, and try to help each other as much as we can to get through this. The API is saying this is directly related to the Iranian sinking of the oil tanker in the Strait of Hormuz."

"Ann, I hate to interrupt, but I can hardly make it back and forth to work now because of the gas prices. I'm not sure I can make it with gas going higher. Is there any way we might be able to work from home, or at least maybe a few days a week?" said Jerry.

"I don't know, Jerry," said Ann. "The Internet has been so in and out, but it does seem to be getting better, and I know we have to do something. With your job, though, Jerry, I don't have anyone that can cover, so I will try to get you some relief to help cover the gas. All of us are getting hit on all sides. Let me see if I can work something out with the board, so we can get through it."

"Thanks, Ann, sorry, I just don't know what to do," replied Jerry.

"It's okay. We'll get through this together. As soon as we get through the run-down, I will make some calls and see what I can do. Let's get through the rest of this," said Ann.

"Actually, the main things that we needed to cover, we have. I just have a couple of other things that came in that we should cover, and the rest can go on page two, or further back.

"The President declared that all of the banks, the stock market, and commodity markets that had been closed at the start of the war will remain closed until further notice. Additionally: he said that, and I quote, 'All food and fuel distribution systems will be expanded to insure everyone will have enough provisions to get through this unparalleled time we are in. Until the nation gets past the shortages that are taking many to the point of starvation and suicide, we must stand together. Therefore, by executive decree, I have put in place an allotment system.'" Ann continued.

"I'm going to shorten this a bit and just summarize the rest of the article. The article later said that the UN has voted on an allotment system to be put in place worldwide because of severe shortages everywhere. The vote failed because they cannot agree on any method of logistics and controls. They are trying to come up with a way to help people across the world. As we have heard, what is happening here with the shortages is much worse in many other countries. The UN is trying to come up with a system that can help globally. Similar statements on food and fuel distribution allotments have been made by leaders of several other leading countries as well," Ann continued.

"I know this is hard for all of us. We all have people we know that are now either gone or dead, but I guess that the paper gives some people hope and a sense of normalcy, as well as giving each one of us here, a diversion from our everyday lives. We also are truly blessed because we do have work in a time where so many are facing no income or hope for the future. Let's make sure that we give the half-full side of the news, and not the half-empty," said Ann.

Ann continued. "At this point, I think we covered what needs to be included. If anyone has any questions, get with me right away, and we will get it to print on time. We have a lot of work to do today, and I appreciate every one of you working together to get it out."

"Jerry, let me know if you're too tight on time to hit schedule. Again, thanks guys. Let's get it done."

When the last of the staff left, Ann began to do a quick mental count of those who have been lost or died in just the last several months. When she added the number of people that were estimated to be gone and the number thought to be killed in accidents, and those in Iran and the Middle East, it was almost incomprehensible. As near as she could figure, between six hundred million and nine hundred fifty million people were gone or dead in ten weeks time! As many as one hundred million people had died each week, and that number was only the start. Many more will die before the radiation stopped taking its toll.

As Ann was reading through the API Alerts, she saw one thing that made her laugh out loud. The President signed into law a federal bill to make it legal for gay's to marry in any state in the United States. *Wow*, Thought Ann. *That's high on the priority list for America. Of all the things to spend time on now, that takes the cake.*

Ann began to finish up what she needed to run tomorrow's paper, and her thoughts went to Sue and what they would do after work. She was thankful they had become such close friends. It seemed now there was no one else she was close to, and she desperately needed a friend.

Ann was running on overload. Her mind wanted to go back to better times to escape the horrors going on all around her. She began to think of a better time when she and her ex-husband, Mike, were walking on the beach of Florida not too far from where she lived now. She remembered the clear water and the beautiful sunsets. Mike told her that he read somewhere that once in a thousand sunsets, there was a brilliant flash of green just at the last second before the sun sets in the water. For a long time, it was a bond between them, and they spent many nights on the beach and many walks, hoping to catch a glimpse of the elusive flash of green.

She hadn't heard from Mike and she wondered if her daughter Patty was okay. Travel was still difficult at best, and there was really no way she would be able to get her daughter back right now. It was the penalty for moving from Michigan to Florida with Mike still up there. Mike really loved Patty, and his new wife, Amy, was good with her. They would take care of her better than anyone else would, and that thought alone comforted Ann in her loneliness.

Stu was happy the movie house was still standing. It had been closed since the people disappeared, but many people had left their numbers and addresses and the places to meet on the door. What he found out was that there was a place where many men were meeting in a large dense woods not more than a mile away. He knew where the place was and decided to go there.

It had been a while since he had gone out seeking sex, but he wanted sex bad. Stu knew it was dangerous, but he went to the woods anyway to check it out. *Amazing how easy it is,* he thought. It almost seemed as though there were more gays now than ever before. While he preferred to be with a woman he had not seen his wife for a long time, and this would take care of his physical needs. Besides, he had forgotten how exciting it was to be with three or four guys a day. Really, if he wanted to wait a while, he could be with three or four men at once. Sex, to him was almost as addicting as alcohol, maybe even more so. Any kind of sex he could want, he could get, except maybe for a woman; they never liked him much.

If there was a God in heaven, then why did he let all this happen anyway? I really was doing good, he thought. The only time I was with anybody but my ex was when she wanted her girlfriend and wouldn't let me close. That wasn't too often. I was too good to have been left behind," Stu mumbled.

Stu began to walk into the woods, and as he got just into the edge of the shadows, he saw two men standing by each other. Stu looked toward them, and one of them motioned for him to come over. As Stu walked toward them, he thought of how far he had fallen from the church and God in such a short time.

"How are you doing?" said one of the men as he reached for Stu. *Going to be a good night*, thought Stu. *A real good night.*

Chinney had a very difficult trip. The motorcycle he bought had only made it a little over one hundred miles before breaking. The last two and a half months, Chinney had mostly walked at night and hid during the day when he was near a city. He found a bicycle near the town of Midland, and it made the trip much easier. With all the problems he was having, he had only made it as far as a small country road outside of the town of Gaylord. Chinney was becoming concerned because he was still a long way from the bridge. It was almost the end of October, and it was getting very cold at night. He knew he would soon have to find a place to stay for the winter. He had already begun to have doubts about having enough time to get across the Straights unless he could find another motorcycle somewhere.

Chinney thought back over all that had happened. He wondered if Jinx was even alive anymore. Chinney figured, as stupid as Jinx was, his odds were less than even for still being alive. *Funny,* he thought, *he didn't even know the name of the boy from school he saw dead on the street. He only recognized his face. Did anyone even pick him up, did anyone even care? He would never know, but it seemed so sad somehow, that life would mean so little now. What had happened anyway? He knew that he would wonder that as long as he would live.*

He missed his mama and Cappi. He tried to rationalize why he didn't spend more time at home with them, but in the end he knew he was wrong and no amount of rationalization would change that. There were some things that he would never know, but he could only hope he would see his mama in heaven. He wondered if he would survive the winter, but he knew in his heart that he was much better off even in the middle of nowhere than he would be on the streets of Detroit.

Other than the motorcycle breaking down, the trip was not as difficult as he thought it could have been. He had been able to find a couple of houses along the way that had no people living in them and he had been able to get out of the rain most of the time when it was real bad. He also found enough food at different houses to keep him going. He was hopeful he would find a place that had enough food and shelter to last him through the winter.

Chinney was riding the bicycle on a country tree-lined road that just took his breath away. The colors of the poplar trees were a bright yellow-gold; unlike anything he ever remembered seeing. All the trees were the same brilliant color, and he was awe-struck by them.

He decided that he would get off the road and walk into the woods and rest. It had been so long since he had ever seen anything as pretty as that forest, and for what seemed like a long time he just walked in it, his eyes bedazzled by the beauty of it. Sitting beneath a tree and soaking in the color, he realized how very happy he was. The lazy flittering of the leaves as they made their way to the ground somehow gave him a sense of peace. For the first time in a long time, Chinney was happy to be alive.

Chinney found a tree that had a couple of large branches broken down on one side, and it created an opening where the sun could shine down on him. It was such a pleasant day, with the kind of warmth that goes right into your very soul. Part of the warmth he was certain, was because of the bright warm color of the trees. *"It's so pretty mama. It's so pretty"* he thought.

Chinney sat a long time watching the leaves flutter to the ground and the squirrels dancing across the treetops. He remembered mama's letter and took it out to read it again. Mama had taught him how to read the Bible when he was a boy, and he again began to read the verses that she had underlined for him. Reading the scriptures again over the last few weeks brought a much clearer understanding of what it said.

He stayed sitting by the tree for some time, and the sharpness of the stirring breeze brought him to the realization he needed to move on. When he got up to leave, he thought that he might have made a mistake by allowing himself the pleasure of the moment and sitting for so long. Walking back toward the bike, he noticed a leaf covered drive that led into the woods and thought maybe it might lead to a place he could spend the night.

Chinney walked to a small crest in the road, and he stopped when he got to the top. Below him was a post-card nice little white house nestled into the side of the hill, and sitting at the edge of a small deep blue lake. Instinctively, he stepped behind a nearby tree to watch and see if there was anyone around.

He watched for a long time before he decided to go closer. He couldn't see any movement at all, but he still approached the house from the backside where there were some trees closer to the house that he could hide behind if he had to.

Chinney crept to the side of the house and looked through the window. The house seemed empty. He wondered if there were people still living here or were they gone? He saw that one of the windows was slightly open, and he decided to chance going in. He jimmied it open enough to crawl through, and entered as quietly as he could into what he found out was the laundry room. It smelled bad like cloth that had been worn too much and not washed. *Jock strap smell, that's what it is,* he thought. Peaking cautiously through the door, he still didn't see anyone, and he began to quietly slip through the house. He was relieved to find there was no one there.

He stood in the living room, and the musty smell was still very strong and bad. It was then he recognized it for what it was. Old-folks smell, he determined that's what it was, old-folks smell. This is the way his grandma's house always smelled.

Gently he opened the doors, first into the bedroom, and then into the bathroom and cellar. Walking through the house, it even looked like old folks. There were two chairs and a couch in the living room, and they were all covered with doilies like he remembered at grandmas. On the walls were a lot of old pictures that probably had been up there since before he was born.

He was sure the people who had lived there had to be at least as old as his grandma was. The fake plastic flowers and knick-knacks all over were just like his grandmother would have. Everything looked old and covered in dust, and the plastic flowers were faded from time. It seemed like when they the put the flowers up, they liked them so much they never took down. When he walked into the bathroom, he could tell there hadn't been anyone there for some time. *Either they're dead or gone*, he thought.

He began boldly exploring the house. He opened the pantry doors and cupboards, and was delighted with what he saw. The old lady was a canner! In the pantry, he found what looked to be enough food to last the winter. He found Ball jars with canned tomatoes, corn, beans, raspberries, greens, and pickles. Besides the home-canned goods they had, there were a lot of other things, including Spam and hash.

'I'll stay here this winter, and I can go north the rest of the way in the spring. I bet that lake has a lot of fish too. I can't believe how lucky I am! Damn I'm lucky!" he thought.

The garage near the back of the property had what seemed out-of-place vinyl siding that someone started to install. Part of what had been installed was falling down. It looked as though whoever owned it had tried to do the siding themselves and did a lousy job of it. When Chinney checked the siding, it almost looked to him like maybe they didn't put enough nails in it, and that was why it didn't hold.

The wind was beginning to blow from across the lake, and it was much colder than he wanted it to be.

Chinney decided to do some exploring to see what was in the garage. The garage was locked so Chinney went around to the back window, and he broke it to get in. When he got through the window and stepped inside, he noticed a terrible smell, that was even worse than in the house.

Yuck, what was that smell, what is it?

As his eyes began to adjust to the dark, he could see a car and what looked like a laughing man sitting behind the wheel. Startled, Chinney jumped. Within a couple of seconds as his eyes adjusted more, he realized that the man was dead. The corpse was grinning, the rotted face of death from behind the steering wheel.

Over the last few weeks, he had seen several dead people, but they had been dead only for a short time. This was the first rotten dead person he ever saw. Chinney tried to cover his mouth to hold back the gag.

As he ran by the car to the front door to unlock it, another quick glimpse was enough to show Chinney how rotten and swollen the body really was. He unlocked and opened the side door, and then quickly opened the overhead garage door before he went outside. He stood a few feet in front of the overhead door to get away from the smell and looked back across the garage, trying to see what was there. The breeze from the lake sweetened his nostrils as he surveyed his new domain. *The guy sure was a packrat,* he thought. *One good thing about it that I know for sure is that this place is empty. He won't be coming back.*

Chinney went back into the house and sat at the old yellow Formica kitchen table. He began to take stock of what supplies he found. With the food that was there, he was sure he would be able to survive through the winter. If he could catch a few fish in the small lake behind the house, he would have some fresh meat besides. He could make it even if the winter was exceptionally harsh. He saw a wood heater next to the car in the garage that might work if he could figure out how to get it hooked up in the house. Getting it moved into the house by himself would be difficult if it was as heavy as it looked, but he was sure he could do it. He'd wait at least until tomorrow to go back into the garage because of the smell.

He wondered what happened to the guy. He thought that maybe he committed suicide because the garage was locked from the inside. Chinney realized that maybe it was a woman in the car instead of a man. He didn't really look close enough to be sure. *Man or woman, it didn't matter. Either way, it sure did smell bad,* he thought.

With the overhead garage door open, he hoped it would air out enough to be able to go into the garage in the morning. *Tomorrow, I'll try to move the stove out and whatever I can find that I can use.*

Chinney sat at the yellow table and then got up to check the pantry to see what he could make himself for dinner. Without electricity, it limited him quite a bit as to what he could eat right now. He found a can of tuna, and some stale crackers. When he opened the refrigerator to check for some mayonnaise, he shut it as fast as he opened it. The smell of the mold inside was enough to convince him there was nothing he wanted in there. He was sure that the mold made that old folks smell he didn't like, and he decided that the first thing he would do was to push the refrigerator out the door and leave it outside. He would fix this house up the way he wanted it to be.

"Yes, this will work very well. I'll stay here this winter and move on in the spring. I'm sure thankful I'm here instead of Detroit, I wonder if Jinx is still alive," he mumbled to himself as he began to shove the refrigerator across the floor.

CHAPTER SEVEN

Woes
Events in the time of Revelation 9

The entire world was in shambles and Ann was thankful she was where she was and did what she did.

Homeland Security sent a representative to reaffirm that the newspaper was critical as a means of reaching the local populations with regional news and food distribution schedules. They were mandated to print the schedules for the food distribution locations for the following day and the requirements needed for eligibility.

Mark Madden was sent to the paper by Homeland Security to review and approve the paper layout before it was run to make sure everything that Washington required was printed. Ann was not happy that the final say on what was printed in the paper had to be cleared with Mark, but she knew it was imperative that schedules and requirements were included daily.

More people had reportedly died of starvation in the United States than soldiers killed during the first and second world-war combined. New York City alone reported that more than 200,000 people had been killed, died of starvation, or committed suicide in the last two months, and that did not include the people who disappeared. Many were killed because they had food, and others died because they had didn't have any.

Ann found herself just trying to contemplate how the world came to this point in what seemed such a short time.

Estimates of the number people who disappeared during what had become known as "the gone," in the United States was estimated as high as thirty million. So many had died or disappeared in such a short time, that most people were already hardened into survival mode.

The people who were gone were already a non-story. People struggling to survive were heard saying that the ones who were dead and gone were the lucky ones.

Ann was not sure why the food shortages seemed to be less than many of the other large cities. She thought that maybe it was because of the many farms in central Florida, and the long growing season put the food supply for the Tampa Bay area closer to the city. The areas in central Florida now supplied much of the fruits and vegetables for the entire eastern seaboard of the country during the winter months. With the gas shortages, and difficulty of getting the food transported farther up the coast into the New England area, there was almost a glut of food in the center of the state. She heard some reports that food was rotting in warehouses one hundred miles south of Orlando for the lack of trucks to move it.

Over most areas of the United States the radiation readings from the collapse of the number four reactor at Fukushima, Japan were lower than expected. However, there were areas of Northern Washington, Minnesota, and Upper Michigan, where even relatively brief exposure was considered extremely dangerous.

The air mass had shifted north, and for several weeks, the jet stream and most of the radiation was pushed high into Canada. Prolonged exposure in western areas of Alaska and parts of Western Canada were considered extremely dangerous, and parts of them had become an abandoned wasteland. The only people who were left in those areas were those who could not, or would not get out.

Ann was finalizing the copy for the next day's run to give to Mark when an interesting news update came through. The pope proposed a joining together of all religions and peoples in order to bring humanity under a cover of peace and love. "In this time of world tragedies it is time to put aside the differences we all have and come together in oneness to bring peace to all," he said at a news conference.

Ann was not Catholic, but she thought the pope was doing a good job. He seemed to have followed Catholic doctrine, and she really had not heard anything negative about him. In fact, she thought his views on contraception, and gays seemed to be a refreshing view coming from the church. She remembered reading some of the prophecies on the Internet some time ago that said this pope would be a heretic, and it was prophesied that the 266th pope would be the last pope. She remembered reading somewhere this pope would work with the Anti-Christ to bring about the world's destruction. *Well, they are too late, it's already happened and it didn't have anything to do with the church*, thought Ann.

The daily morning recap meeting was about to start. Frank and Jerry were both wanting to go over a couple things that had been a problem the last few weeks.

Normally, they had at least an extra week of paper stock in the warehouse. They had been running dangerously short, and twice in the last two weeks they had to shorten the ad pages to print the news.

"Hey, Ann, good morning," said Jerry as he walked in.

"Morning Ann," acknowledged Frank as he came in behind Jerry.

"Good morning guys. Hope it's going good so far this morning. We have a few things to go over this morning. I know you both had mentioned the paper shortage and I've talked to Mark about it to see if he had any ideas about how we can get a few days of inventory ahead, because as we all know, the ad base is what keeps us going," said Ann. "Mark told me he made some calls, and he found some extra paper rolls. We have a truck picking them up late today in Orlando. A small paper closed a couple months ago, and we're getting the stock. This is over and above our normal allotment, so we should be good for some time."

"That's great news, Ann. It will really help us, and a couple of companies have wanted to increase the sales ads, so we'll be able to accommodate them," said Frank. "I really appreciate your help on this."

"That goes double for me, Ann. It's become almost impossible trying to balance what we are trying to print to what we have to print it on," said Jerry. "Thanks Ann."

'I'm really glad Mark found out about that paper being closed, and having stock in their warehouse," said Ann. "It's probably a good thing that we have some extra paper coming because it seems the news on the world scene is so profound that we can't possible print it all. For my part, I'd like to see us only print the good news; it's almost depressing with all of the crap that the world is sinking into now. It's pretty sad isn't it that we can hardly find uplifting stories now. Sorry, guys, I digress. We do have a couple of stories that will need to share the front page. I'm going to start with the good news first, and that's starting with the Middle East war, and what's taking place right now."

"It's the best news we've heard for a while regarding the war. We did get an 'Alert' from API, and it seems there is a breakthrough on a formal peace agreement in the Middle East. The UN announced that the newly formed New World Government voted in a couple of weeks ago, was immediately thrust into the middle of the peace negotiations between Israel, Iran, Syria and surrounding countries. The Alert states that the G20 worked together with religious leaders including, surprisingly to me, the former Black Pope of the Jesuits, to help bring about the seven-year peace plan and lasting peace to the region."

"I need whoever is working on this aspect to get more background information on the Black Pope, and how and if he is part of the Catholic Church," said Ann.

Ann continued. "One of the key issues of the settlement provisions was an agreement to allow the rebuilding of the Temple of Solomon on the temple mount. The former Black Pope brought forth an impressive proof through studies done over many years, proving the generally held idea of where the Temple of Solomon was located was wrong, and was off by forty feet. This would allow the Temple to be built without disturbing the Muslim masque. The back wall would be built to within thirty feet of the masque that is standing at the site."

"Israel would receive a portion of the surrounding area outside of the outer court area to act as a safety buffer in order for them to be able to worship in peace. The buffer area is to be patrolled by United Nations troops with an unusual mandate of using deadly force if necessary to keep order. In return, the Masque is not touched, and the area directly surrounding the masque will remain as it is. The Palestinians will keep the rest of the West Bank and the remaining land previously agreed to by Rabin, including the Golan Heights."

"That is probably the best story we have today, but unfortunately it's not the only one. It seems the war has come here. You may have already heard this, but they have proven the black outs we heard about yesterday, have been proven to have been caused by sleeper cells setting off bombs in strategic locations throughout the United States. There are some reports saying they set off bombs in a number of locations in Europe as well."

"We all know what happened in the United States and the deaths of thousands in many of our cities because of the riots and food shortages, especially in California, but there is more to it if you read further," said Ann. "So much for the liberal political correctness crud against Islam phobia. It turns out that the people saying that we shouldn't be concerned about radical Islam in our schools and cities were wrong. We finally have word on what really happened, and it's sad to see how destructive the whole "We can't hurt anyone's feelings crap has become." I'm going to put the article up on the screen so we can all read it, and then we'll discuss it. We need to get this out today, because the people need to see it. The authorities want everyone to be on the watch and report any unusual activities. Read the article, and see how we can put this into a format that can be used to heighten awareness of our readers so we can, hopefully, keep it from happening here without the political correctness police jumping on us."

- The Israel-Iranian war devastated the United States at home in a way that was unprecedented. Iranian sleeper cells were given standing orders that if Iran was attacked with nuclear weapons, they were to retaliate against the United

States with dirty bombs. Bombs were set by the sleeper cells in New York City, San Diego, Washington DC, and Los Angeles, and explosions occurred in twenty-two central electric power plants. The reports indicate that at least one of the bombs set in NYC and LA were dirty bombs, and all of the affected areas are currently under evacuation mandates. The President who was not in Washington at the time along with his staff have been moved to an undisclosed location for the immediate future. Power grids over much of the country are out and it may take months to restore some of these areas.

"As we all know much of the United States is still subject to brown-outs and blackouts." Ann Continued. "We just got an alert saying that mandatory rolling brownouts have been issued over large areas to curb electric use until the downed electric grids can be brought back online. It is estimated that over twenty-five percent of Americans will be without full-time electricity for the foreseeable future."

"The bad news keeps coming in from California. The Southern California state water project, and the Colorado River project which supply water to southern California, were heavily damaged by the bombs. Twenty-two million people in southern California are without access to water and electricity. State officials are unsure when the repairs can be made but is feared that it may take months." said Ann. "I can't even comment on the article. We are all going through more than we can even imagine, and to be under attack this way is almost incomprehensible at this point.

"In order to save time, I am going to send a recap on the remaining updates to your computers, but the two major stories we covered need to take the top spot on the front page. Put the rest of them as lead-ins on page one, if you can fit them," said Ann. "I repeat, it's imperative that we make the bombings as major headlines. I know it may start a war within the country against the Muslims, and not all Muslims are bad, but it has to go out because a lot of people will die from these terrorist acts, and it could affect us as well.

The FPL power plants are on high alert, and have armed guards at all of the plant locations and relay stations. We need to make sure the people are aware of what happened and they need to report anything unusual. Hopefully, we don't have the same thing happening here."

Ann was nearly finished for the day when Jack from the tech department came in. He never said anything. He looked down and shook his head, almost in shock. He gently, mechanically, put a news release on Ann's desk and walked out.

- A huge earthquake, and a cataclysmic volcanic eruption, has devastated Hawaii. Preliminary reports are showing a 9.0 quake caused wide-spread destruction. The number of dead is not yet known. It is believed more than a thousand were killed, and the injured number in the tens of thousands. Honolulu was hard hit, and several volcanoes are erupting at nearby islands. One of the volcanoes was on the island of Kahoolawe. The blast when the volcano erupted was so great that shock waves were felt as far away as California. First satellite photos show the island was completely destroyed.
- A tsunami wave created from the blast hit parts of northern Mexico with seventy-foot high waves. The area hit the hardest was a very low population area, and fortunately the death toll was not as high as it could have been.

Ann felt as though the lower death toll was the best news she read all day.

Back in the eighties when Mt. St. Helens erupted, the sunsets were a brilliant red. If there were any good in what happened at all, it would have to be the sunsets.

A knock on the door brought her back from the deep thought she was in.

"Hi, Ann, how's it going?" said Sue, as she stepped through the door. "I've got these articles you wanted to look at on the New Age movement. Have you talked to Jon Pierce about the article you want to do? I bet he could get some good back-up information for you."

"Not just the propaganda stuff but he's got the history of the movement since it began a number of years ago," Sue continued. "Actually, Jon said that it's been around for several decades now, since the mid-sixties or so. Jon said it's becoming real strong because of the people disappearing and that God has weeded out the undesirables. Those of us who are left are to begin anew the work of putting the world back to what it was intended to be before Eve sinned," Sue continued. According to Jon there's still a weeding out that will continue to take place and when all that are not going to accept are gone, the peace will begin. Anyone not working to bring about peace and order will be eliminated by God, just as those who disappeared were. Have you heard that there are still a lot of people, mostly Christians, who continue to cause problems and are really working to destroy what God wants to do, and the peace he wants to bring about?"

"Boy, has he ever got you brainwashed, are you falling for that stuff he's shoveling or what," laughed Ann.

"Ann, I don't know if you heard yet, the new Pope said it is imperative that the world comes together under a one-world religion," said Sue, in a serious tone. "I remember an article we did saying that the 266th Pope will be the Pope who is called the false prophet in the book of Revelation and will work with the Antichrist. This Pope is the 266th Pope, and that's kind of a scary thought."

"I'm pretty swamped right now with what we need to get out," said Ann. "I'd like to do something on the New Age movement you pulled the articles on, but I can't get to it today. I've, got a lot to sort through, so maybe we can go through those articles tomorrow afternoon, and see what we can put together."

"Sounds good," said Sue.

"Not to change the subject, Sue, but I need some R&R. What are you doing tonight, anyway? Any plans?" asked Ann.

"No, I don't have anything. What do you have in mind?" asked Sue.

"I thought maybe just a quiet night and maybe a walk, or some roller-skating, would be good. Would you like to come over?"

"Sure, what time is best for you, Ann?"

"Seven-thirty or so works for me," said Ann. "But you call it."

"That sounds good to me too. I'm going to the break room. You want me to get anything for you?"

"Coffee would be great thanks," said Ann, as she looked back down to finish her reading.

Ann began to think about what Sue had said. *What if the Pope brings the Catholic Church into the one-world church, what will happen? What does it mean if the Pope is the false Prophet anyway? Things could not possibly be worse than they are right now. I wonder if anything better will come out of it now if there really is a one world church.*

The so called "religious right" and Messianic Jews are beginning to grow strong again in some areas, and what they're saying is totally different from what everyone else is saying. And what about those two prophets in Jerusalem making all of that negative news and making people feel worse and causing conflict, I wonder what that means?

The New Agers, the New World Order, and now the New World Church are saying that if you do not obey the government and follow the new mandates, it will be considered anarchy. Boy, I wonder who's going to win this one.

Ann was hearing a very vocal group of Messianic Jews and Christians saying Jesus came for his church. The reason they say they were left is to bring the Jewish people who would listen, to a saving knowledge of Jesus Christ.

Isn't it bad enough that we have everything else that took place but now we have a stupid holy war of some kind brewing, and both sides squaring off to fight about it? Everybody is saying that God is on his-or-her side, and who is right? If the Vatican and Muslims join with the New World Church it will bring billions of people together. You would think that with the millions of people gone and the millions dead and dying from War and starvation that everyone in the world would want to work together for peace. Why would anyone riot or promote differences and anarchy through, and, under, the name of religion? It's pretty obvious that someone has to be wrong. I wonder if the Pope, being the 266th can bring the many factions together.

Sue stepped in. "Here's your coffee Ann, if you can consider it coffee. With the shortages that we have I guess we're lucky to have this. Has it only been a few months since this whole thing started?

"I know, it seems like a lifetime doesn't it? The whole world has collapsed almost overnight. I find it hard to even imagine some degree of normalcy. Sometimes, I want to scream because of all the bad news, said Ann. Damn, I wish things were the same as before. And I digress, it's a little crazy, I know, but I want a man so bad I'd even take Jack in the shop. He smells bad, and his teeth look like they've never been brushed, but he's male."

"Ann, if that's all you want is a male; my neighbor's got a big German shepherd that's not fixed. He smells better than Jack, probably bigger too."

"You're bad," said Ann. "If something doesn't happen pretty soon, I'll take you up on that."

"Just as long as I get to watch," laughed Sue.

"I'll see you tonight Sue, I may be a couple of minutes late, it depends on how long it takes to get outta here, but I'm planning on leaving here early."

"Later," said Sue as she walked from the office.

Brenda was walking down the back hall to the emergency room. She had been told by the chief of staff in the directors meeting that the crucial supplies they had run short of would be replenished by the end of the week. The problem had been the logistics because of the gas shortages, but he had been assured that they would get the supplies they needed. Brenda responded by telling him they needed those supplies at any cost because she was at the point where more lives could be lost by not having what they needed. Without the supplies of drugs and antibiotics, the hospital might as well shut the doors and send everyone home.

In the last two months, many people had died because they did not have enough staff and supplies at the hospital to handle the caseload. Management had discussions on what would be needed to begin sterilizing needles and re-using them because they were running dangerously short. Everything inside her wanted to scream out against it, but without additional supplies they truly could see no alternative. Most of the supplies had fared better, with the exception of several of the antibiotics that she used most often were no longer available. The pharmaceutical company where they were manufactured had an explosion and resulting fire, and they had no other source available that could provide them.

Brenda's good friend, Dr. Spitzler, the emergency room doctor in charge at night, took his own life the week before. He was working late as usual, and for the past few months he had worked unceasing to try to help everyone he could. He said he was going out to his car for a cigarette. When he got there, he sat in the passenger seat, took a gun from the glove box, and ended it.

No help, no supplies, no place to put the patients, and now they were asking them to go back a hundred years in their care of the patients and re-use needles. *It's not right that we risk their lives with used needles, after we struggle so hard to save them, it's just not right*, she thought.

Another critical shortage was anesthetics, and Brenda had been in a morning meeting where they discussed using ether for surgery again if they could not get the needed drugs. There were far fewer serious surgeries at the hospital due to the of lack of supplies, and fewer doctors who could do them.

It seemed just a short time ago, she was constantly pushing for increased use of testing, and now no nonessential tests could be performed. People, it seems, have become expendable, and she had been placed into a position of having to make decisions that affected the lives of those who came into the hospital for care. Brenda's innermost being hurt from the gut-wrenching decisions that they were forced to make.

As Brenda made her way down the patient-filled hallways, she was thankful that it was better today because there were no people waiting outside under the overhangs.

A slight tear filled the corner of her eye because she was asked to compromise everything that she was taught and believed in, and she knew that she would.

Janice was really happy that she had met Jon Pierce. Finally, she had something to focus on. Finally a purpose in her life, and she could be something she never thought she could be before. Everia was right because these past few months had definitely changed her life. Now that the new age had begun, Janice would enter into it with thanksgiving in her heart. Thanks to Jon, she was finally beginning to understand how much everyone needed to be working for the common good.

"That is the only thing that makes sense," said Jon. "Your husband will be reborn, and will have the chance to redo his life through a new body. He will have the opportunity to redo his life as the god within us all wants us to."

It was still difficult for Janice to understand why there hadn't been a baby born since the people were gone. The *Sun* did an article on what happened when the people disappeared. The babies about to be born who were still in the mother's womb were taken out. One moment the woman was pregnant, and the next, the baby was no longer there. All the young children were reported gone. There were a few reports of some children since everyone disappeared, but she hadn't heard of any children younger than ten or twelve.

Damn, I still miss Jennifer, she thought. *Would Jennifer be reborn again to her?* She heard that Kate Poosins, who lived in the next block from her, was nearly seven months pregnant at the time, and her baby left from inside her. Her neighbor told Janice that Kate never got over it. She said, "Kate just sits in her chair and stares, I think Kate's the lucky one," her neighbor said. "I wish I didn't know what was going since this all started."

Why were all the babies taken if those that were left needed to teach them how to live in the new age? she thought. She had asked Jon Pierce about it at one of their meetings. He said it was time to take back the power. Those and only those who were in tune with mother earth and their own spirit guide within would ultimately rise up and make the difference in the new world order of things. The wave of power had passed over the earth, and many, such as Janice, had received power because they were sensitive to their spirit guides. By taking hold and cleansing herself of the old like she did, she would be a great leader. Jon said children would not be born again until the purification process was complete, and then they would be born only to those who would learn to be gods.

"A great leader, he said. Me!" she mumbled. Jon said it and so did Everia. Everia said she was going to be a great teacher and leader for the people.

Her spirit guide had also demonstrated her great call. Sometimes now, she would know things even before they happened. Everia was teaching two days ago, and Janice knew what she was going to say before she ever spoke. Her spirit guide told her! She had begun to hear her guide more and more. Often now if she wasn't paying attention to her crystal, it would begin to dance, and she knew that her spirit guide wanted to talk to her.

Everia and Jon both said that she was beginning to receive from a higher spirit, and that she was now beginning to hear from her higher angel. They both told her that it was rare that anyone so new, would be given the gift of communicating with an angel that way, it was rare indeed. She would be great in the new age, when she learned to fully accept that power that was being offered her.

She found out through Everia that her angel's name was Alex. When she asked her crystal, it would begin to dance to let her know she was right. *Alex is a funny name for an angel, but he's my angel,* thought Janice as a smile crept across her face.

CHAPTER EIGHT

Woes, Start of 1/3 of the people are killed Events in the time of Revelation 9

Jim was pleased with the cabin and he was sure he could survive even an extended winter there. He had worked cutting wood and had put up enough wood to last through the winter. Now that the snow was knee deep, he was thankful he had enough stacked wood next to the cabin to keep from having to leave the cabin for long periods of time to cut more.

Standing in front of the warm fire brought back thoughts of long ago when he was a young man and he and his friends would build a fire on the beach along Lake Michigan. He lived two of his high school years near the little town of Manistee. He reminisced about the many beach parties that they had and about how much he enjoyed those rare nights when the air was so crisp, and the fire would warm him enough to take the chill from his bones. He never was in any serious trouble, but those days were always full of turmoil for him nonetheless. It seemed that, in his mind, he remembered his youth as being so frantic and always rushing to get somewhere and do something, anything.

Even after he married, he always wanted to do and see new things, and it was a sore point between him and his wife. When they went on vacation, Jim was always on the go and his wife's idea of a vacation was to be sitting by a pool or at the beach and relax. When she died several years ago, he had never found anyone whom he really could see himself marrying. It was easier for him to accept being single at this point in his life. Jim doubted that he would ever find a woman that he could let himself become that vulnerable to again, like he was to her.

As he pondered the last few years, he realized his ideas really changed when his wife died, and he was so lonely without anyone to keep him balanced, and be his sounding board. He would have to find what he had lost, and he knew that it was only through the Bible and prayer that he would be able to find where he went wrong. He would have to go back to some of the things he had taught before, and he knew that he must find what he missed.

He knew one thing in his heart, and that was that he did not do what God wanted, he did not call sin for what it is, and he was wrong. Instead Jim let those who came to his church accept and think that they were all right in whatever they wanted to do. God loves the sinner, but he hates the sin, and homosexuality, adultery, and following false religions are all sins in the eyes of God. Jim did not teach them the right way, which was as great a sin as any other, and he knew he was not in heaven because of it.

Jim had repented, and he needed to be in God's word until it filled him to where he would know that he was standing in God's perfect will.

One thing Jim did not bring was a calendar. He didn't really need it, but it could help him gauge how deep the winter was still going to be. He knew that he was in the first part of December and that winter had come very early this year. Already the snow was two and one-half feet deep, and he thought it might be attributed to the Middle East war or the volcano in Hawaii that he heard about over the car radio.

To keep the car battery charged, Jim would start the car and run it for five minutes at six o'clock every evening to listen to the local news headlines.

Jim knew from his studies that there would be two more major wars. The war of Armageddon will take place at the end of the seven years of tribulation, and Jesus will defeat Satan's army. Then, the final war as written in Ezekiel 38 and 39 of Gog and MaGog involving

Russia and the Middle East, will take place at the end of the thousand years.

Jim was amazed at how clearly Scriptures were being fulfilled right in front of his eyes. He knew that every word written, and even what was not written would be fulfilled. Even the current state of Egyptian rule and their willingness to nullify its prior peace agreement with Israel was shown clearly in Psalm 83:6-9. In Isaiah 17, the final destruction of Damascus, which started with the civil war a number of years ago, was clearly shown.

The radio had been giving a smoke index on the six o'clock news every evening. With the respiratory problems he had for years, he needed to keep abreast of the smoke index as much as possible. For the last few days, he had not heard the report, but he was sure that he had to be getting some smoke from fires or something else at the cabin because he had been so wheezy and his breathing was so labored. Jim put wet rags and towels under the doors and windows to keep at least some of the smoke out, and it seemed to help.

No matter what, the Bible is very clear that this tribulation time would last seven years. The time frame of what events would happen and when during that seven-year period was not quite as clear to him, but he was sure that with study, his understanding would become clearer. Jim thought that in the spring, there would be some who would come seeking to escape from the cities. The coming persecution would be unlike anything the world had ever known. Those who profess to be Christians, or even someone who is critical of liberal government policies, will do so at the expense of their very lives.

Sheeple – that's what they want are sheeple who blindly follow them to hell, thought Jim. The government mandated and promoted policies where everyone would be treated equally for the common good. Jim was sure so much of what has happened over the last few months, other than the people who were gone in the rapture, was deliberately brought about to subdue and control the people.

For a few short years the Lord gave the United States a reprieve with the last administration. The conservative President managed to right many things that the government put in place through the liberals reign. When the rapture took place, however, it was an almost immediate transformation changing back to the destructive liberal agenda, and the New World Order movement.

Every person in the United States is now expected to blindly believe and accept the oneness and humanism doctrines that would treat each as one, and all as one. People who refuse the government mandates were considered racist and anarchists. Jim knew there would be many killed for professing their beliefs. Never before in history and since the beginning of time would so many die, and people who kill Christians were brainwashed to think that they are doing the world a favor. He expected there would be a flood of Christians and others coming north in the spring seeking escape from the persecution in the cities.

This winter had already been good for Jim. He found what he had been missing was the same Jesus he had been preaching all these years. What he needed to do and did was to truly ask Jesus into his heart.

The Holy Spirit revealed to him why he was spared. Jim was to finish what he was called to do, and in the way he was supposed to do it. One thing that Jim knew for sure, and that was that he would tell everyone what is needed to survive eternity and go to heaven. He would show them the road to salvation as long as he had a breath within him. He would not fail again by telling people only what they want to hear no matter what the cost to him. As long as he had a breath of life within him, he would not fail to speak out.

Jim was surprised that he managed to shoot two deer and a porcupine to eat. He never did do enough hunting to consider himself to be a good shot, and he felt blessed to get enough meat to last the winter.

With the small ice-fishing pole, he did well fishing on the small lake in front of the cabin. He found that about fifty feet out from shore, just a hundred yards south of the cabin, was a sharp twenty foot deep drop off. Jim found it was good fishing there, and he had caught several walleye and a twelve-inch long yellow perch just in one day. As cold as it was he hung them from the porch ceiling, and they stayed frozen until he was ready to eat them.

He had really begun to look forward to the ice fishing, especially after he made a small portable wind block from some old lumber and cardboard he found in the shed. Keeping the wind off his back while he was fishing made all the difference in the world. Jim found that he had gotten to where he would look forward to the briskness of the cold in his lungs. For some reason that he couldn't understand, the cold seemed to let him breath better. He couldn't remember why he got away from ice fishing for so many years. It had always been a pastime he enjoyed, but over the last few years he let the enjoyment slip away from him.

Two days before, Jim had hooked a real big one. *Must have been at least four or five pounds,* he chuckled. *It was the big one that did not get away,* With the fish and the venison, it would be a comfortable winter.

Looking out of the window Jim watched the first rays of the sunrise begin to spread across the frozen lake. The pink sky and the reflection off the snow merged into a oneness in glorious color.

Jim began to pray out loud as he took in the beauty of the sunrise. "How many people are seeing this beauty for the last time today? How fast the world is falling apart around us. So many need to hear your word, Lord and what you are saying before it's too late. You Lord, have given me this second chance, and I won't let you down again. Greater is he who lives in me than he who lives in the world. To be out of this body is to be with you Lord, I praise you Jesus for your mercy on me. Father, I promise you that I will not again fail those that you lead to me to hear your word. I will preach your loving salvation, to a dying world with everything within me. Thank you Jesus for this second chance."

As he watching the sunrise over the ice on the lake, he realized that one of the reasons he never really liked Michigan at this time of year was not the cold, but rather the lack of sunshine. *How many weeks has it been? How long has it been since I saw the sun? Three or four weeks anyway. Praise God though, that I've seen the light today,* he thought to himself. And Jim smiled.

He thought that it was more overcast than what he remembered. So much dust was in the air now that there were several days that even the clouds had turned a deep red color.

Jim did not understand everything about what was taking place, but the Lord had given him revelation through the reading of his word, and Jim knew that the time was rapidly drawing to an end. Over one-half of the people in the world will die over the next few years, many facing an eternity of damnation not having that blessing of heaven. Hell is real, and heaven is real. It is only by the grace of God that you are saved, and it is free for the asking. It is very common that people spend twelve to twenty years in school preparing for work from which they retire at age sixty-five. Most people, however, don't spend any time at all preparing for their eternity. Often if they do spend any time seeking God, it is only one hour a week, on Sunday.

Many people seem to think they've made such a big sacrifice for God by going to church for an hour a week. God is like a lover and he wants you to seek him and come to him. No matter how much he loves you, he still wants to be acknowledged in your life. The only sin that Jesus did not die for was rejection of himself. In that time alone with the Lord, Jim knew beyond any doubt that the lines had been drawn in the sand for the last ultimate battle between good and evil. "I'm glad I read the back of the book, and I know who wins!" Jim yelled "Thank you, Jesus!"

Ann was lying in bed and going over some of the events that took place the last few months. She had tried to fall back asleep, but for some reason when she would awake, even after sleeping for a short time, she would be up for the day. That had always been a problem with her, even when she was young. She quietly lay on her side of the bed so as not to disturb Sue.

Ann let the barrage of thoughts go through her mind and sort itself out in the between-sleep-and-awake time. The entire world had changed, and her personal world had changed in many ways she was unhappy with. What had started out to be a tremendous opportunity to report the news as it took place had turned to now only printing what the government has declared to be important. While the government had alleviated much of the food shortages with the food lines and better distribution, they had otherwise begun to rule with an iron fist in every area of their lives.

In the beginning, Ann could see the need for government intervention and control on all levels of her life because of the mass chaos and the anarchy that had run rampant in St. Petersburg and most large cities. Now, though, it seemed the government had set an almost Gestapo rule over everything, and everywhere, and the unknown "they" were controlling every area of peoples' lives. The new world wide implementation of the G5 system seemed to fit, and was now used by the government to monitor even the everyday lives of people. There were so many regulations and rules smothering everything. She wanted to scream. She remembered the book *1984* that she had to read in high school and thought that what they were living in now was *1984* on steroids.

Damn, thought Ann, *I can't put anything in the paper that has not been cleared by Mark, and, why does he have to be armed in the office? When did it start anyway? Yes, the world was in a chaotic state, but she still should be able to tell the truth about what was happening throughout the world. It seemed as though any value that was highly prized before had now become useless and obsolete.*

News reports on the Patterson Street massacre downtown was even off limits, and they were put under a "gag-order," except for printing generalities. Few people outside of the *Sun* staff and those that lived nearby really knew what happened there. *God, how could they do that anyway?* The police cordoned off the area shortly after the latest riots had begun and tried to restore order by strong-arm control. They did it by keeping people from going in or out of the area. Most of the buildings were burned in the riots, and those not burned were looted and destroyed. *What they did with those people was wrong, it was wrong,* thought Ann. There were at least ten thousand people that lived in that area of the city, and the rumor was that the government troops shot many in the standoff.

When the government troops and police went into the area and they tried to move people onto buses to ship them to a government-run camp, all hell broke loose. Some of the people began to move back, and when one of them broke and ran, the first shots rang out and it became a slaughter. The people who resisted were shot-just shot, no trial, no being thrown in jail, just shot. The collateral damage was overwhelming, and Ann was told that at least twenty-two minors were killed. That entire area had become one that the police said they could not control, and they said they needed to move the people into the camps set up in the center of the state to bring order back into the city.

So many had died, and this is America? she thought. Since the United States was moving to a vote to be united with Europe and the one-world governmental system, things were beginning to move in a direction which Ann was sure could have never happened before. Even though there were first-hand reports of atrocities that took place in St. Petersburg, she couldn't report it. With the court gag order, she couldn't even report what had happened in her own town. *What a bunch of crap the government is dishing out*, she thought. *I'm so tired of being without everything. It's been months of this now. I just want some kind of order back in my life. I'm tired of my life the way that it is. I can't even do my job any more without doing what that government jerk wants and gives me approval to print.*

I can't believe how much my mind is wondering, thought Ann. *It's not even seven o'clock yet, and if I keep daydreaming this way I'll never get to work on time. I guess it really doesn't matter though, does it?* As Ann was thinking she was barely recognizing how cynical she was becoming.

Ann was doing better, though, since she and Sue began sharing her condo a few weeks ago. They had pooled their limited resources, and by living together, they managed to get by better than they had been by themselves. It was nice too, to have someone to be with and have someone to talk to. It helped to take away some of the anxiety and fear that she had when she lived by herself.

Sue had turned out to be a reasonably good roommate. While they didn't agree on everything, they did agree on most things that were important. Ann was scared, and she really couldn't tell anyone but Sue.

Sue was easy to get along with. Ann had not ever had a female room-mate before, but she was happy about having one now. Actually, Ann thought, she just never had been with a woman before. Physically it helped a lot to have Sue with her. While neither one of them considered themselves to be a lesbian, the physical release they found together would do until one of them found a man to be with. Ann never thought she would be with a woman, and before Sue she didn't see how anyone could enjoy this kind of relationship, but Ann admitted to herself that a man never did as much for her. She reached over and lightly caressed Sue's back and then began to get out of bed.

Ann began the mechanical movement of moving toward the kitchen and the coffee pot. The smell of the coffee would wake her. *Amazing how some habits die so hard,* she thought. Coffee had been extremely hard to get lately, and the last two-pound bag she got, she had to work out a deal with one of the guys at the government overseer's office. She knew she probably would be paying for that for a long time to come. With the way things were she would do whatever bargaining she had to, to get those things that were important to her, and so would Sue. They would do all right, and by the time things were straightened around they would come out ahead.

"Damn, I hope that the water is hot," she murmured to herself, "I hope that the electric wasn't cut back again, I really want a hot shower this morning."

Ann brushed her teeth and let the shower water run, at the same time hoping it would be hot this morning. As she finished brushing her teeth, she thought that she had better wake Sue or they would be late. As she reached into the water in the shower, she let out a loud "yes!"

It was going to be a good day……

Bill Homebecker sat in his chair on the fourteenth-floor penthouse deck, crushed from the events of the last few months. He had built his fortune from nothing, to an empire, by clawing, scraping, and destroying everything and everybody in his path to make it to the top. He looked back and remembered the weak, stupid people he had cheated and lied to the last few years, and he had to admit to himself that he could not remember them all.

Bill was a powerful man who had grown up in the construction industry, and had made a fortune by manipulating sub-contractors, and the women in his life. He built his empire by himself, in his own way, and he was proud of what he had done. Bill stood over six-feet tall and had a rugged complexion. He prided himself on looking good in a suit or coveralls, but in the last few years, it was most often in a suit that he made the most money.

Bill was one of the few who found a way to capitalize on the government backed bailouts, and became wealthy in the process. Even though most money sources dried up during the 2008 housing meltdown, he found private sources that allowed him to make both him, and them money.

He was very creative and developed a way that he could back projects with collateral he built up over the years in order to protect his money people. His sources made a high royalty, and he got the construction contracts. It wasn't perfect, and it was a lot of work, but he was one of a few that made a good living even through hard economic times.

He finally reached his dream. He finally was a multimillionaire, and at least he could still say that even though he could not get to his money from the bank. The news from his private banking sources, though, was crushing to him. The money stream had been cut off, the notes he had with them were called, and just like that he was bankrupt. His bank had not reopened, and he no longer had any access to his money, and no one had the foggiest notion when it would be freed up again.

If only he had not put so much into the Applegate Commerce Industrial Park complex. A sure winner, he thought, a sure winner. He had tentative contracts for enough sales to cover everything he had put out, and he let it all ride on the next project. *Just one more project, I always needed just one more*, he thought.

The money had brought him everything he ever wanted: a cigarette boat, sports cars, power over people-everything. He had beautiful women who would come at his beckon call, and he was known as the most eligible bachelor around. With all that façade, there was no one who knew how very alone he was. What he found out was that without his money, and his things, he was alone and hollow inside. He had a good life, he had it all. Who was it that said, *"The one who dies with the most toys wins?"*

Bill walked to the edge of the penthouse wall and looked over. Many of the buildings he could see in the distance were ones he built. Much of the town was his, but now, he was, in a few short months, totally bankrupt, and he could see no way back. *It isn't fair, it just isn't.*

Bill slowly surveyed the town, and looked back across the deck. The blacks of his eyes flinched just so slightly, and a darkness that could barely be seen, gently, quietly, covered him.

He didn't hesitate. Just one step….. and it was over.

Brenda was breathing a guarded sigh of relief because she was feeling they had gotten over the worst of the medicine shortages. The past months had been a living hell, and finally, they had gotten over the hump and were beginning to see a shining light on the other side. So many people had died in such a short time, and she was beginning to feel the long-term effects of the never-ending people looking to her for their healing.

They were so short of everything, but it was the normal shortages that they had gotten used to. Brenda was thankful though, they didn't have to sterilize the needles and reuse them as they thought they were going to be forced to do just a short time ago. A shipment came in before they had implemented the policy.

The patient loads they were getting in now were more like what they had before the world fell apart. They had begun to see an increase, however, in the number of people that were having difficulty in breathing because of the large amounts of smoke and dust in the air. Thank God they were not in an area where the fallout was bad, that would only complicate things and make them worse. The older patients were by far the worst off. They typically had the most breathing problems anyway, and the number of respiratory problems had been increasing daily. The policy hadn't changed yet, and until the supplies increased and the patient load greatly decreased, they would still be under a no heroics policy for anyone over sixty. So many elderly would not come to the hospital to seek treatment.

What concerned Brenda more than the respiratory problems they were seeing, was the outbreak of cholera. They had three new cases of cholera in the last week alone. In all her years of being a nurse, she had never seen even one case of cholera. She knew that if the water supplies and food situation did not improve, then this was only the beginning of what was to come. Cholera......... Cholera who would have ever thought there could be an outbreak of cholera looming in Clearwater, Florida?

Brenda had long ago given up on having what others considered a normal life. After her husband, Doug, died a few years ago, she had never remarried and it had become her work that kept her going. She had several chances to remarry, but she never was excited over any man enough to want to give up her life for the sake of his. She had gotten where she actually preferred to live alone. Now she was lost in this never-never land in the hospital that was a self-imposed trap that she enjoyed more than anything else in her life.

The hospital treated her well, and she was fed well at work. She didn't even have to go out of the hospital for anything, which was just as well. The mess and masses of people coming in from the outside world had convinced her that the most normal thing there was in life was to be in the hospital. There was nothing that even resembled a normal life anymore outside of the emergency room.

Several of her staff had disappeared in the gone, and they had been short staffed since. She was so glad that now, they seemingly were going to be ok if the supplies could keep up with what was needed in the emergency room. When the administrator would authorize it, she would hire the nurses she needed to bring the staffing back up to a normal balance. If the smoke from Hawaii let up and the water lines were repaired, Brenda knew they could make it through the crisis and they would soon be all right.

"*Cholera, who would have believed it?*" she thought.

CHAPTER NINE

Three plagues of fire, smoke, and sulfur
Events in the time of Revelation 9

Janice was beginning to stir. She had a difficult time sleeping. She sealed off the door and window bottoms with wet towels to keep out the dust, but it still seemed to find its way in. The continuous dust and smoke seemed to be bringing back the touch of asthma she had as a child and was causing her breathing problems.

"Damn, no man, no food, no kids, no electric, no car, no nothing. I'm sick of this. I need a change. Alex, I need you now!" she spoke out loud. When she spoke, the crystal in the window began to dance. *Thank God there's something I can rely on,* she thought. At least Alex wouldn't let her down.

Everia took Janice under her wing to teach and train her. She told Janice she was given the gift that's for sure, but she still had to learn how to use it. Janice went to a few meetings with Everia, and Everia was showing her the ropes. "There is so much to learn, Everia told her, and I'll teach you one step at a time." That was like Babe Ruth teaching you how to bat. She would learn from the best!

When Everia couldn't go, she would go with Jon. Jon was a big help as well. He told her he appreciated the fact that she was so eager to learn and he would be happy to teach her everything he could. What Janice found out from him is how broad based the New Age movement really is. There were so many areas of belief that seemingly jelled together to make a whole, and make sense. Janice met several people who were like Everia-psychics and clairvoyants. The list of talent at the meetings was tremendous, and many of the people she met were incredibly gifted and versatile.

Janice was being taught how to read tarot cards with accuracy, and how Alex, her spirit guide, would help her learn to read them better. She was excited because she was learning so much about so many different areas of the spirit world. The meetings offered the backdrop of diversity for what she wanted to learn. After many hours, and much study, Janice was beginning to better understand what would happen to the world in the very near future.

They often began by praying to Mother Goddess Earth. Janice learned the planet is a living intelligent being, which is in communication with the hierarchy of ascended masters of the universe. The humans, who accept their god within, are sensory extensions of the living planet. Janice was excited to learn there really is reincarnation, and because of that, death is very insignificant. Dead souls are recycled and come back as another sensory extension of the living earth.

All of us are part of god, she learned. If one says audibly, "I am god" the sound vibrations align the body energies to a higher attunement. You are allowed to say "I am god" as often as you want, and to love yourself is to love god, we are our own creators. Everyone is god. *There is so much to learn,* she thought. Each soul is its own god.

One night, late into the fair, Everia took her to see a very special man, a Bhutanese Lama who began to levitate above the ground by a supernatural power. He went into a deep trance for nearly thirty minutes and then began to rise off the floor. Everia told her he was in tune to his higher unlimited self, his higher unlimited soul. He was tuned in to the unlimited one who teaches and guides him into a higher-and-higher plane of consciousness, through each reincarnation. According to Everia, he was born many, many times, and unlike most of us, he learned from his past lives. Rayule was his name.

Rayule was to teach the next day, and Janice was excited about going to the class. She asked Jon if he would take her. Together, they learned so much. Rayule knew the very depths of the beginning.

"Reality is whatever you imagine or desire it to be," Rayule said. "There is no right or wrong. There is neither good nor evil. Even murder is not wrong or evil. The person who commits murder, doesn't need to be punished by being put into prison, he is going to be punished for eons to come because he is going to live with that guilt, and it will set him back in his evolvement for many ages to come. Man is divine and the master of his own destiny. Who needs worship? Indeed you do, and who needs to save you? You do, and indeed who can answer your prayers? You can." Rayule went on for hours with his teaching, and Janice grasped at everything he said in her eagerness to learn.

Janice found out that what happened when the people disappeared happened so the ones who are left can get on with ushering in the New World Order. Even the new economy that is being put into place now will be one where all people will be treated fairly. Janice found out that the new world would be run in a fair and equitable way through humanism philosophies, and recognizing the value of every human being.

"Reality is what you imagine or desire it to be, Rayule said. There are some, though, who cannot still believe what has come forth for this time, those will need to be aborted like a defective child so the result will not be a monster. Evolution is good but not nice. Only the good can evolve, those who can believe they are gods can evolve and change. Those who are lower, and are not god centered will not survive to inherit the powers of a universal species. The destructive remaining ones must be eliminated from the body. We come to bring death to those who are unable to know god, for if they do not recognize they are gods they must be taken from our midst before they destroy the new age and the mother planet. Those who, as a group, pose the biggest threat to the world at peace are the Christians and Jews. Those who believe a higher force created them, and would seek to push their views onto the rest of us-are to be feared. When they are destroyed, you will see a world the way it was intended to be. Peace and harmony will reign, and every person will have a fair economy to work from."

Rayule told her he could see that her spirit guide wanted to teach her much. She would lead many if she would let her guide lead her to all things. After he said his good-byes to the others, she and Jon left.

"I have so much to learn, Jon," she said, "so much to learn." Her mind drifted in thought to a day long ago, when she and her husband, Jerry, brought their daughter Jennifer home. She remembered how quiet that first moment was when Jennifer first slept through the night. She still missed those quiet moments.

Jim walked onto the lake to spud a hole in the ice. *Sure is cold,* he thought. *The smoke, I would think the smoke would make it warmer but it doesn't.* Jim cleared out the loose ice and put his favorite jig popper on the line.

He was thinking about the last few months as he automatically began to move his line up and down to attract the fish. It wasn't long before a fish tugged on his line and Jim instinctively jerked the pole upward to set the hook. *It's a good one,* he thought. As he pulled it through the ice he saw a distant lone figure walking toward him from the south. *It begins. It now begins. The battle has now started,* thought Jim.

The clouds were so gray and the man so black against the snow.

The man strode closer. The dirt and the cold and the never-ending smoke in the air streaked his face. He was tall and lanky, and the hat he wore appeared two sizes too small, revealing his balding blond hair. The sadness and hurt the man had been through clearly showed in his eyes. Jim could readily see he was hurting and the sunken, hollow look of his face showed he had not eaten well for a while now.

"My name is Jim," he said to the man. "A couple more of these, and we'll have enough for supper if you would like to stay."

"Thank you. My name is Chris, and I would be much obliged. I'm really hungry and cold. Any help would be a blessing."

Chinney woke early and was up for the day. The last eight months were very hard, but he was doing okay. Winter was early and very cold. The food from the pantry, and the fish he managed to catch through the ice was enough for him to get through the winter, and he was very thankful.

He looked forward to the daily ritual of going onto the lake and fishing through the ice. It was only two weeks now that he really trusted the ice as being thick enough to walk on. He usually managed to catch enough fish so that he could eat fish nearly every night. He felt proud of himself for learning how to fish and because he knew he was doing well for a homeboy.

Chinney figured out what to do and how to hook up the chimney flue to get the wood stove working. He found a metal cover in the kitchen, which he thought looked like an old pie plate covering a hole in the chimney behind it. He hooked the stovepipe from the back of the stove to it, and it worked.

Getting the stove in the house from the garage was the hardest part because it was so heavy. He guessed it weighed close to a hundred and fifty pounds. He finally moved it inch-by-inch by putting a two by four under a corner and prying it up. Even using the leverage of the two by four, he could only move it three or four inches at a time. It took him almost two hours of struggling to move it into the kitchen. He was not at all sure why the stove was in the garage, but he was glad it was there, and it worked.

The old man had enough wood stacked up to easily last the next two years or more. Chinney was thankful he didn't have to spend all his time gathering wood. He found the stove gave off enough heat to keep the entire house comfortable when he closed the bedroom and porch doors.

He liked sleeping where it was cool, so the cold bedroom felt good to him. He wasn't sure why, but he always liked to sleep in the nude. His habit was from no particular reason he was aware of, but it was more comfortable to him to sleep without clothes. Even on the coldest days, the house was warm enough to be comfortable without a coat.

After the garage door was opened for several days, Chinney finally got past the smell and went to see the man in the car. As near as he could tell, the man must have killed himself. The car key was in the on position, and the garage door was locked from the inside. Chinney wondered what happened to the old man. He thought maybe his wife was one of the ones who were raptured or maybe she died and the man couldn't stand being alone. He had no way to be sure.

By the old mail he found, Chinney knew the man's name was Emil and his wife's name was Brenda, Emil and Brenda Longley. Chinney thought of trying to bury him, but instead he just covered the car with an old tarp he found in the corner of the garage. Emil was old, but it was so sad the way he died. He had to be all alone and full of hurt. He could understand how hurt Emil could have been if his wife disappeared because of how much hurt he still felt when he thought of Ginna. He still missed Ginna more than he could ever imagine possible.

The time he was alone was good for Chinney, and he learned a tremendous amount this winter. His mother was right. He now knew how right she was. He read the Bible through once from Genesis to Revelation, and he read the New Testament through three times already. It took a while, but the more he read, the more he understood of what mama tried to tell him when he was growing up. He knew now what she said was right. This was the time of the end, and he would have to do a lot to be able to see mama and Cappi again. He was sure Jesus came for them. His mama tried to explain everything to him as best she knew. What she said was the Antichrist was on the earth, and he would probably be the leader of the one-world government. The Antichrist would have great power over the richest nations especially, but would be an influence and in control worldwide.

Chinney felt that he needed to try to get where he would be with some Christians if he could find any who could help better explain to him what God would have him do in these times. Until he found other Christians, his mama told him to read his Bible all the time and pray for guidance, and God would help him to understand through his Holy Spirit. Mama told him very clear that he had to take one step to God, and God would take one step to him. God's steps are big steps though, and if he kept reading and praying, very soon he would begin to know God, and Jesus would be his friend.

Mama said, "What Jesus wants is what any good friend needs, and that is time with him. Jesus wants you to be so vulnerable to him that you have to depend on him, and trust in him for everything just like you would your closest friend. "Remember Ginna?" she said. "Remember how you trusted her with the deepest things inside? If you tell your deepest things to Jesus then he will tell you things too, and you will become friends, close friends like you were with her. Remember too that, just like Ginna, if you don't treat Jesus right, you can hurt him. He can be easily bruised and you can hurt his Spirit like you could with Ginna, and Ginna could with you. When you find the friend in Jesus, you will never be alone again, and you won't have to worry about being led wrong because Jesus will guide you, and his Spirit will show you all things to keep you safe. You need to take the first step and ask him to show you and teach you, and he will."

"Chinney, Jesus said to seek first the kingdom of heaven, and that is what you must do. When you do, you will see clearly nothing else matters. Seek him first!"

Chinney was reading the Bible by candlelight, and his mama's words echoed in him. He was feeling so lonely. All the reading he was doing was good, but still he had a desire to talk to someone. He said out loud, "Are you with me, Jesus?"

The voice of Jesus almost yelled inside him and said, "Yes, I am here, I will never leave you nor forsake you Chinney."

Tears of joy streaked unashamed down Chinney's face. From that moment on Chinney would never be the same.

A mighty wind of God was blowing through the land, and the people who refused now would have no other chance. Just as strong as the fire of God which burned on the inside of the people who accepted

Christ, there were many openly condemning anyone who believed. A clear line was drawn between good and evil.

The persecution of the church was growing louder each day. There were many people accusing the churches of serving illegally stolen food, and were saying the church was subverting people to anarchy. The government and many outside of the church blamed the churches for everything that had gone wrong with the world. They blamed them for the Middle East war, the lack of food, and everything the government was not providing. In many areas churches went underground because of the open attacks, and murders of the churchgoers. New York and southern California were especially dangerous. He couldn't imagine the horrors of what must be taking place there.

Throughout all the reports though were the underlying great expressions of joy and peace that the Christians were showing, even when they were persecuted. Jeremie and all who were born again knew that to be out of their body was to be with the Lord.

The angel of the Lord came to him again three nights ago. Jeremie wasn't sure if the angel came to him in person or in a dream. The angel told him to appoint three who had been shown favor by the Lord Jesus. He was to set up a schedule for them to teach and preach in shifts around the clock. All who would come would hear the word of the Lord, and the Jewish community needed to know Jesus was the Messiah they had been waiting for.

One of his assistants, Franklin, was one of the chosen. He was not as knowledgeable as the other two, but he more than made up for it with his enthusiasm and excitement. Several had come to know the Lord through him. Jeremie was very pleased because many who were coming were from the Jewish community, and what he was called to do was being accomplished.

As word of the hope of salvation through the Gospel of the Lord Jesus Christ began to spread, the number of people grew daily.

Jeremie knew he was fulfilling the word given him by the angel of God.

Ann was thankful her life was finally beginning to take on a somewhat normal everyday feel. There were areas she had struggled with that she could actually see were beginning to improve. The food allotment she and Sue received was increased slightly and raised from what had been just enough to keep alive, and they had hamburger last week. With Sue's and her allotment together, they could actually vary their meals.

The problems the United States faced in some of the larger cities, was no comparison to what Russia had become. The border countries could not handle their own hungry and injured, and found it impossible to deal with the Russian emigrants. The people from Russia who came to the border for help were not allowed to enter, and it was reported they were brutally shot if they tried.

Ann picked up the paper from the day before and looked again at the picture of a boy who was burned so badly that all his skin hung in layers from his body. He was stripped of all his clothes, and was clearly starving. The boy had clearly been burned and was trying to climb a barbed-wire fence into Europe to get help and was shot down by the European-border guards. The boy appeared to be about twelve or thirteen years old. As hardened as everyone became over the past eight months, the picture of the boy hanging from the barbed wire broke her heart.

Ann was happy Washington's media Czar's appointee Mark, wouldn't be around trying to run the paper for the next two weeks. She was relieved that he was sent to a two-week seminar and training program. Finally she could see they were doing what government people have always done best-nothing. *"I'm glad that control freak is out of here,"* she thought. The only government functions the paper contended with now were to print the food-line times and the rationing schedules. Although few people had work, the food lines and government work programs were helping most people survive.

Ann thought back to what she remembered reading about the government-work programs of the thirties. From what she remembered about the old CCC work programs, the new program Washington had put into place was very similar.

The government announced they would open all the land currently in farm food banks, and anyone who needed work would be given food and temporary housing on the farms. Farm co-ops were being set up throughout the United States, and to Ann, it seemed that, that was a good thing and could help with the severe food shortages if they could logistically get the food to market.

Jerry interrupted Ann's thoughts as he stepped through the door.

"Hi," said Jerry. "I've got this copy you wanted."

"Thanks, Jerry, I think we'll be able to use it in today's issue. How's Sandy doing?"

"Not too good. She's really paranoid about the fallout from Japan, and she's got the house sealed off from top to bottom with everything we own. She's really been freaked about it. She won't listen to me about most of the radiation being way up north and just falling on the northern most states. You know, and I know, Ann, not much radiation is falling here, but she won't listen to me."

"Yeah, we're pretty lucky, we'll always have the possibility of radiation, but it looks like we're safer here than anywhere else in the United States," said Ann. "At least we're as safe as anyone can be now. Did you hear they think that some radioactivity will be spread throughout the world in a matter of two years? Even in Alaska and northern Canada it doesn't look as bad as what they thought it would be initially. The reports released by Washington say people can survive even the worst radiation if they don't go outside for extended periods of time. We just published that the amount of radiation a person gets here in Florida, is no more than it used to be with the old radon watches from the fifties. It's really pretty safe here. And if it's not safe, what can we do about it anyway? I'm more worried about the riots, or being shot by some crazy than I am about radiation."

"Me too," said Jerry. "But Sandy is not doing well with it. She can see robbers, and that bothers her, but she can't see radiation, and that frightens her more. I guess everyone is spooked about something now."

"Hey Jerry, you heard the one about the farmer's daughter?"

"You're bad Ann! So you're the one who started that, you mean the one with the watermelon patch, don't you? I knew I loved you for a reason!" laughed Jerry.

"I wish you would, said Ann. "But I somehow don't think Sandy would be too happy about that! If any of your friends are single and horny, give them my name, will you? It's always the good ones who are married. I'll tell you in advance, though, that I'll just about settle for anyone right now."

"Ann, I'll do you one better than that. I'll write your name on every john wall in town. You'll be famous before your time," Jerry chuckled.

"Well, the way I'm feeling right now, if I'm not famous yet, I want to be. Thanks Jerry!" said Ann.

"You got it kid," Jerry laughingly said as he left the office.

"Cute butt, it's too bad he's married," thought Ann. *But the good ones always are."*

Ann began to read the copy Jerry brought in.

The United Nations and Palestine have agreed to allow the rebuilding of the Jewish Temple of Solomon, on the Temple Mount in Jerusalem. It was part of the peace agreement but the details took a while to complete. The Temple is to be located on the original site, which is some forty feet away from the outside wall of the Dome on the Rock. The space between the two is to be under the United Nations jurisdiction through the newly created Council of the Court of Coexistence – the CCC. The CCC will bring all world religions together under an interfaith movement in order to break down the religious divisions that are further exasperating the World's massive problems. The Roman Catholic Church would be the first oversight leader of the Council, and the board has leaders in place from every major religion. Every four years, the council will vote in another leader.

All religions within the world will be brought together to create a spirit of oneness and harmony. They were brought together to help bring about the peace the world will need for its very survival going into the next millennium. Instead of focusing on differences, the common oneness was stressed. At least three hundred thousand people died in the 16 day war between Israel and Iran. The world will never really know the real number of dead, but it is felt this peace accord will ease the tension, and keep it from escalating again.

At a joint UN council meeting the CCC spokesman made the following statement: "The new age has dawned. The world has under gone a change of mystical proportions, and now the gods of the universe have joined together all who are left, to rebuild the world in peace and harmony."

"Whew, powerful goofy statement," thought Ann.

Ann couldn't believe that the new official office of the new CCC created by and under the UN officially sanctioned the statement. It was the most bizarre statement she had ever read from a church.

The article went on to say the world would be filled with joy going into the future. The people would begin to learn of their own divinity and rule over their own destinies. Even the Roman Catholic Church endorsed the Council of the Court of Coexistence as being truly what God intended. The pope stated that the new CCC formed a bond between all nations and peoples to express the love of God in their own ways and in peace, and he endorsed the oneness and unity of mankind entering a time of peaceful co-existence with God as the head.

Ann began to remember a piece she did on the Chrislam movement a while back.

"Seems eons ago," she thought. She tried to remember what it said, and what she remembered it was very much the same as what the CCC was doing. She remembered that when she first read about Chrislam, she thought that for some reason, they took out the cross when they removed the T from the name of Christ but left Islam in it without any change. To have the Roman Catholic Church joined with Muslims, Buddhists, and every other religion seemed a real far out idea.

"I don't care what anyone wants to believe, I hope it brings peace to the world," thought Ann. *"I'm so sick of the way things are right now. I am glad about one thing though, and that's the stupid appointed government media jerk Mark, we had in here for a while is gone. If the government stays away from me, I can print every version of every religion that comes across my desk, and everyone can believe what they want to believe."*

Ann's thoughts were interrupted when Sue knocked on her doorjamb.

"Hi Ann," said Sue. "Gotta minute?"

"I got a bunch of minutes for you, Sue. If I can get out a little early, would you like to take a walk on the beach? It looks like we'll have something other than rain for a change. It's been a while since we've had a dry day to walk on the sand, and the smoke count is way down today, so we won't choke," said Ann.

"I'd like that! I'd like it a lot! It works for me!" said Sue excitedly.

"Great! I'll try to get out of here by four-thirty or so. If you go back to the apartment and get my suit, and come back for me, we can leave right from here. Maybe we can even get something for dinner and cook it at the beach. I know! The little park on Sand Key has a shelter with a charcoal cooker, I mean grill, and it's got a great beach," said Ann.

"Yeah, I'd like that! said Sue. "I'm going to leave in about an hour. I'll stop back with the stuff and pick you up."

"Great, what was it you wanted to tell me anyway? I got so excited about thinking of getting out of here I didn't give you a chance to talk," said Ann.

"Wait until you hear this! said Sue. "I picked up a treat to share, something we haven't had in a long time. John in marketing traded me chocolate for the can of cherries we have in the cupboard! Hell, we don't have anything to make a pie with anyway, and I can't cook, and you don't like to. He had a whole bag of Snickers in his cupboard! Can you believe it? It's been so long time since we had any chocolate. We have desert for our picnic!"

"Leave it to John. Are you sure all you had to trade was that can of cherries? He never has impressed me as someone who will be a nice guy for nothing," said Ann.

"That's all, I swear it!" laughed Sue. "Course, I don't have it in my hot little hands yet either!"

"Just get the Snickers any way you have to, and leave me so I can get back to work before I get too frustrated to do anything. Get outta here!" Ann laughed. "Let me finish this up and I'll see you later."

Ann quickly went back to her reading to finish up for the day.

CHAPTER TEN

THE CABIN
Events in the time of Revelation 10

Jim was pleased the stranger came. His name was Chris Kerner and was originally from Toledo.

He was traveling with two others to try to get away from the death and fighting and find a safe place away from the cities. They made it as far as Mackinaw City near the Bridge and separated to search for supplies. Chris went one way, and his friends went the other.

Chris had little success finding anything they could use because most of the businesses were closed and boarded up. The few stores he found open had little he could use, and he walked back to meet his friends again. As he approached the corner where they agreed to meet, he could see police had stopped both of his friends for questioning. He watched from a distance as they were loaded into a police car in handcuffs. He never saw them again.

He walked away trying to be as inconspicuous as possible and saw a semi being loaded that was heading to Northern Michigan. Chris went to the driver, and they made an agreement for passage, and Chris paid him everything he had left to go across the Mackinac bridge to St. Ignace. He stowed away behind some boxes. The driver of the truck pulled over just outside of ST. Ignace and let Chris out. Chris thanked him and walked quickly into the woods near the road. The driver told Chris as he was walking away to be watching overhead because the government had drones in the area, and to keep away from the towns.

It was the first of November when he first found the cabin across the lake from Jim's. He lived on what he found in the cabin and what he could steal from the small town five miles away. His food supplies were nearly gone, and when he saw Jim on the ice he hoped Jim might be able to help him.

Jim began to cook some of the fish he caught, and he was extremely excited and happy to have someone to talk to. They were both happy being together and talked constantly. Jim was glad he had caught a number of fish and had a can of corn to go with it, because Chris was so very hungry. Chris and Jim both needed to talk, and they talked without stopping throughout the evening. Being able to just talk to another human being was something Jim needed, and missed so much.

Chris was an architect in Toledo, and had worked for the firm of Johnson and Carl Inc. for the last four years. Chris was unsure why he and his friends decided to come to Upper Michigan after the people were gone. Chris just knew they had to get away from what was taking place in Toledo. He told Jim many stories about what he saw and what happened to him. What he told Jim convinced him even more the rapture had indeed taken place.

"Jim, my wife before she died, was in her ninth month of pregnancy, and I took her to the hospital because she began to go into labor. She was full term, and the baby was coming no matter what. We went to the hospital emergency room, and they took her to the delivery room as soon as we got there. I went in with her, to be with her when the baby was born. That was about two o'clock or so in the morning. Peg was in labor for somewhere around three hours, and the contractions were getting closer and closer to where the baby was ready to be born. The doctor told her, 'Just a little more. Just a little more. Push again,' he said. Push again!"

"Then this bright light filled the delivery room, and the baby just disappeared! Right from inside her body! Jim, Peg just began to scream and scream. She finally went silent and for days wouldn't eat, she wouldn't say anything, in fact she never spoke again. That's when all hell broke loose. I'll never forget what happened then. They came in about nine o'clock, or so and said I had to move my wife home, she was stable and she would have to go home to recuperate. They said there were so many injured people coming in they needed the bed. It was a case of extreme emergency. They gave me some pills to help her rest and helped me get her into the car. The hospital was so overloaded by then we could hardly get down the halls because of the people hurt and dying. Peg never spoke again.

"After I got her into the car and took her home I put her to bed. I thought she was asleep. I went to the couch and lay down to try to rest. When I got up a couple of hours later, she was dead. Peg must have got up and found the pills the doctor gave me, and she took the entire bottle. I called the ambulance and they told me it would be at least two or three hours before they could come and if she was dead, I would have to wait for them for at least twenty-four hours. Jim, the baby was just taken out of her body!"

"I know," said Jim." I know. Your baby is one of the blessed ones. The baby is with Jesus."

"I want to believe that." said Chris. "The whole world is upside down, and now with this damn smoke in the air all the time. Did you hear Iran and Israel got into it, and Israel never once got any major hits? Iran never even hit Israel with even one large missile. If they did get any missiles up, the Israeli defense system took them out. They figure Iran got hit with at least three nuclear missiles, and some of them appear to have had multi-warheads. Iran is still smoking. The fallout is what we must be getting now and is a combination of Hawaii, Iran and the Japan nuclear reactor. I'm sure that this must be radioactive."

"Yeah," said Jim. "We need to stay inside to keep away from some of it as much as possible. I'm allergic to smoke, and I've been having a lot of problems breathing. I have to be careful when I'm outside, and I've only been going out on the days when the smoke index update from WKLZ is low. A lot of smoke we have right now, though, they are saying is the smoke and debris from the island off Hawaii."

"Do you think we can survive this at all?" asked Chris. "I'm so tired of my life this way. Everything I ever cared for in my life has been destroyed. Peg was everything to me, and our baby, I never even got to hold it. I never even knew if it was a boy or a girl. We told them when we had the ultra sound done, we didn't want to know the sex, and wanted to be surprised."

Chris was clearly shaken by the last few months, and Jim knew he needed to talk out his deep hurts. Jim knew Chris would have to go through a healing process, and he would just let him talk over the next few days and let that healing process begin.

"Chris, there is a way we can survive eternity, but we may very well die before this is over. We can, however, help a lot of others before we do die, those who are going to come the first of spring. I'm going to tell you what happened, and, Chris I'll show you how you can be with your baby and Peg, God willing, once again. You see Chris, the four horseman of the apocalypse are on the earth right now. Have you ever heard of them?"

"Yes," said Chris. "I think I heard about them in church. My wife and I would go sometimes. Actually, we only went Christmas and Easter and some-times in between, when her parents would visit. Just before my baby disappeared, the pastor was talking about Jesus coming soon and we needed to be ready. He always seemed like a nice guy and had a good service."

"And what happened to the pastor, Chris? Do you know? Did you ever see him again after your wife died?" asked Jim.

"No, I tried to get hold of him after the baby disappeared, and he was gone. I guess he was anyway, I went over there, and his house was open, and no one was home. When I got there, a man from the church told me it was empty and they thought he and his wife disappeared."

"Yes," said Jim. "Where do you think they went? Did the man at the church know where they were or where they had gone to?"

"No, he didn't. He was pretty upset too. Apparently, someone in his family disappeared as well. That's where I met Josh and Sammy, the two men I came up here with. They convinced me we needed to get away from Toledo before it got worse. That's how I ended up here," said Chris.

"Chris, everything I've heard leads me to believe we are in what the Bible calls the tribulation period. The Antichrist will be in power shortly, and the four horsemen have been released to run across the earth. Do you know who the four horsemen are?" said Jim.

"No," said Chris. "I never studied the Bible. I do remember the pastor said one of them was death."

"That's one of them," said Jim. "The first Horseman is the Antichrist. The Antichrist rides the white horse. He has been loosened on the earth to bring destruction to those who would follow him. He is the leader of the New World Order and the first world leader. In Revelation Chapter 13 and Chapter 17 the economy and the events, which will give rise to the Antichrist is clearly described. When we read it you'll see what is being described is similar to the European socialist type of government monetary system. The European Unity agreement is a prototype of what is being set up across the world under the New World Order system."

"I only have the news I get from my six o'clock news radio report, but I know I'm right. The new European Unity is encompassing the old Roman Empire, which is what it needs to be according to the Bible. At the head of that empire is the Antichrist, he is the one who we will find out brokered the peace agreement with Israel and the surrounding countries after the war with Iran and Syria ended."

"Chris, we probably won't know for sure who the Antichrist is until he goes into the temple in Jerusalem and declares himself to be god, unless we hear one of the leaders, dies or is killed, and miraculously rises from the dead. The Antichrist is described in the Bible as a very smooth statesman who will woo the people who are tired of war and are desperately seeking peace.

Jim continued, "Halfway through the tribulation time the Antichrist will go into Israel and declare himself to be god in the temple that will soon be rebuilt in Jerusalem. When the Middle East war broke loose it set the stage for the Antichrist. He is one of the leaders who structured agreements for the peace accord."

"The second rider is the one who comes on a red horse. This is the ability to make war. There will be wars over the earth for the next six-plus years. We've already seen the nation of Iran, and Syria destroyed, and there will be others as well," said Jim.

"Reports on Iran, which have been pretty limited, are that nearly all major military sites in Iran are now completely unusable. Tehran is nothing more than a large crater and many military strongholds were totally destroyed as well. Iran, for all her military might, could not stop any of the Israeli attacks and missiles from coming in. Israel on the other hand, never had one of the large Iranian missiles hit their soil. That small country by itself totally destroyed one of the strongest countries in the Middle East!" said Chris.

"Yes," said Jim. "Many of the wars and conflicts going on now have started because of the third rider. The third rider is Famine, and Famine rides the black horse. The reason there are so many wars and conflicts world-wide is, at least partially, because people are desperate and are starving to death. Food, in the middle of a famine is worth more than gold or silver. It's amazing how hunger brings everything into a different perspective. If you don't have enough to eat, everything else you do have means nothing."

"You're right," said Chris. "Sitting across the lake with no way to fish and very little food, I was getting close to being totally desperate myself.

"The last horseman is the one you probably heard about, the rider on the pale horse," said Jim. "The rider is Death, and he is accompanied by Hell. You can see what he has done all across the globe. How many millions of people do you think have died since this whole thing started, since your baby was taken? Millions, hundreds of millions, maybe even a billion or more? Death is running rampant on the face of the earth, and you will not see an end to death until the end of the seven-year tribulation, when Jesus returns to rule the earth."

"The war that will take place towards the end of the seven-year tribulation is called the battle of Armageddon. It will take place before the tribulation time ends."

"The Bible says Jesus will return with those who were raptured, and for the next thousand years will rule the earth with a rod of iron. We are seeing the end of the world as we know it unfolding before our very eyes. According to the Bible, over one-half of the people will die in the next six years time! Chris, that's about *three and one-half billion people* in this seven-year tribulation time. It's because of the rider on the pale horse, and with him comes Hell. Chris, many of the people who have died will go to hell for all eternity, all eternity!"

"Chris, I was a pastor, and I didn't make it! The word tells us we must be born again, and Chris, I was not. I spoke the word, but I didn't believe a lot of it in my heart. I believed anyone who would come to my church would be saved, and I never preached about anything but a loving, all-forgiving God. He is all loving, and forgiving, but there is also something he wants from us and something he expects from us. He wants us to seek him as we would a lover. Chris, if you lived with your wife, and never spoke to her or got to know her intimately, what kind of relationship would the two of you have had?"

"Not a very good one, I'm sure," said Chris. "I always thought my wife and I had a really good relationship. I mean we didn't fight much, and I loved her more than I could ever imagine loving another person. She was everything to me."

"I know she was," said Jim. "Imagine what it would have been like if you didn't love her enough to speak to her or to take time with her doing those things you knew were important to her. Would you have had any kind of relationship with her at all?"

"No," said Chris. I suppose it would have been pretty fruitless to even be in that kind of relationship. Really, we wouldn't have had any reason to be together at all if we didn't communicate."

"Well Chris it's the same with God. If we don't take the time to know him and what he likes and wants from us, we cannot expect to have a relationship with him that would be meaningful to him or us. God does not hate a person who has sinned against him, but he hates the sin and those who would continue to sin after they declared they accepted Jesus as their savior do not develop that relationship like you did with your wife. Jesus wants to have you seek him and love him just like you sought after your wife and loved her. The only way that happens with God is when you read his word and study it, and communicate to him through prayer."

Those who were raptured were the ones who learned to love God for the love he first gave them. Those who sought him in every way they could, those who loved him and were re-born and whose spirits united with his, were the ones who were raptured. The Bible says we must be born again to enter into the kingdom of heaven, and, Chris, the good news is we still can do that!"

"The highest form of communion with God is communication, direct communication. It begins by prayer and develops into a wonderful relationship, if you first seek him."

"There is so much I have to do and part of what I have to do is to show and teach others where I made my mistakes so they can be saved too, continued Jim. Chris, there is going to be another rapture in the next few years and I don't want to be left here again. What the world has gone through since your wife died, is nothing compared to what will happen after the Antichrist openly declares he is god."

"Chris, what we know is that what took place is commonly called the rapture of the church. I have been studying everything I had for reference and studying my Bible since I came up here. I really missed it, but I can show you where I believe the Bible says we are to be in another rapture or taking away in Revelation 15. I want to be on that ticket out. I missed it once and God willing I'll not miss it again!" Here, let me read the scripture. Jim opened his Bible and turned to Revelation to read:

> [2] And I saw what looked like a sea of glass mixed with fire and, standing beside the sea, those who had been victorious over the beast and his image and over the number of his name. They held harps given them by God [3] and sang the song of Moses the servant of God and the song of the Lamb: (NIV)

"Chris the victorious ones, the people who are victorious over the beast and its image and the number of his name is us. We are in that time along with the Jewish people right now. The Word says those who are victorious will sing the song of Moses and of the Lamb. The reference to the song of Moses, I believe Chris, are the Jewish people whose eyes soon will be opened and realize Jesus is the Messiah they have been waiting for. Those who sing the song of the Lamb, which refers to Jesus, includes the saints who survive the tribulation time, and do not take the mark of the beast," said Jim.

"The last few months have been a blessing for me, and Chris, what the Lord is doing is nothing short of a miracle for me. The time I had alone to meditate and study God's word, and to seek him, and be with him, and adore and worship him, has already made a tremendous difference in me. The most incredible thing now is God, through his Spirit, speaks to me. To hear his voice guiding me is so beautiful I can't even describe it. He has guided me for hours through the scriptures and has shown me that I am forgiven, and what he wants me to do in the time remaining for me here. He has shown me and given me a better understanding of what will take place in the next few years."

"I better understand what I need to know about the Book of Revelation and of some of the Old Testament books of Daniel and Isaiah among others. What the Bible said of the end times is happening right now! What we are going through is the final battle between good and evil. It is drawing to an end even as we speak. Do you know Jesus, Chris? Do you know him as your personal savior, as your friend, as one who would speak to you and guide you? Have you ever given your life to Jesus and asked him into your heart?"

"I went to Sunday school when I was a kid, and like I said, my wife and I sometimes went to church. Do you really believe this is the end of the world Jim?" asked Chris.

"No," said Jim. "The world as we know is ending, but the end of the world will not be for a while, at least one thousand years. What is happening right now is the four horsemen of the apocalypse have been loosened on the earth and one-half of the people who are left on the earth right now will die within the next six and one-half years. Chris, those who were raptured are with Jesus right now. You'll be on the next trip out, Chris, if you only believe enough to allow Jesus into your heart."

"Chris, the Bible says now is the time for your salvation, now is the hour. Chris, you did not come here by chance, you did not survive to be here by chance. Chris, what is taking place right now in the world can only make sense and can only be survived by going into eternity through the love of Jesus. Why God has brought this to pass is because the world as a whole has rejected his great love, and has rejected the love of his Son Jesus who died for our sins, every sin," said Jim.

"There is no sin you could possibly have done that will not be forgiven when you ask God to forgive you. Absolutely nothing will not be forgiven-not murder, adultery, stealing, lying, absolutely nothing. Chris, there is nothing you have ever done that will not be forgiven if you ask Jesus into your heart. If you ask forgiveness in the name above all names, it will be granted. The only thing now that will keep you from going to heaven and being saved is to reject the one who died to save you. The Bible tells us you'll be washed clean by his blood, and will be born again as a new creature in Christ. What has to happen is that you ask him into your life and into your heart. The scripture tells us that God so loved the world he gave his only begotten Son who died for us that we might live. Jesus died on the cross for us that we might have everlasting life with him."

"It is a change in your heart that needs to take place, a turning to Him in trust and commitment, and then you will see even the deepest recesses of your heart come alive and free."

"Jim, please," said Chris. "What do I have to do? What do I need to do to have what you have?"

"Chris, let me guide you, I want you to repeat after me. Lord, I am a sinner, I have sinned against you."

"Father, I believe that you sent your Son, Jesus, in the flesh to die on the cross for my sins."

"I ask your forgiveness for my sin, I ask to be washed clean by the blood of Jesus, which was shed for me, a sinner."

"Jesus, I ask that you come into my life, I ask that you come into my heart."

"I thank you Jesus that you died for my sins, I thank you that you saved me, and I thank you for your love."

"Jesus, I thank you that I am born again, thank you Jesus."

"Lord, I ask that you fill me with your Holy Spirit, I ask the manifestation of the Holy Spirit and the power of the Holy Spirit to manifest in my life."

"Thank you, Jesus."

Chris repeated the prayer as Jim led him and tears of joys began to fill his eyes.

Jim and Chris talked continuously of the things of God. Jim took the time to explain to Chris those things, which were going to take place in the next three years and beyond to the end of the age as described in the Bible.

"Pastor Jim, can you teach me what the Bible says about where we are, so I might fully understand what is taking place? I know we talked about so much. I want to learn everything I can, in every way I can. There is so much to learn," said Chris, still full of excitement.

"Yes, Chris, we will begin tomorrow morning. It's been a long day and I'm really tired. We still need to get your room ready, and get you settled in. You are at the start of the most incredible journey of your life, and I need to be wide awake to begin the class," and Jim smiled.

CHAPTER ELEVEN

Seven Thunders Sealed
Events in the time of Revelation 10

Janice was beginning to stir. She still had problems sleeping. She could not understand why or how the dust could continue to get in when she sealed off the windows and the door bottoms with wet towels. Her breathing was a problem from the dust that was always in the air. If she could, she would consider leaving the Tampa area, but there was no place in the country any better, and with the limited travel ban still in place, she wasn't sure if they would let her through anyway. At least here, there was no radioactivity like there was to the north. She couldn't even imagine anyone living with radioactivity on a constant basis.

She would try to locate a room air filter, and she was sure the filter and some sex would help her sleep better. Maybe with the sex, she wouldn't care if she slept or not, and a slight knowing smile crossed her face. *Sure has been a long time,* she thought, and her mind wandered to better times.

Janice grew tremendously in her gifting over the last few months, and she got to the point where many people were calling on her for readings. She had the gift. Everia told her few received the spirit world as she did, and Janice, in her reality, could affect many people for good as few ever could.

Everia continued to show her and to teach her of the things of the new age. Janice was going to be one of the most gifted psychics of all time. She would be able to help many who would come to her and bring them in contact with the higher being inside themselves. She would be able to put them in contact with those who had passed to the spirit world. Everia was going to train her to take her place in the near future for she knew her time was drawing to an end and she would soon die so she could help those being reborn to come back over to this side. She said Janice was the one who the spirits have called, and Everia would train her well. Everia, from the time she knew of her calling, looked forward to walking totally in the spirit world. She was passing the gift to Janice. It was a tremendous responsibility, and Janice would not take it lightly.

Yostock was elated. The report of the seven-year peace agreement between Israel, Iran, Syria, and the Islam leaders spread rapidly throughout Israel. To Yostock and the other rabbi, the news was what they had prepared for. The Temple of Solomon could now be built and would prepare the way for the Messiah.

They had finished enlarging the opening of the cave. The Arc of the Covenant was ready to be moved to the temple as soon as the Temple construction was completed. Few outside of the Jewish community knew that the Temple would be built in as little as ninety days from the time they broke ground. Every piece of the Temple was pre-made, every stone was cut, and every timber was finished and numbered to go into place.

Millions had died in such a short time, and the news of a peace agreement was a call for optimistic celebration.

Jeremie was running on empty. He had been up nearly twenty hours straight. There was a fervor building that was beginning to sweep the land, and many people were beginning to turn to Jesus. Others who did not, were becoming more evil. A division between good and evil had been clearly drawn. It was a war within a war. It was time to begin setting up a camp near the center of the state. One of the leaders had six hundred acres in the center of Florida, away from the big cities and much of the scrutiny and government controls. The government under Washington liberals, the ACLU, and even the newly formed Council of the Court of Coexistence had branded fundamental Christians as promoting anarchy because they were derisive in their beliefs. Many Christians were being arrested for no other reason than believing the Bible.

The gathering of people in the Tabernacle had grown to where there was over four hundred night and day, and often, there was standing room only. With the men who were preaching and those who were helping, there was a continuous service and praise for what God was doing for the people.

God was providing their needs, and they implemented an ongoing serving of meals and food distribution for the starving people in the area. *How many would continue to stand through the persecution, which was being poured out against anyone who professed Jesus as Lord only God knows,* he thought.

Many would pay the supreme sacrifice for their belief in Jesus Christ as the fullness of the Antichrist policies are implemented. Believers will be tested, and martyrdom will face many before the harvest of the earth. Jeremie knew his purpose was to let them know what was going to take place, and then it would be their choice that they would follow, just as it always has been.

Jeremie could visually see what was taking place all around him. No longer were there any gray areas between right and wrong.

The gathering of people continued to grow, and they were bringing others with them in ever increasing numbers. Just four weeks ago, he had sent his leaders out as the Angel of the Lord instructed him to do, and they started groups in three new nearby locations.

Jeremie now alternated between the home groups, going from one to the next. He appointed believers to be at all the various locations to order to keep the locations opened day and night. "The services must not stop, he told everyone. The time grows short, and we will not lose even one who might come.

One of the groups was meeting in a large Messianic Jewish Synagogue and it was filled to capacity nearly all the time.

"Praise God for his mercy and grace!" thought Jeremie.

The gathering of the believers were covered by the power of God. Many were healed and blessed by the power of God manifesting during the services. Jeremie never saw so many people alive and happy and full of life as those who were now in the church. So many people came because there was no place else to go that was so happy and full of life, instead of death.

While Jeremie tried not to focus on what was taking place away from the church he was concerned about the events happening within the United States, and the collapse of order and anarchy running rampant. He knew the events had to happen because the United States was not to be a world player in the final countdown, and even the non-mention of the United States in the Bible had to be fulfilled. The totalitarian regime of Washington had been allowed to prosper to where it would destroy the very essence of the country. Under a thinly disguised government slogan of "FORWARD TOGETHER" was a government bent on destroying everything that was good in America.

It sounded as though revival fires had started in every major city in the world, and although there were many who were gone from the first rapture, he was certain that there would be many more this time. He was set aside, and sent, for this very moment in history when the Lord would return in glory with his church.

Jeremie knew that those who accept would be taken out in the harvest sometime after the Antichrist sat in the temple, and desecrated it by saying he was god. The greatest moment of all time was about to be played out. All that come to Jesus will be taken in the great harvest written in Revelation 15: 2-4, just before the wrath of God will be poured out on those remaining on earth.

"I pity anyone who will remain, and there will be many. Thank God for his mercy, he has brought more in today. Lord, help me that I may be tireless," he prayed. "Help those you have called to find their way here."

An angel of the Lord appeared to Jeremie again as he knelt praying. When the angel began to speak Jeremie was startled. Jeremie bowed his head before him, and the angel said; "GET UP! I am a servant just like you. The Lord has sent me to tell you to send three elders to an old Christian church called, the New Tabernacle on 77th street in Sarasota, to open those doors for the people in that area. There is an old caretaker named Mann there who will open it up to them. He is expecting the elders to arrive. The time grows short, and there are many yet who will come."

Just as soon as the angel came he left.

Jeremie called the elders together and told them what the angel had told him, and sent three of them to the New Tabernacle to open the doors. When they arrived the caretaker was there as the angel said he would be. Many people began to come in shortly after the elders arrived, and the congregation grew almost overnight, just as Jeremie was told.

Throughout the world, the same thing was beginning to take place everywhere there were congregations of Jews and Christian believers. He was told that in New York, amidst the starvation, riots, and killings, the church was flourishing, and food was being provided through what could only be described as divine intervention.

Chinney was pleased. The winter was well under way, and now that he was settled in the house, he really enjoyed it. He had been able to survive, and he knew he would have enough food to last the winter. *Not bad for a city boy*, he thought.

Rummaging around in the garage, he found an old fishing spear that he sharpened to a razor edge. He used the spear to chip a hole in the ice to try his hand at spear fishing. He covered himself with an old blanket. *Colder than a witch*, he thought, but it did keep the wind off.

The first day he got two northern pike-one was barely fourteen inches or so, but the other one, Chinney thought, must have gone thirty or more inches long. He had never in his life caught a fish as big as that pike, or seen water as clear as it was below the ice. It was like looking through a giant aquarium. The fish were everywhere. He remembered the water in and around Detroit and wondered if it was that clear before it was polluted so bad. Detroit was always so dirty looking. "It's a real armpit," his dad used to say. Chinney knew he was right.

Chinney had gotten very good at keeping the fire burning continuously. Most of the time he was warm enough in the house so he could sit and read with a light blanket over his shoulder. He always slept better when the room was cool, and he slept well this winter with the wood stove being the only source of heat. Before stoking it up in the morning he usually found ice in the water jug he kept in the kitchen.

He was happy with the way the house looked. He had never had a place of his own, and he was looking forward to spring breaking here. He wondered if the bushes around the house were the kind of bushes that always got the rose bugs in them in the spring. He wasn't sure what the bugs were called, but he remembered they were so plentiful at his aunt's house in Dearborn in the early summer. He remembered finding them on the rose bushes and the white flower bushes like he thought these were.

It was beautiful-looking outside with the snow covering everything now, and except for the constant cloud cover, he liked it. *Maybe I'll stay here and have this for my own house. I really like the way it turned out for me,* he thought.

The living room, once he got rid of those old folk's doilies, looked pretty good. He moved the couch over by the window so that when he sat in it, he could look across the lake. He found that he especially enjoyed the early mornings.

Man, what's happening to me? I never liked this stuff. Maybe it's because Detroit was so bad. The last time he could remember anything pretty at all in Detroit was walking down by the river just as the sun was coming up and looking across to Canada. Too bad when the sun rose, the view lost much of its appeal because of all the garbage. He always enjoyed Trappers Alley but he didn't get down there often. There was a place that his dad and mama took him to called *Pegasus*. The food was different, they had cheese that they set on fire and pickled octopus Chinney really enjoyed. It was the only place he ever ate Greek food, and he remembered how much he enjoyed it.

He began to wonder if the restaurant survived or if it was burned down like a lot of Detroit.

"I wonder if anything's there any more, or if it's all gone. It's been so long since I've heard anything that I might be the only one alive for all I know," he thought.

In a lot of ways this winter has been the nicest I have ever known. I really miss mama, but I guess when I was there, I really didn't pay too much attention to her and sis. I was too busy doing my own thing to take time with them. Now I have time, but they're gone. I wonder if they're walking on streets of gold that it talks about in the Bible. It sounds so pretty with the giant pearl gates and the river of living water running by the trees of life. It sounds so much like the golden trees here this fall. I have learned so much this winter, so much, he thought.

"Mama, I want to be with you," he said. "I want to be with you Jesus." Chinney heard a gentle voice inside him say, "You will be."

He had read the entire Bible through again this winter and was now starting on the New Testament for the third time. He opened his Bible to John Chapter 11:25-26 and began to read about the death of Lazarus. As Chinney began to read, a verse jumped off the page at him, and he felt a tingling sensation all over him when he began to read it out loud.

> [25] Jesus said to her, "I am the resurrection and the life. He who believes in me will live, even though he dies; [26] and whoever lives and believes in me will never die. (NIV)

It was as though the words spoke only to him. "Yes Lord, thank you," he said. "I believe."

"And you shall live and never die," the voice within him spoke.

With tears of joy welling in his eyes, Chinney believed then beyond any doubt, that he would see his mama again.

CHAPTER TWELVE

Seven Thunders - scene in Heaven
Events in the time of Revelation 10

Janice was beginning to get over the jitters that she had throughout the day about leading tonight's meeting. Many of her followers and even some who had met her for the first time, were coming up to her, and their smiles were beginning to place her at ease.

"So young in the gift and yet so strong," one woman told her.

Most of the people came because they had heard about how extremely powerful she was and how she was supernaturally walking in the psychic gifts.

The events scheduled for the evening were about to begin, and since it was her first speaking engagement, Jon set up the meeting to be with a small group of about twenty people to allow Janice to be comfortable and not be overwhelmed.

Many belief systems were represented at the meeting, but they all shared one common thread, and that was that, they believed that through them and their commonality, the world would be saved.

One couple who stood out to Janice practiced witchcraft and Satanism. They were both quick to point out that they only practiced white witchcraft, and as they began expounding on their beliefs, Janice realized that their beliefs closely dovetailed into the rest of the group. It was their reality that they were following, and it really was very close to everyone else's at the meeting.

It seemed to Janice the only group that no one identified with was the right-wing Christians. Not even the liberal Council of the Court of Coexistence accepted the principles of Christianity which excluded other religious groups.

The right-wing growing Messianic-Jewish Christian groups would not accept anyone else's belief system and, in fact, openly attacked everyone else's beliefs. They declared there was no way to salvation except their way through Jesus Christ. Some Jewish Christian leaders openly criticized the president and his destructive policies that brought the United States into the New World Order and placed the United States into the new world wide monetary system. It appeared as though the President in return would be made the first president of the new North American Continent region, of the New World Order.

She could not understand the people who openly criticized the government and were pushing the country toward civil war. She did not like the check points and the shortages, but they were necessary to bring things back to normal. The rising resistance movement and pockets of fighting for old values and their perception of the constitution was helping no one, and many people had died because of it. Janice knew the government leaders were doing what needed to be done to help bring the country back from collapse.

Washington leaders are the only ones who had the information to make any sense out of what was taking place. They, among others have taken a world totally shattered by the events in the last months and turned it around to where there, at least, seemed to be some hope of returning to a functioning society. There actually would be a new world, and it would be a better one under their leadership.

The world events were clearly bringing about the Age of Aquarius, and it would become the age of peace and prosperity as never before in history. The time was at hand. It had arrived and she was proud to be a part of it.

The one who gave the psychic power to her was now in control. Those at the gathering heard the voice of prophecy being spoken through Janice. Janice was beginning to be considered a psychic of the highest order because of her unique insights into the spirit world.

Janice didn't understand it, but even her voice changed to a much deeper, almost manly voice, when she gave a reading.

The voice within her spoke out and said: *"The dark one comes."*

Janice continued: "What the world has waited for is at hand. Yes, even all creation has waited for the time of the unveiling to occur. The dark one is here. Those that have no compassion, those that do not accept the divinity of man, they will perish. They who will not accept will be destroyed, and peace will rein eternal. Those that have a narrow view and will not accept will be destroyed. It is the duty of every enlightened one to work for the elimination of those who would seek to alienate others from the god within. Christians and Jews with their exclusionary views are the problem with what is wrong in the world. Christians have caused most of the wars, and even now would seek to divide the world with their views that their way through Jesus is the only way to heaven. Heaven is here. It is now, and we are the gods who will change the world for peace, but we must eliminate the insurgents from the face of the earth. When they are reborn, they can then be retrained in the way they should be."

Much praise went up after she spoke the word. Jon was pleased, and Janice was, at that time, proved genuine.

"I don't know why you were so nervous," said Jon. "You were great. You have a sensitivity that few have to what the spirits are saying."

"Thanks," said Janice. "I needed that vote of confidence."

"You're welcome Janice," he said. "Speaking of confidence, would you like to get together at my place? Maybe we could have dinner. I don't have a lot to offer for dinner, but I would be good company. I have enough gas that I could take you home later, and I really enjoy your company."

"I would like that too," said Janice. "It has been a long time since I have had dinner with anyone, I'd really like that a lot. I have been alone since my husband died in a car accident when the people disappeared."

"Yeah, I heard that, and I didn't mean to make you feel bad. I didn't mean to bring it up."

"That's okay, Jon. I mean, I'm over it, and I have been doing well with it, but you need to realize that I haven't been with a man for a while, and I'm real lonely inside. You might not be able to handle me. I might very well be the woman your mother warned you about."

"Don't you just wish?" Jon laughed. "It's been a while, but I don't remember too many complaints."

As Jon laughed at his own joke, Janice felt a deep appreciation because the two of them seemed to be finding some common ground. As she looked at him, she realized how nice looking he really was. He had strength about him that she liked. At what she guessed to be over six feet tall and with a ready smile for her, he was going to be fun to get to know.

I really want him tonight. I really need him, she thought. *I want to start making love watching the sun go down and finish making love watching the sun come up. He'll never know what hit him.*

Ann slowly reread the Alert that had just come in. Los Angles had been nearly destroyed by a huge tsunami resulting from an undersea earthquake. The epicenter was located about fifty miles off the central coast of California. First indications were that thousands had died. Heavy damage was reported as far north as San Francisco and as far south as Mexico, but the greatest damage was concentrated in the L.A. area. The tsunami was by far the largest on record in North America.

Not since the tsunami that hit Japan over ten years ago had anything of that magnitude been reported. The wave was estimated to be over eighty-feet tall and traveled over two miles inland in some of the lower areas. Reports were sketchy at best, but it appeared that most of the coastline was destroyed in a matter of minutes. Ann shuttered to think of how that was going to affect California because of the rampant food and water shortages they were already experiencing.

Ann picked up the phone and called the print room.

"Jerry here," he answered.

"Hi, Jerry, could you come up here please? We have some changes this morning; we need to push a headline if Mark agrees."

"Sure," said Jerry. "I'll be up in about five minutes. I need to finish this set."

"Thanks," said Ann. *A wave eighty-feet high who would have ever thought it?*

As Ann got up to walk to Marks office, she continued to go over the current news reports. His door was open, and Ann knocked twice and stepped in.

"Hi, Mark, I just got a breaking news story on a tsunami in California, and LA was virtually destroyed in a matter of minutes. I wanted to make sure you are okay with me running it today."

"Hey, Ann. Yeah, I just got off the phone with FEMA and you can let the story go. Run it, but keep it as light as possible and try to play it down. Make sure you put in how FEMA and Washington have declared the entire region a disaster area and are pulling out all the stops to save as many people as possible."

"Sure, Mark, I will. Is there anything else that I should concentrate on as far as the earthquake goes?"

"No, I think that if you put in how far the epicenter was from the coast and keep away from how extensive the damage was, it will help lessen some of the panic for people who have families there."

"By the way, Ann, the article on south St. Pete becoming stable again and how the people are being fed and the articles on the governor helping to stabilize distribution was great. I got great response from it. Thanks," said Mark.

"Glad you liked it, I'll let everyone know," said Ann as she walked from Marks office.

Ann was thankful that her world seemed to be at a point where it was somewhat survivable. As she sat down at her desk, the phone rang and Ann was brought back to reality. She picked it up and was pleased it was Sue.

"Ann, we've got a story that you should see," said Sue.

"Bring it in," said Ann.

Sue came in and brought the copy. "Ann, I thought you should see this. I thought things were finally going to be getting back to normal. Just a short time ago, West Virginia and parts of North Carolina were hit with hailstones weighing up to ten pounds. Leesburg Virginia was especially hard hit. The authorities have no idea how many have been killed, but they are sure it numbers in the hundreds, maybe thousands. Some houses were flattened by the sheer weight of the ice. The authorities have not been able to get to the area because of the roads being impassable."

"You know, I can't even imagine where to go to hide from those hailstones," continued Sue. "They said they just came right through some of the buildings. What would we do if it happened here? Are we going to hide under a table or a desk? They said that the hailstones were so big there was no place to hide."

"Do you think this will ever end, Sue?" asked Ann. "We're still much better off than most people, and if we weren't working here we would really be up the creek. Is there any place open that maybe we can go to tonight just to get away?"

"None that I can think of that would be safe. Hell, I guess that there is not many places that would be safe anymore," said Sue.

"Yeah, you're right," said Ann. "Dumb idea. It just would be good to get out."

"Sue, you didn't hear this yet, but it just came in that LA is totaled now too. We just got word that an eighty-foot-high tsunami all but destroyed the West Coast. LA already was bad, but there can't be anything left now." I can't even imagine what is going to happen to the people who are left alive there," said Ann.

"You know what Sue? We have been hearing that Las Vegas is still going strong. It seems there are enough people left with some kind of money. It must because people still want to be there to keep their minds off everything else. What do you say we head over there and become girls of the evening? I really need to get laid, and to be paid for it would be a dream come true".

"Might not be a bad idea, I mean you're great but to get with a man right now, would be awesome. Maybe we could get some glitter too. It works for me. I got to tell you, though, Ann, I would go down for a candy bar right now. I don't think I would be enough of a business woman to keep us eating right".

"Yeah, you're right, Sue," said Ann. "I'm not so sure any more if what we have to offer is even worth anything, it seems like most of the men are gay around here. The ones that are not gay are like Jack downstairs, and he doesn't have anything to trade. In fact he scares me. But I have to be honest. Even with him, if he waved a candy bar in front of my face, it would probably be enough".

"I know. Me too. I guess I shouldn't complain, but everything is so damn messed up right now. I want to go out and get a hamburger and fries, and get laid by the first man I see that's got two legs and a smile".

"You and me both," laughed Sue. "You're great, but I really want a man between my legs."

"I know. I know. Don't remind me. Just that when you find one, let me know, and let me have seconds, will you? Just make sure you leave him breathing, and I'll do the rest".

"No guarantees about that," said Sue. "At least not right now anyway".

Nearly out of breath, Jerry knocked on the door. "What is it that you need Ann?" he asked.

"Sue and Ann both broke out laughing at the same time. Timing is everything." Ann laughed. "Timing is everything."

Just two blocks away in a neat row of condominiums, Harriet Barns was beginning to stir from her afternoon nap. As usual, Harriet was sleeping later than Frank. After being married for forty years now, he knew her well.

They retired six years ago and had saved their money very prudently so they could enjoy their golden years. When the bank shut down and everything crashed, they had been driven to the point of despair. All the regimentation that they had put into their lives, to raise a family, save their money, and get set for retirement-everything that meant something to them-had been taken away. They did everything right, the way they were supposed to, and this was their reward.

Frank had been crippled some years ago by a stroke. Not enough to be placed in a care program but enough to make some things difficult to do. The growing resentment and the general feelings against older people had brought him to despair. He no longer felt as though they had any control over their lives, and if he was sent to the hospital for any reason now, Harriet would be left alone.

Frank pulled the drawer open and pulled back the shirts to uncover the Colt .45 that his father had brought home from World War II. He had not talked to Harriet about what he was planning, but he was increasingly distraught over the lack of control over their lives. Throughout their marriage, Harriet had depended on him for everything, and what he had to do he would do, without her knowing. They had no food, and the streets were running rampant with crazy people.

Why had this happened to them? He often had asked himself that. They should be taking that cruise to Alaska they had planned, and they should be enjoying their grandchildren and children right now. Instead he was loading his Colt and had a resolve to end what had become a living nightmare for both of them.

He did not understand why the children were gone. Why when he and Harriet had gone to church all their lives, would this happen to them? They had been good churchgoers for thirty years now, since the children were born. They had been going back to church even more often, nearly every day now, when they could get gas, and it still didn't seem to matter. The priest told them that they had to continue to pray to Mary and that things would be alright. Still, it was everything that they could do to survive, and all the prayers did nothing to get their money back. Everything that the priest told them to do didn't help, and he had begun to doubt that there really is a God. It was either starve or die with a quick bullet to the head.

He finished putting the bullets in the magazine and pulled the safety off. Harriet would never know, and he was sure with his resolve, he would not hesitate to use it on himself. With tears running down his cheek, he put the gun to the back of Harriet's head and pulled the trigger.

Chinney was ready for spring to arrive. He made a backpack, and packed it with as much as he could carry. He survived the winter, and it had been good for him, but being shut in all winter was making him restless. He had made up his mind that he would leave as soon as the ice began to melt so he could reach the Upper Peninsula early enough to get settled and plant a garden.

He felt the biggest treasure in the house might be the large stash of seeds and some books on gardening he found in a box under the steps in the basement. Chinney was hopeful that he would find a place where he could plant the seeds in time to grow a crop to help him to survive the next winter.

Chinney needed the company of others and to be able to share with other people what the Lord had been showing him. Jesus was his best friend, and he felt he would bust open inside if he didn't share that with other people. He was hoping that there would be others that would be close to where he was going so that he would not be alone in the months ahead. He was thankful for the place of Emil and Brenda Longley and the use of it over the winter, but he knew that it was time to move on, and he was ready for what lay ahead.

Now that the snow had pretty well melted, he would leave. It was sad in some ways to walk away from the house because it was the only home that he had ever had on his own. He knew, though, he had to leave early to get to the cabin and lake to plant some crops and get established.

The nights were still pretty cold, but he had a warm sleeping bag, and he had a small water-proof tarp to cover with to get out of the weather along the way.

So much in his life had changed so fast. He had really learned in his heart how very precious he is in the eyes of Jesus. Mama had underlined many things in the Bible for him, words that meant so much to her and now to him as well. He read and reread the New Testament over and over again, and the words were becoming part of him. Jesus is the word for it says that in John. He found out that by getting the word in his spirit, by reading the word, he was growing stronger and stronger in understanding the things of the Lord. Now when he prayed often, words and thoughts from the Bible would come out of him. He was so thankful that he knew he was saved.

Chinney shut the door and took one long last look around, and then began walking up the hill towards the road.

As he walked along the long drive, he was amazed how much smoke and ash seemed to be in the air. He had spent most of the time this last winter inside, and this was the first time that he was out for an extended length of time. He put his extra shirt around his face and tied it off at the back of his head to try to filter some of the smoke. While the air was not choking him, he didn't like the taste of it, and it made his eyes water. After a few miles, he realized how long a trip it was going to be.

The bike that he found last year had two flat tires, and as much as he wanted and as hard as he tried he could not get the tires to blow up without a tire pump, and he was forced to leave it behind. *I'm going to have to find a bike to use that has air in the tires, and maybe even a helmet for a motorbike with a face shield to keep some of this smoke out of my eyes. It would be great if I could find a motorbike somewhere,* he thought.

Except for the smoke and irritation, Chinney was enjoying the walk along the countryside. There was a ditch along the road he was on that had spring water in it. The road was great for Chinney because it was gravel, something he really wasn't used to and just walking along it gave him a good feeling.

The clouds opened slightly, and the sun coming through was so warm and so enjoyable that the unexpectedness of it exploded out from him. "Thank You Jesus!"

It had been a long time since he had seen the sun. It seemed like nearly all winter it had been overcast. He felt so at peace and full of joy that he sang out loud as he continued his journey.

He had been walking two hours before he realized he had not seen a car or any signs of life anywhere. He really wasn't sure if there was any life left, but him. He would have to find some kind of transportation to get across the bridge to where he wanted to go. A bike, or car, or anything would really help.

He began to think why he had never learned to drive a car. He wasn't even sure he knew how to start one. He would try to learn though if he found one, he just hoped that it would be an automatic.

As mid-afternoon approached, Chinney was on a road that bent to the right in a large sweeping curve. He could see in a hollow near the end of a long drive what appeared to be an abandoned house. Maybe there's a bike or some extra food there he thought, or at least something that he could use. He started down the drive always on the lookout in case someone might be there.

It was an old house. *Probably not lived in even before the people disappeared*, he thought. From the appearance of the house, he could see that most of the windows were broken or knocked out long ago. Surprisingly, the front door was locked, but the picture window was broken in the living room and he climbed through. He went through the rooms one by one, looking for anything that he might be able to use and always looking for any extra cans of food.

He found very little that had any value to him. He found a couple of cans of vegetables and some really stale crackers, but someone else had been there before him, and there was no other food in the house. He did find one treasure though, a Swiss Army Knife in a drawer. He was sure that, it would come in handy. Chinney had heard of Swiss knives before, but he had never seen one, and with all the attachments on it, it was a real find.

Chinney went to the stand-alone garage at the back of the house and found an old mountain bike hanging from the dusty rafters. It had a basket in the front and a headlight on the fender long since rusted beyond fixing, but the bike was solid and the tires looked good even though they were flat. He began going through all the junk in the corners, and by the accumulated dust, he knew that all the stuff had been there for many years. It had not been moved, probably since before he was born, he was sure of that. Finally, he found what he was looking for, an old-style tire pump. *Yes,* he thought. *Just what I needed!*

After a very short time of pumping the tires, they felt firm, and he began to pack the bike for the long trip. With some rope he found in the garage and black electrical tape, he used a large cardboard box and cut it in two to make saddle bags to hang on the back fender. *It's sure going to beat trying to carry it all,* he thought.

"Praise God! Thank you, Jesus," he said out loud, and he began to sing songs onto the Lord.

Chinney spent most of the rest of the afternoon readying the bike for the journey. By the time he finished getting it ready, it was late afternoon, so he decided to spend the night there. The bed upstairs had a mattress, and with his sleeping bag he was comfortable.

The sun was just getting ready to set, and it was the first sunset that he had remembered seeing in a long time because of the constant overcast sky. He was determined he was going to make the most of it. Chinney went in the house and got an old chair from the living room and brought it out onto the front porch. It was nice to be on his way. In some ways, it was almost like a great adventure for him. To be moving again and starting on the journey to the cabin he remembered from the family trip was exciting. Sometimes he found that the first step was the hardest; after that, the steps often take care of themselves.

He watched the sun slowly begin to set over the hillside to the west of the house, and it turned to a bright red color before it settled behind the trees. *So beautiful,* he thought. *My life is rough right now, I miss mama and sis, but in a lot of ways it has never been better to me than right now.* "Jesus, I love you," he said out loud.

"I love you too, Chinney," said the soft voice inside him in a gentle, firm way.

CHAPTER THIRTEEN

Scene in Heaven
Events in the time of Revelation 10

Jim and Chris spent the winter in deep study and prayer. Finally spring broke through with a beautiful freedom of warmth that they relished. The leaves were budding, and the fresh new green of the first buds were on the trees.

The first of the spring flowers were just beginning to bloom, and when the sun was shining through the clouds, it seemed to match perfectly the yellow flowers on the bushes next to the cabin. They were the flowering bushes Jim loved seeing in the spring, and they were always the first sign that spring arrived. Along with the flowering bushes, the daffodils were pushing through last year's leaves along the roadside leading into the cabin. To look at the countryside now, you would never know the world was under the death throes of change. The blanket of green along the lake edge and the clamor of noise from the frogs in their spring mating rights filled the air.

Jim had developed a constant cough, and he assumed it was from breathing the smoke. The smoke was lighter now, but the cough seemed to be getting worse and never let up. Chris was very concerned because Jim's lungs did not seem to be getting better, and he had no idea if he could physically carry Jim to a doctor. Chris was doing the heavy work because Jim was so physically drained with even the least amount of exertion. Jim would begin to wheeze when he did any kind of physical labor.

Chris learned fast during the winter months. Jim was especially pleased with the enthusiasm Chris showed for learning. They planned to go into town as soon as Jim was feeling better to begin preaching, and teaching anyone who would listen. They planned to teach until the next rapture came, and they would take as many with them as they could. Both of them knew all they could do was to proclaim the Gospel. Some would listen, and some would not.

Chris, even though he still had much to learn, was going to be a real help to those he would come in contact with. Jim told him that when spring comes and they begin to have church services, he wanted Chris to begin preaching as soon as he felt comfortable. Chris would preach, and Jim would teach. There were two reasons Jim felt this was the direction they should go. One was because Chris needed the training, and the second was because Jim was physically exhausted. The constant coughing was draining him of his strength, and teaching was less physically demanding for him.

They planned on going into town a week ago, but Jim's condition prevented it. Without any medicine or access to doctors in the area, they were pretty much on their own. It felt better to Jim if he stayed inside and out of the outside air as much as possible.

The fishing seemed to slacken off some when the ice left. Even with the rowboat Chris didn't seem to catch as many fish as he was when he was fishing through the ice. The ground was still too cold for him to dig any worms which he thought might be better bait than the ice poppers. The ice fishing poppers were the only thing he had small enough to catch bluegill with. The red-and-white Dare Devil lures they found were too big for the pan fish, but Chris decided to give them a try anyway.

It turned out to be a good day for fishing after all. Chris managed to get a bass close to two pounds with one of the Dare Devil's, so they would eat well tonight.

They found in the Gibbons book on what wild things you could eat, that cattail roots were a good diet substitute for potatoes. Fortunately, they found many cattails along the edge of the lake. They did not taste too bad, but they were pretty bland without salt and pepper.

Chris was sure Jim would be happy with the bass he caught. Chris brought the fish back to the cabin and cleaned it. By the time he took it inside for supper, Jim had the rest of the meal nearly ready. Jim finished boiling the cattail roots with some fern sprouts that added a slightly nutty flavor. The fish would not take long to prepare. They set the table and Chris said the blessing over the food.

They did not finish cooking the fish before the knock on the door. Chris got up and quickly went to the wooden door and opened it. Standing on the front porch was Chinney, skinny and exhausted from the long bike ride to the cabin.

"Hello," said Chris. "Come in!"

"Thank you," said Chinney. "Thank you!"

Brenda was very distraught over not having enough supplies to help the many people coming into the hospital. Government programs and regulations had devastated the medical industry. The hospital seemed to be getting most of the supplies they needed, but over the last two months they again started to run short again.

The past months had been a living hell for her in the emergency room. Brenda was meeting with the head of purchasing to see if there was any trade off of supplies she might be able to accomplish. As she tried desperately to procure what they needed, a Code Red Alert came over the loud speakers.

CODE RED, E.R.!, CODE RED, E.R.! Blared the speakers.

Every available person began scrambling towards the emergency room.

Police were coming in the emergency room through the outside entry, and the commanding officer asked to see the one in charge.

The unusually hot weather and the loss of electric power to many parts of the city brought the people to the brink of anarchy. Massive riots broke out across the city. The worst of the rioting was moving towards the hospital, and the anger of the people was so intense, the police were forced to pull back. Forty police officers were outside the hospital, but a large mob was moving towards them, and were smashing cars and setting buildings on fire.

Officer Todd told Brenda additional troops were on their way to the hospital to help. They had been given orders to "shoot to kill." He told her that there were many dead just a few blocks away.

Brenda could hear gunshots, which sounded close by. Panic and fear was electric and contagious throughout the hospital as it was put under lockdown.

The idea of treating people who were shot was so far removed from the shots themselves that she had never in her life had to put the reality of the act with treating the patient. They were always separate from one another. Now she was faced with the two realities coming together.

Shots echoed from down the corridor, and the commanding officer ran towards them. More shots and screams of dying men filled the halls. Through a broken door in the south side of the building, rioters were streaming into the hospital and unleashing their anger at anyone who seemed to be in their way.

Instinctively, Brenda began yelling orders at those nurses nearest to her to seal off the ER from the rest of the hospital. They put all the doors on emergency lockdown from the inside, and six policemen stood near the outer glass entry doors in riot gear and shotguns.

She ran to one of the officers and asked him about moving an ambulance around to the sliding glass doors and back it in tight to block the main emergency room entryway. The officer quickly ran out and backed the ambulance up to the sliding door as tight as possible.

More shots came from down the hall! Brenda thought that maybe instead of keeping those out who wanted in, they cut off their own only means of escape. Machine gun fire filled the halls near admittance, and then there was silence inside the hospital, except for the police yelling commands. It was over. The people left as fast as they came.

Brenda was overwhelmed nearly to the point of tears. It was not out of compassion for the people who were killed but rather what seemed now to be the hopelessness of it all. No matter what she did, no matter what the hospital did, there was so little they could do which seemed to make a difference.

Until now, one thing the hospital afforded Brenda was a way for her to put her head in the sand and not face the reality of what took place over the last year. Last year when everyone disappeared she could hide any opinion and any feelings she had about the disappearances by burying herself in her work. She was always one who would not face life directly but blamed everyone else for her misery and her situations. By concentrating totally on her work, she had the mental out she needed. Now she no longer had the luxury of hiding from the world; the world had entered her domain.

Six were dead in the hospital alone, and another twelve in the parking lot. The people lashed out at everything wrong in their world. No food, no money, no jobs, no God, no nothing, and like lemmings they went collectively running off the deep end together.

Several of the police were injured, and only a few of the insurrectionists survived. Brenda would do what was needed to help the injured, but she knew in her heart this was only the beginning of a long hot summer of riots and murder.

"I really need to get out of here, but where could we go?" thought Ann.

Ann began to read through an article she was told to print.

The article said that the government placed restrictions on travel. The migrations of people coming into the southern states, from the west and north, were causing massive problems. The southern states were being overwhelmed. The infrastructure couldn't handle any more people. Even Mexico shut their northern border to block the United States immigrants.

Strange, she thought. *The liberals fought to let all the people come across the southern border, and wanted open borders for everyone, but are now blocking US citizens from moving to a safer area of the country. The only thing really being said was the government itself was no longer in control of the country.*

How quickly things changed. As she thought about it, she could only think back through sadness at the change. It wasn't only the total loss of freedom she felt, but everything seemed so false and under a façade of the old government slogan of "Change you can believe in!" She could only believe the slogan if she reversed it to, "You can believe in the Change," but she would now be adding "or else" to it.

Pockets of resistance groups were growing, and it was looking like it would turn into an all-out civil war across parts of the United States.

Sue knocked and stepped through the door.

"Hey Ann, what's it looking like on the time getting out tonight? Jan asked if we could come over for dinner and cards with her and Andy. We haven't done that in some time."

"Yeah, I would like that very much. Let's do it."

"Good, I'll let her know, see you at five," said Sue as she walked out.

The phone rang. It was Mark.

"Ann, could you come in for a minute? I have some things we need to go over.".

"Sure, I'll be right in," said Ann.

As Ann began walking to Mark's office, she was wondering what new rules would be added to getting the paper out. She knocked on the door that was partly opened, and stepped in.

"Hey, Ann, sit down," said Mark matter-of-factly.

"Washington just sent some updates and new regs for us, and we have to go through them together."

"Because of the problems caused by the insurgents, now, whenever you print anything they are to be referred to as terrorists, and in no way can they be called insurgents or get any legitimacy added to what they are doing. They are anarchists and deserve to be executed on the spot when they are caught. From now on, there will be nothing printed that will give any encouragement or credibility to them. The Internet, e-mails, texting and the newspapers, as you know, are already under strict monitoring by Homeland Security, but they now want us to not print anything about what is going on with their group. World news is okay, but we are to print nothing on the insurgency. Also, and this is important, whether we get notice of bad news or not, we can only print that things are improving and Washington has everything under control."

"What about the natural disasters, are we to print that?" said Ann.

"Yeah, we can still print about the weather related articles, in fact we can expand on that, but make sure every article says how much the government is doing to help the people recover. We need to make sure people know that their government is for them and keep that to the forefront of the news. I want to make this clear, while we often have breaking news stories that come through just before we get ready to print; from now on *nothing* other than local updates gets printed unless I personally sign off on it. Is that understood? said Mark in a commanding tone.

"Yes, I understand. I'll let everyone know. Is there anything else that is changed? said Ann.

"Just one more thing, Ann, and this is on a personal note. From what I have seen you have done a great job as editor, and I want you to know I realize that the issuance from Washington steps on your toes somewhat because I have to take some of the decision making away from you, but it is not my choice. Washington decided that it is for the common good that no information that could encourage national terrorists is to get out, and I have to agree with them on that."

"I realize that. We are all in this together," said Ann.

"Exactly," said Mark. "If you even look at the gun confiscation laws Washington was pushing for, you know how many lives would have been saved if they would have been able to pass and enforce those laws? We wouldn't be having this conversation right now if there were no guns in the hands of the terrorists that are trying to overthrow the government."

"Looking objectively at it, the problem really started with the Republican challenges to Washington on lots of issues and especially issues they say went against the Constitution. The NRA put huge legal blocks against some of the previous administration's attempts to take away their guns, and look what we have now-mass chaos and murder in the streets. Do you know, Ann that because of the terrorists, much of the budget is now taken up by security measures? We could be using that money to feed the people instead of putting boots on the streets, so to speak. I can't believe anyone would rise up against the government the way they have, when they are trying to do the best they can with the hand they were dealt," said Mark.

"Anyway Ann, from now on, everything that is not directly related to the community has to come through me, and there are no exceptions. Any doubt on any release, call me, even if it is a weekend or after hours to review it. Again, *no exceptions*."

"Understood," said Ann. "I will make sure that everyone knows, and I will not let anything go through to print without your approval."

"Good, I knew I could count on you," said Mark. "It starts today."

"Anything else?" said Ann.

"No, we're good to go for now. Thanks, Ann."

"Not a problem," said Ann as she rose to leave the room.

I need to get us away from here if Sue will go. What good am I doing here if I can't have the dignity of at least letting me feel like I have some worth, she thought.

What the hell is the difference whether you die from starvation in the mountains, New York or here in Tampa Bay, or die from a tidal wave in LA, or being blown to bits from a volcano in Hawaii? Dead is dead! No ifs, ands, or buts about it. Dead is dead, graveyard dead is graveyard dead! Hell, the whole world is dying, and dying in a hurry. No matter where you are, no matter what, whether you were rich or poor, it doesn't matter. If you have food, now you may be killed for it, if you have gold you may be killed for it. There are still laws but few law keepers, and everyone does what they want. From the beginning of time to now, there is no difference. People do what they need to do to survive.

Maybe if we go into the middle of the state we could find a place where we could grow our own food and survive.

As Ann continued to think about what Mark said he wanted her to do, Sue stepped in.

"Ann, do you think we should try to take something over tonight to Jan and Andy's when we go over to play cards? If we get to the house early enough, I could make a small pie with the few apples we picked up last week," said Sue.

"If you want to bake a pie, it sounds really good to me. Are you sure you can really bake the pie?" laughed Ann.

"Don't laugh. I'll just follow the cook book directions on the pie," chuckled Sue. "What could possibly go wrong? I think it should be relaxing getting out for cards tonight, and just having some fun."

"I think so too," said Ann. "We both need a break from here. See you at five."

CHAPTER FOURTEEN

Two Witnesses on Earth
Events written in the time of Revelation 11

Ann was going through some of the articles that were on her computer, to wrap up what she needed to get finished before she left for the day. An article caught her attention as she was going through the updates. Two apparent prophets appeared in Jerusalem, seemingly from nowhere. They were saying that the people needed to repent of their sins, and prepare to leave Israel. The prophets said they are to go into the desert, because God was bringing everything to a rapid conclusion.

The prophets are telling them, "The judgment of the world is about to take place. Woe to the city, and woe to the people of Israel, because the evil one is coming. The temple is nearing completion now. Soon after the construction is complete, the Antichrist will enter the Temple and desecrate it by declaring he is god. Prepare to leave now into the desert, prepare now," they were saying. "The end of the ages is upon us, and every prophecy written by Daniel is about to be fulfilled. The eyes of the Jewish people have been closed for two thousand years, and now you will see that Jesus, who was crucified, is the Messiah you have waited for."

The article further went on to say the prophets have supernatural powers, and the rioters cannot touch them. Several people were so upset they tried to stone them, and when they attacked the prophets- they were burned to death. Anyone trying to hurt them cannot get close, because fire comes out of their mouths, and they are burned alive. Some of the Messianic Rabbis said the two are the witnesses written about in book of Revelation. They were sent by God to be witnesses to the people, to reveal the truth of what is to come.

Great, that's just what we need, thought Ann. *They finally have a peace agreement in the Middle East, and now these two are trying to start another holy war of some kind.*

Janice was beginning to get ready for the night's meeting. She was having a difficult time understanding what was taking place within her and how it affected others. She was becoming sought after more and more all the time. She did not know why she was chosen by the spirits to be used as a channel from the spirit world. It was a great honor to be used by the spirits to bridge the gap to the spirit world.

The spirit Ramel would speak with a deep man's voice from within her-his voice-and would speak through her when she would totally surrender to him. She found that by relaxing and calling on him, and meditating, she would begin to speak with his voice and begin to call out things in his name.

Ramel was a spirit guide of the highest order, and she felt excited and proud to be used so mightily of and by him.

He said that the new age had come and those who resisted must die. Ramel was a spirit visitor from the Planet Zor, and he would soon arrive in the flesh to herald in the new age of peace and prosperity on the planet earth. Man is deity and god Ramel would teach those with a teachable spirit all things needed to bring about the blessed age to soon come.

"Do not resist what appears to be evil, but instead, evil will work itself out when those who commit wrong are brought to the realization of what they have done wrong when they are reborn. They will then come back to learn from those who have taken it upon themselves to learn what the spirits are teaching them," said Ramel.

"Do not be afraid, but follow the instincts given you by the spirits," continued Ramel. "The only spirit to fear is the one that proclaims, 'I am all-powerful, worship me.' Do not worship any spirit that proclaims to be higher than you for you are a god, and all gods are equal in the universe."

Jon Pierce had become her staunchest ally, and finally they had moved in together. Jon wasn't very good in bed, but it sure felt a lot better than being alone. She and her husband always had a lot of problems that they constantly struggled with, but when they did have sex, they were always good for each other in bed. *Jon sure looks good though, I guess I can't have everything*, she thought.

The meeting was just about ready to start. Normally, there were a number of followers who would be led to ask questions of the god Ramel, and he would answer them through her. It would be a good night tonight because she felt such a strong presence within her. Once, she had seen Ramel with her eyes, he showed her a shadow of himself. He was seven feet tall and was a dark shadowy figure, which stood away from her. Jon said it's very rare that anyone would see a spirit that way, and that he was making himself known to her, to prove he was going to make himself and his presence known on earth.

Ramel did not look like what she thought he would look like. He was huge. Really, if she thought about it, he was frightening in some ways to see. He was dark, almost a shadow, and his eyes were yellow, and cat like. She did not see him very clearly, but she knew that it truly was a great honor to be used by such a great power.

Janice and Jon walked into the room that had been reserved for the meeting at the rear of the Radisson. They were immediately greeted with stares of admiration from the people that had been waiting there in anticipation of the nights reading.

Jon whispered in her ear; "You are becoming famous, and your fame is going before you."

Janice could feel a tingling of excitement as she began to greet people that they were introduced to.

The mixture of people in the room was incredible. Other psychics, mediums, famous people from all walks of life and backgrounds, and even some in the entertainment industry were present.

There was an expectation that several famous movie stars would arrive soon as well. Great people were beginning to show up. It looked as though the seating for two hundred was not going to be enough. The energy within the room was beginning to rise to a feverish strength and pitch. Janice could hear and feel that the movement was growing in strength and stature. Slowly, they worked their way to the front of the audience, shaking hands with everyone and greeting them along the way.

The opening speaker was Ron Prescott, and he began by beating on the side of his glass to bring the meeting to order.

A falling hush came over the room.

"Ladies and gentlemen, we have a very important news story to open with. For those who have not heard already, just a few minutes ago, I was informed that the United Nations and, indeed, the world now has ratified the Council of the Court of Coexistence, and the coming together of the religions of the world. No longer has the world system chosen to remain segregated. Now, we will be united with all major world religions, and the Age of Aquarius has officially begun. In Europe today, the world religions, including Humanism, Muslim, Islam, Buddhism, and Catholicism, have united together to celebrate our oneness to bring about a new age for humanity. The entire world has joined together to bring this to pass and have vindicated our stand on the oneness of god within us. The new age has begun let us rejoice in it!" said Ron.

Applause broke out across the room, and one by one, those in the room rose to a standing ovation.

"Now without any further ado, I want to introduce our new woman of the hour, and we believe of this century, Janice through whom Ramel speaks. Janice," he said as he put his hand out to welcome her to the podium.

Janice rose from where she was seated with thunderous applause and walked across the stage toward where the podium and microphone had been placed.

"Hello," she began as she comforted herself behind the podium. "I am pleased to be here. What Ron has said is good news indeed. Let us all rise to our feet and rejoice in it."

Again, those across the room rose to applause.

As the applause died down, she began to speak. "Some of us who have gone through our many other lives have waited a long time for this day. We have waited a very, *very* long time for this. Very soon, even before the end of the next five years, we will see the coming of global peace. Our one-world government will work to end all the weapons stockpiling, and now with the true unity of the one-world church we will have peace across the land. We will witness the coming of the old ones to teach us the way to eternal peace and prosperity. No longer will there be rich or poor, but all of us will have abundance through a fair and just economic system created in the way it was intended to be. The gods, when they come, will show us how to let the god within each of us come out, and will bring a peace that will never be repealed. The peace that comes will be forever."

The crowd roared its approval, and many of them stood to their feet. Janice waited for them to stop before she continued.

A hush came over the room almost as if thick oil was flowing across the people. Janice felt the flow of Ramel coming over her. He lived within her; Janice could feel him.

One of the people at a front table asked her, "Who are you?"

Janice felt the answer coming from Ramel, and it excited her because she knew that she had given complete control of herself to him.

"I am the higher self. I am Ramel of Janice," the spirit of Ramel said. "I am her unlimited soul. I am the unlimited one in her, who guides and teaches her through each reincarnation."

At this, Janice began to rise from the floor and levitate over the stage, and the crowd jumped with glee and awe.

"I am he who comes to guide all who will listen, all who are enlightened to their own spirit guide within, and I have come to teach you the mysteries of the ages."

Most of the people had never seen anyone levitate and were in awe and amazement at what was taking place.

Only those very close could see the yellowing in Janice's eyes and her eyes take on an almost catlike appearance. Only the closest few could taste the slight tinge of sulfur from the pit of hell as Janice floated three feet off the ground. The crowd stood mesmerized by the moment.

No one saw Janice flinch as the demon Ramel stepped further into her body to complete his possession of her soul.

Ann decided to get away from the condo for a while and picked up her skates to skate on the condo trail. The condo association put in the walking trails when the condos were built and the trail was totally in the protected compound. She was thankful they had armed security hired to walk the grounds to help keep the owners safe. It had been a long time since she had just gotten out of the house alone, even for a short time. She donned her skates and began skating down the trail.

She had to get away from Sue for a while and away from everything else that seemed to hold her in bondage. As dangerous as it had become to even get out of the house alone, she felt safe on the walking trail.

No longer could they go anywhere alone. Although the problem was minimal where they lived, anarchy and total lawlessness pervaded everywhere.

She began to go over in her mind an article that was sent by an anonymous author that made a lot of sense and put a degree of understanding about what had taken place over the last few years. Much of the information she received was filtered by the government and their parrot, Mark. It surprised her when she received the article in her in-box. When she got it, she quickly printed it to read when she was out of the office, and then deleted the e-mail. She hid the copy because she knew she would be in trouble if it was found in her possession.

It seemed anything that criticized the government was now considered subversive, and it had now become commonplace to hear someone had disappeared with no trace. She heard rumors that when someone went into the camp run by the government in the center of the state they would not come out.

She tried to make some sense of what it said. The e-mail said it was written in March 2019, and she felt if it were true, it was almost prophetic in what it said. She heard rumors about a secret governmental department that was set up to monitor and take control of every activity of the citizens for "their protection."

The reality of the government "nanny state" appeared much more oppressive, and worse, than anyone could have imagined it could be.

She tried but it was hard to remember back to when she felt free. The G5 technologies was the controlling backbone that made it so she felt constantly watched, and that she had to be careful in everything she did. There was a level of security from it, but also a feeling of no longer being in control of her life. It almost seemed to her that she was in a prison without walls, and she was beginning to hate it.

As Ann began to read the article, a slight breeze rustled the leaves above her.

Over what she estimated was more than a billion people had died, and now she was fearful of even reading a non-approved article.

The writer said that after the people disappeared much of what the government was doing was deliberately engineered to put in place the New World Order.

Ann finished reading the article and tore it into small pieces, and then buried it deep in the ground covering it with leaves.

She sat on the bank for what seemed a long time. As much as she really appreciated Sue, she was so thankful to be alone. Ann sat there letting her thoughts of the good times she missed so much, play in her mind. .

Sue was not a lesbian before, at least that is what she said, but now, she had become so jealous and so demanding. Sue had become almost relentless in her desires for Ann. But even with all that, Ann still felt lonely deep inside. She wanted so much, and longed so much, to be back to a time forever lost.

As darkness approached, she reluctantly set out for the condo. She was glad she had treated herself to the luxury of being alone with her thoughts. She wasn't sure why or how, but sometimes she felt less alone when she was by herself. When she was by herself, there was no pretense of talking just to be heard and no false meanings to what were said.

Boy, am I turning into some kind of nut case or what? she thought to herself as she skated back toward the condo, and an impatiently waiting Sue.

Jim's breathing problem was becoming worse. The weakness he had with his lungs had begun to fester and give him a lot of pain.

Chris and Chinney were becoming good friends. Jim was pleased to see their love in the Lord was growing at a phenomenal rate. Between the two of them they were evangelizing to the people in the immediate area, and twice a week went into the small town of Jenkins eight miles down the road.

They had grown so much in such a short time, Jim thought, and he was happy to see it. Last month, they started having two services weekly in Jenkins, and Bible study three times a week.

Two days ago, two more people had come from Lower Michigan and were now living with them. Their names were Andrea and Tom, a married couple from Southern Illinois. Tom's background was in construction, and he immediately volunteered to take over the expansion program that Jim and Chris had talked about.

Chinney really enjoyed being at the cabin. It was everything that he thought it could possibly be. The cabin was great, but what meant so much more to him was meeting Jim and Chris. Jim was clearly the leader, and Chris, had learned from Jim and was now teaching Chinney. Jim was sick a lot of the time, and Chris took over much of the ministry work, even in teaching. Chinney really liked the gentle spirit Chris had, and it was so good to have someone he could laugh with again. It just made him so happy to have a friend.

They searched some of the old houses in the area in hopes of finding a piano for music at the camp. Chris knew how to play a piano, and Chinney really wanted to learn to play one. Jim said that if they could find some musical instruments in town that they could learn and practice during the long winter months.

They had a CD player, but batteries were hard to come by. They were concerned that when they ran out of batteries they would not have any music at all, so the quest was made to find a piano and some other instruments.

"Music is good for the soul and God likes a cheerful heart. In this time of sorrow for the world, music will bring people faster than anything else, and it is good to sing onto the Lord." Jim said.

The material gathering for the new cabin was going well. They felt that with good weather, they should complete it by mid-July or so. The increased space would allow for cots and living for twenty more people.

They had become one growing, thriving group, and Jim, while the leader on most things, had taken a back seat to Chris on the building, and the preaching. He was too sick from the smoke and dust in the air. The others did not seem to notice the smoke anymore because it was less intense than it had been. With Jim, however, the smallest amount of dust in the air was enough to start him coughing.

Jim knew that his call from God was to teach the others what to do and, as important, what not to do in their walk with the Lord. God wants those who seek him. He extends his mercy to anyone who would ask forgiveness, but after that salvation experience, he wants those he loves to love him back, and give him the praise and the love that he desires from them.

A successful Christian walk is a two-way street, God loving you and you loving God, and respecting him enough to make him the focal point of your life. Do that, and the Spirit of God will lead you on the path you are to go. In fact, the Bible says that God will make that path clear and will smooth it for you. When you take a step toward God, he will take a step toward you. The difference is that God's steps are big steps, and when you find him, you will find an incredible reality that you never could have imagined.

Chinney impressed Jim, not by what he said or did but in that he could see that God had begun a work in him. He could tell from talking to him that he had a terribly hard life growing up in the ghettos of Detroit.

Chinney had totally sold out for God, and showed he loved God with all that he did. Chris was teaching him, and he was learning fast. He was so happy that God had given him another chance, and he thanked God for his mercy every day. Every day he prayed that God would allow the seed in him to be on fertile ground.

Jeremie was preparing for the service. He was to speak at St. Johns Roman Catholic church. There were only a few people there, and he did not know if they were Catholic, or what their background was, but the time is short.

Jeremie went to the Lord in prayer and sought his council and his comfort. He had done everything God wanted him to do to the best of his abilities, and with great rejoicing he danced before the Lord. He knew that the Lord was even now going to bring those who will open their hearts and listen.

He knew that in a short time he would soon be called into heaven.

Jeremie received word that the two witnesses were now in Jerusalem proclaiming God's judgments coming upon mankind. They are walking the streets in great power, and some of the people are heeding their proclamations and warnings to leave because of the coming Antichrist. Most of the people, though, are choosing to ignore the witnesses because their eyes have not yet been opened. For some time the Messianic Jews and Christians have been telling the people what will happen when the Antichrist enters the Temple.

The two witnesses will continue prophesying about what is to take place, until they are overpowered and killed by the Antichrist. Throughout the world, television teams will continuously broadcast their bodies lying in the street, while many people celebrate their deaths. Three and one-half days after they are killed, people worldwide will see them rise up from the dead, and ascend into heaven.

Jeremie would continue to preach on every corner and in every church until he was taken up to be with the Lord Jesus. He rejoiced for that which he was shown by God that, even now, God still had a plan of salvation in this final hour for those who would call upon him.

He was to stand in the services and speak out the Word of God, and the Holy Spirit would give him what he was to say. Only a few now would accept, but he would not be harmed. They would want to kill him, but they would not be able to. He was to go from church-to-church, and speak.

The scales on the eyes of the Jewish people were being lifted and they would finally see that Jesus was the Messiah they had been waiting for. God even now would not have any perish.

The service had been in progress a short time and at the point in the service where it came time for the reading of the Bible a hushed silence came over the congregation as Jeremie stepped to the podium. There were only 34 people at the church and Jeremie could see the shadow of desperation covering them.

Jeremie walked forward to the podium and began to speak. His voice filled the air and the light of the Lord surrounded him when he spoke. The people who were there remarked among themselves later that he looked like an angel.

The Lord spoke through Jeremie: "Those of you who are here this day, I will read from Joel 3:14 for this is the word of God to you."

> Multitudes, multitudes in the valley of decision! For the day of the Lord is near in the valley of decision.[15] The sun and moon will be darkened, and the stars no longer shine.[16] The Lord will roar from Zion and thunder from Jerusalem; the earth and the heavens will tremble. But the Lord will be a refuge for his people, a stronghold for the people of Israel. Joel 3:14-16 (NIV)

Jeremie continued: "Joel speaks of the Day of the Lord, and he spoke of this time in history. The day of the Lord is here and the time of decision is drawing to the end. You are in the valley of decision that have to decide who they will serve.

What is done through ritual will not bring you into the presence of the Lord. To worship anyone, a saint, and yes even Mary the mother of Jesus, will not be heard. You can come to our Father only through his son Jesus.

The beautiful buildings and ritualistic prayers that are not said from the heart are not what the Lord is seeking. The Lord looks at your heart, the heart of a man... not the beautiful buildings we look at as being holy but rather how your heart is inside as being holy. You say you are rich but yet your riches are as filthy rags to him. You are neither hot nor cold and you will be spit out of his mouth. Seek him as one who you would seek to be in Love.

The time for you to make a decision of who you will follow is closing, and those who would seek him even now will find him. God loves you and he would have none lost. He will not turn you away, and there is nothing you have done that will not be forgiven you right now, but know this, that those who refuse to repent now of their wickedness, refuse for all eternity."

Jeremie continued; "I want to read again from Joel 2:12-13."

> "Even now," declares the Lord, "return to me with all your heart, with fasting and weeping and mourning."[13] Rend your heart and not your garments. Return to the Lord your God, for he is gracious and compassionate, slow to anger and abounding in love, and he relents from sending calamity. Joel 2:12-13 (NIV)

The service lasted a short time and he ended the message by leading them through the salvation message and the assurance of salvation. The thought of the people who accepted the Word and those that he had seen so readily accept salvation through Jesus brought warmth to him.

"Now is the time for your hearts to be turned to the Lord your God, and now is your time of salvation," declared Jeremie. "I want all of you to come forward and I will pray with you. It is time to make your peace with God for he wants none to be lost."

As the people came forward and he prayed for them, the power of God overshadowed them and they gently fell to the floor.

Jeremie continued praying with them over the next 45 minutes and then left to go to the next church. There were many who asked God for forgiveness and mercy in Jesus' name, and God heard their prayers.

Jeremie knew the Antichrist would rise to power in a very short time. He would rise to become ruler of the world just before the three and one-half year period from the time the people were taken out. The Antichrist would go into the soon-to-be-finished Temple of Solomon in Jerusalem and declare himself god. All of heaven would come against the world in the time following. The people who think they are going through difficult times now do not yet realize it has only begun. What the world has gone through has been relatively calm, compared to what is to come.

At the end of seven years the world will witness the final battle at Armageddon and in that one battle alone over two hundred million people will die. Jeremie knew that those who were being persecuted would be fleeing from the cities and the rule of the Antichrist.

A huge wave was building, not a wave that could be seen but a wave in the spirit world, one that already has unleashed the forces of evil.

When people make the choice of taking the chip, which the New World Government would soon mandate, they will be proclaiming allegiance to the Antichrist. The Mark of the Beast spoken of in Revelations is the act of placing your belief in who will save you, and who you will serve. It is part of the Antichrist system.

Jeremie had asked several in the congregation to go to the center of the state and find a place away from some of the government oppression. They found what they wanted in an old camp, a former "dude ranch" near Avion that had a large enough facility to house several hundred people. Twenty volunteers were already on site beginning the process of getting the camp in order, and to plant food and gardens.

Jeremie was increasingly concerned about those of his church who had reported being attacked by non-Christians. The attacks were beginning to increase in regularity. The Lord told him that it was to be expected, that the walk with him did not mean that they would be free from all trouble and persecution, but rather since they were persecuted for his namesake, to rejoice.

Before the time of Jesus' return, there would be many who would die and be martyred for the sake of Christ's name. Many times the Lord spoke to Jeremie guiding him and letting him know there would be some who will listen and some who would not.

All over the world there were others just like Jeremie, some stronger, some weaker but all bringing the same message of Jesus being the Messiah. The time is near. Still many would not listen to what was said. Even with the rapture having taken place, many still did not listen or choose to hear the gospel of their salvation.

Brenda felt like she was under constant criticism from the people she worked with. She had to make some incredibly difficult decisions about the care level that was to be given to those who came through the door, and no matter what she decided, there were many in the front office who were not pleased.

They were running short on supplies again, and the entire north wing of the hospital had become nothing more than a place for people to come and die. They simply did not have even the most basic supplies to help them any longer. Even the infrastructure supplying the hospital was collapsing. The main sewer system had backed up and was unusable-not because of collapsed pipes, but because the main pumping station for the area was burned during the riots and the pumps were shut down. It allowed the sewage to back up all the way into the hospital lines, and necessitated setting up Porta-Pottys in the parking lot.

The electric service had become intermittent over the last several weeks, and without the emergency generators, they would have had no electricity for the hospital at all. The concern right now, though, was that one of the generators was down and they were running with the back-up. The generators were old and were not of a large-enough capacity to run all the electrical equipment throughout the hospital. The electric was being rationed to keep the main services operational, but they were very close to not having enough capacity to keep even the essentials going.

Brenda ordered a cut back on all non-essential electric use and that extended even to the parking lot areas. The police who had been sent to keep order for the hospital were very uneasy with that decision. The entire situation at the hospital had deteriorated to one of priorities. The constant pressure to put out the most immediate fires and the lack of staffing and supplies left very little room for proper treatment for the patients.

She had to issue mandatory age-requirement guidelines for treatment, standard triage treatments, and non-heroics based on survival probabilities for everyone. Basically, they were not to treat anyone who had less than seventy-five percent chance of survival without treatment. It was not a popular decision with the staffing, but they had little other choice considering the gravity of the situation.

Brenda would not be at all surprised if the hospital would soon shut down. The government issued a mandate that it was to remain open, but as is often typical with the administration and the Government mandates, they did not give them anything additional to work with. They had very limited supplies, and they no longer had any sanitation or electricity on a regular basis.

Washington said that the hospitals were to remain open, and that supplies would be sent. It seemed to her that all they were good at was the constant flow of bull.

She was told that the main pump had a cracked housing casing from when the pumping station was burned. The pumping station was not reopened and repaired because there was no one who could repair it. The contractors who normally would be able to fix it had gone bankrupt and out of business long ago with the collapse of the economy. The government for all their empty promises had no one who could handle the job or get the equipment and pumps needed to make it operational again. She understood the only company making that type of pump casings was closed as well.

So here she was working in what the government said was an essential public facility, and they had nothing to work with. The hospital had become nothing more than a motel for people waiting to die. The moaning in the hospital was painful to hear.

Something new, which had been added to the hospital duties, was the euthanasia ward. People would come in to get a shot and be put to sleep. Euthanasia was another new government regulation. Anyone wanting to die could come in, sign a consent form, and receive a shot and never wake up. There was no longer any hope for many people, and the despair that most faced with this new age was more than they could handle.

Brenda found herself thinking that the only things the government truly accomplished were the things of death, and not life.

CHAPTER FIFTEEN

Seventh Trumpet Sounds
Events in the time of Revelation 11

After much delay, the Temple of Solomon was completed, and Yostock was chosen to be one of the rabbis who would carry the Arc of the Covenant to its resting place in the Holy of Holies. The Temple was beautiful in both the original design, and the execution of the craftsmanship in rebuilding it.

The Temple could not have been rebuilt without the signing of the peace accord following the Middle East war. An additional agreement between Palestine and Israel gave up some West Bank land to Palestine in return for the rebuilding of the temple in its original location, and allowing them to build it on the Temple Mount next to the Dome of the Rock.

The leaders of the United Nations, the New World Government, and the Council of the Court of Coexistence agreed with the studies done over many years. The studies proved that the generally held belief of where the Temple of Solomon was located was wrong by a distance of 40 feet. By rebuilding the temple on the original historical location, it allowed the temple to be built without desecrating the Dome of the Rock Muslim Masque. The ground between the two was agreed to be symbolically occupied by the Council of the Court of Coexistence, as a symbol of peace and acceptance of both major world religions.

As part of the agreement, Israel would retain much of the surrounding area outside of the Outer Court to act as a safety buffer in order to be able to worship in peace. The Palestinians received much of the rest of the West Bank, and the remaining land previously proposed by former President Rabin, with the exception of the Golan Heights. Following the example of the United States, several other nations moved their embassies to Jerusalem in a show of unity and promotion of world peace.

The time leading up to the return of the Messiah, was the most exciting moment in history to be alive. Yostock knew that the temple being rebuilt could begin the time of the ages prophesied in the Scriptures.

As they raised the pole, which carried the Arc to their shoulders, to Yostock, because of the excitement of the moment the weight of the Ark almost seemed to be non-existent. Thousands-upon-thousands of people lined the streets as the procession made its way to the Temple Mount.

As Yostock, and the other Rabbi carried the Arc they knew that Israel, and indeed the entire world, would be forever changed when the Arc of the Covenant entered into the Holy of Holies, and the veil was put in place.

Ann wasn't sure if the paper would keep going because the readership had greatly fallen off over the last few months. The Internet, cell phones, and most television news channels had been restored, and the newspaper seemed to once again be heading into oblivion.

She was lost in thought when Mark called.

"Ann, come in here please," said Mark. "I have some things I need to go over with you and Jerry."

"I'll be right in," said Ann.

She picked up her notebook from her desk as she walked to the meeting.

"Hi, Mark. Hi, Jerry," she said as she stepped in the door.

They both acknowledged her, and Mark said, "Good. You're here. Grab a coffee, or water if you want. It may be a long meeting. We have a lot to go over."

"Thanks Mark. I'm good for now," she said.

"One thing we do want is to make sure that we print articles that show Washington has the heart of the little people, and is bringing the isolated revolt under control." Mark continued, "There seems to be a slowdown in the attacks and Washington is feeling that the terrorists are finally being brought under control. Even in St. Pete and Tampa, there is a lot less violence taking place over the last few weeks. I want the new stats constantly put before the people so everyone can start feeling better about what is being done."

"What about the insurrectionists that are hiding in the Everglades, have they been able to bring them under control?" asked Ann. "I know they said they do not have enough security forces to roust them out of there. They said last week they would 'starve them out' and cut the food distribution into the area instead of sending in large numbers of troops. It's reported that drones were sent in to minimize them. Should we continue to follow it?"

"First of all, I want to remind you that they are to be referred to as terrorists. Keep all references to them at a minimum and just constantly tell our readers that the government has everything well under control and are working to bring their lives back to normal and put the rise of terrorism down. By the way," Mark continued, "Washington leaders just approved using armed drones to track and destroy their camps where they lack resources to directly get in, so that whole problem should be coming to an end soon."

"Another thing you need to keep in the public's mind is that because food production has increased the food shortages are beginning to lessen."

"What about the bomb that exploded in the St. Mary Catholic Church in Miami yesterday, and killed more than fifty people. Should we print it?" asked Jerry.

"We believe that a far right-wing radical Christian or Messianic Jewish group that disagrees with the Pope and the CCC is responsible for that bombing, and yes, you can print it. The prepper group hiding in the Glades is most-likely responsible for it, and we want the people to know who their government is fighting against, and how dangerous they really are," said Mark.

"What is your interpretation of far right-wing?" asked Ann.

Mark looked at Ann almost in a condescending way and began to almost lecture to her. "The far right-wing is the same group of people that started opposing Washington's policies a number of years ago, and they have not let up yet. You can begin with the Evangelical Christians, Al-Qaida, Hamas, and the Messianic Jews. All of them have one thing in common, and that is that their way is the only way to heaven. Combined, they have caused more deaths and grief to the human race than any dictator or leader ever has."

"So we are going to push the idea that the bombing of the church was done by the preppers, I mean terrorists? I mean, should we use that as our lead-in or should we continue to just keep it as an unknown?" said Ann.

"Keep it as a lead-in and pretty low-keyed," said Mark.

"Jerry, keep the scheduled distribution schedules, advertisements, etcetera as normal, and, Ann, let me see everything before it goes to print," added Mark.

"If anything else comes up, let me know, and I'll do the same. Thanks guys," Mark concluded.

"If I could, ask one last thing Mark. What should we say about the large numbers of Christians that are being murdered throughout the world? I mean, the report we got two days ago said that a large group of Muslims in Paris killed more than one hundred Christians in their homes when they went on a rampage throughout some of the neighborhoods, on what appears to be a Jihad. Shouldn't we say something about it and be reporting on that?" asked Ann.

"No, leave it. We do not want to push or acknowledge a war between the Christians and the Muslims. Just leave it be."

"Ann, e-mail me the copy before you get it to Jerry. I have another meeting, so unless there are some other questions, I need to go," said Mark.

"I'm good," said Jerry.

"Me too, I'll forward the front page draft as soon as we have it," said Ann as she stood to leave.

As Ann walked back to her desk, she began pondering some of the events that they either were no longer allowed to report on, or just were considered to be of non-importance enough for the paper not to mention.

The last year had been relatively calm compared what they had been through the last few years. It seemed as though Washington had finally restored some order over the rioting and the anarchy that was spinning out of control.

The United States had only begun to come out of the severe depression that they had been in the last three years. The rains finally fell over the Midwest states and increased the harvest to ease the famine. The rich lands that were released from the land banks were helping the US slowly come out of the depression. She would make sure they stressed that in the editorial for tomorrow's paper.

Ann began to reminiscence about her life changes over the last months. Why she still was with Sue, she wasn't really sure, but they had managed to work things out. Sue didn't seem to want to be with anyone else, and she was not subtle about that in any way. She assured Ann, however, that she would not stand in her way if she found someone.

Ann worked through the negative feelings that had been driving her about their relationship for so long. She realized how lucky she was compared to so many other people. The two of them had actually made some headway in their relationship and in life in general. The city had expanded the bus line to run by the condo and into downtown, which made it much better for them. The city of Largo also started Friday-night concerts in a secure city park, and they loved the freedom of being there and out of the condo. It made a world of difference to both of them to get out and be with other people once in a while.

Aside from an occasional fight breaking out, it was a very pleasant way to spend an evening. Ann guessed that the reason that there were so few problems was because of the large numbers of police that were always present. While she hated the feeling of constantly being watched, she was thankful for the added protection.

Chinney and Chris were increasingly concerned about Jim. He had grown worse in the last few weeks, and now he was bedridden most of the time.

The group had grown into a commune of sorts, and each had a different task. The group had grown to a commune of sorts. To Jim it was like a time-out of the sixties.

There were over twenty believers living in the camp, and Jim was still considered the leader of the group. They decided to call the camp Spiritual Life, and the majority felt it was a good name.

Chris was ordained as the senior pastor, and Chinney as his assistant. Chinney had grown in so many ways. Tomorrow was his turn to preach, and he was nervous, but at the same time, he was looking forward to it.

"You'll do well tomorrow, Chinney, God has given you an enthusiasm that is contagious, and the people respond favorably to you," said Chris.

"Thanks for all of the words of support, I really need it," responded Chinney.

"It's okay, we all go through it, and I'll be there to help if you need it, but I don't think you will. Just tell the people what God has shown you. Let them know that, even in this time we are in, it is in God's perfect will and his desire is for all of us to move closer to him. He will bring them peace even now in this tribulation time," said Chris. "Everyone needs what we have found, and they need to make that choice. Again, you will do fine."

The next day, they had a group meeting in town, at an outreach center. There were not many that morning, and it helped put Chinney at ease, and after just a few minutes, he began to relax as he preached.

The radio reported the smoke levels as being dangerously high that day, and some of the regulars stayed away from the meeting because of it. Sometimes even at the mid-week evening meetings, they would have thirty-five or forty people turn out. They had services every night in town, and many of them would be there rain or shine, but when the alerts were high, a lot of the people would not venture out.

The regular town members would help with gas and with some food when they could. The people staying at the Spiritual Life all took turns in the food gathering and in the sharing of the duties and things that needed to be done. There were two who seemed especially good at hunting, and they had fresh venison several times a week now.

About the only information they received on the radiation count was a noon radiation report on the local radio station. They were told by the local newscaster that anything over 150 mSv's was considered extremely dangerous for extended exposure, and it was recommended they stay inside as much as possible.

Jim continued to get worse, and he had become very weak and steadily began to decline. The others in the camp felt that he did not have long to live. He told them that he wanted them to have a celebration when he died and that he was thankful to the Lord that to be out of the body was to be with him. Jim was ready to be with the Lord now, especially since he had become so sick over the past few months. The bleeding of his gums and overwhelming weakness he had along with some hair loss was a sure sign that he was dying from radiation sickness.

Chris had done a great job on designing the camp buildings. There's not much you can do with old log architecture Chris said, but Chinney was impressed. The main meeting house they built was beautiful. They finally found a piano for the meeting place, and Chinney was quickly picking up on playing it. He would play during services, and a man named Joseph would play the drums that they picked up in one of the abandoned buildings in town. It was fun and the best time Chinney could remember in a long time.

He wished that Gina could see how he was doing now with his life. She always believed in him, and he wondered if she ever thought that he would be preaching and playing in the church band. Chinney was sure that was what she meant when she said that she knew that he would be more than he ever thought possible. He would be happy with himself when he began to see himself as she did. He remembered what his mama told him, Behind every good man is a better woman," or something like that. Before, he always thought that mama said that only because she was a woman, but now he wasn't sure.

Spiritual Life had grown tremendously in such a short time. The new people that came were real nice, and it was more like a close family than most of them had ever known. The people did not have a lot of competition between them, but rather a tremendous trust and respect for each other.

The two married couples, who had arrived over the last three months, had their own little cottages set off to the side. The cottages weren't much to look at, but it gave them the privacy they needed.

The only person Chinney didn't get along with real well was Mr. Chaveeti. He was older, at least in his sixties, and pretty set in his ways. Chinney guessed that he just didn't like kids at his age, but he was OK to be around for short periods of time.

Everyone in the camp was busy preparing for winter. They knew that they needed to get enough extra put up in case others found their way to the camp. They were working steadily on the extra provisions, and it had been going well.

The seeds Chinney brought with him had been the Godsend that produced some of the food they needed to make it through the winter. The food they grew and harvested provided enough to feed everyone.

They decided that they would try to build at least one more cabin before winter, bringing the number of buildings to six plus the two small efficiency cabins for couples. The overall feeling at the camp was one of extreme optimism that they would be prepared for the next rapture, and there was a frantic pace about the camp to bring as many as they could to the saving knowledge of Jesus.

One of the men, Jerry, an older man with white hair from near Chicago, was teaching one night and what he said tickled Chinney. He said; "When the time for the next rapture comes, I want to be holding on to two non-believers and tell them, 'Believe or I let go.'" Not real funny, but it made Chinney laugh, and he had gotten to the point where he really enjoyed his life for the first time in his seventeen years.

Everyone was given their chance to teach classes. Jim said that there was nothing that taught a person so fast as to have to prepare yourself to teach others, and so they all took their turn. Sundays were reserved for Chris though, and on rare occasions, when Jim was feeling up to it, he would bring the message.

The time was growing short, and there was almost and electric feeling in the air when they would get together to pray and to talk about what to do to spread the word to as many as possible.

Jim called a meeting because he wanted to share with the camp an article he felt was extremely important to everyone. He felt it was relevant because they heard on the radio a couple of days ago about the chip the news said would be voted on in the next session of Congress. He felt it was absolutely critical to everyone that they understand what is taking place, and what will take place over the next couple of years.

The government was debating a law requiring everyone to get a RFID chip based on their social security number, to get a food allotment and medicines. The Bible was clear that this would lead to permanent, forever damnation. The scripture in Revelation 13 shows the mark of the beast would not happen until after the Antichrist enters the Temple in Jerusalem. Shortly, the Temple will be completed because they are rapidly approaching three and one-half years since the people were raptured. Jim was quite sure the RFID chip they were talking about mandating was the Mark of the Beast referred to in Revelation 13.

Jim pulled out an article that had an interesting chart computing the number of the Beast in Revelations, which was in one of the magazines he brought with him from Ft. Wayne, and passed it around so everyone could see it.

A	B	C	D	E	F	G	H	I	J	K	L	M
6	12	18	24	30	36	42	48	54	60	66	72	78

N	O	P	Q	R	S	T	U	V	W	X	Y	Z
84	90	96	102	108	114	120	126	132	138	144	150	156

C	O	M	P	U	T	E	R		
18	90	78	96	126	120	30	108	=	**666**

> **Rev. 13:16** Also he compels all [alike], both small and great, both the rich and the poor, both free and slave, to be marked with an inscription [stamped] on their right hands or on their foreheads, [17] So that no one will have power to buy or sell unless he bears the stamp (mark, inscription), [that is] the name of the beast or the number of his name. [18] Here is [room for] discernment [a call for the wisdom of interpretation]. Let anyone who has intelligence (penetration and insight enough) calculate the number of the beast, for it is a human number [the number of a certain man]; his number is 666. (Amplified Bible).

Jim began to tell them that they are near the mid-tribulation time, and that this chart was something he came across several years ago. He told them the beast is not the computer because the Bible says the beast is a man, but the beast system could only work by using the expanded computer systems developed over the last decade, and the new technologies that have been recently implemented, like the G5 system.

"I want each one of you to study Revelation 13, because that is the time we are about to enter. Many people will go to a Christ-less eternity, because they take the mark of the beast as a way to survive the times we are about to go through," said Jim.

"I believe the chip the government is going to vote on is the mark of the beast, as is described in Revelations. The computer systems, and chips mandated by the government fit the "how" of making the whole system work. With the world-wide reach of the new technologies, and the interconnection using the Internet of things, and the G5 delivery system, you can understand how quickly they can make it impossible to buy or sell without it," said Jim.

"The little news we are getting is that the chip implants are now voluntarily being implemented, and it sounds as though a number of people have already gotten them. Most are accepting them as being an absolute necessity to survive the failed monetary system, and the authorities are saying once it's fully implemented it will be difficult to survive in most metropolitan areas without one. The Messianic Jewish community and Christians in the larger cities are very vocal though, saying they would not take the chips for religious reasons. The Council of the Court of Coexistence, and the Roman Catholic Church, however, are saying that the chips are the only way to restore order to the world," said Jim.

Jim continued, "The chip is being touted to help the government make sure everyone is being treated equally, and are given enough provisions to survive."

Jim continued to talk and had everyone turn to Revelations 14: 9-11, to help them better understand the mark of the beast.

"I want you to take a look at Revelations 14:12 because the Word tells us that: "This calls for patient endurance on the parts of the saints who obey God's commands and remain faithful to Jesus." That is us, and we must remain faithful, and not take a chip, and please, everyone we must let anyone we meet know what will happen to them if they take the chip.

"It is only a matter of time when anyone professing to be Christian will likely be put to death for their belief," continued Jim. "According to both the news, and the Bible we know the Antichrist is now on the earth. He is a world leader and my guess is he probably is part of the European Unity nations. Many millions will die because of him."

"There is another chart that should be of interest that shows what the Antichrist needs to have in place to fully come into power. I think most of us can see that these things have taken place over the last few years," said Jim.

<u>There are only three things needed for the reign of the Antichrist:</u>

- A one-world government – now being established into ten regions
- A one-world religion – under a "Universal Earth" covering with the 266th Pope being the leader
- A one-world monetary system – Already being put in place"

Where we are right now is probably the safest place we can be because the G5 tracking technologies are generally focused in the metropolitan areas. In order for the G5 to work well, the relays need to be spaced very close together because of the short wave length, and the reach of the system. Here, as we all know, pretty much everything is bartered for, and we eat what we grow and hunt. That helps us survive, and keeps us out of the system. It is important for all of us to go into town as soon as we can, and to the people we know, and let everyone know they "*must*" not take the chip for any reason!" said Jim in an almost too loud a voice..

Jim had been talking ten minutes and began coughing uncontrollably, so he motioned to Chris and Chinney to take over.

Chris motioned for Chinney and several of the others to come up to pray for Jim, and then they helped him back to bed.

When they came back into the room, Chris began to speak: "Let's continue in the book of Revelation where Pastor Jim left off."

Jeremie had to marvel at what God had done in such a short time. He oversaw three hundred leaders now, who rotated to make sure that every church had coverage twenty-four hours a day. Time is short and there was no time to lose. So many had come to an understanding Jesus is Lord in such a short time they knew it was only because of the Lord's protection and intervention.

In the time since the rapture of the believers, more than twenty-thousand Messianic believers and Christians were meeting constantly in many of the old churches with more coming in daily.

Jeremie was given an article to read by one of the leaders. The article questioned the pope's stance and questioned the argument that the pope had laid out that seemed to lay the groundwork for the Antichrist to come on the scene. The article questioned whether the pope could be the false prophet spoken of by John the Revelator. The pope shook the religious community when he declared that *everyone* was redeemed through Jesus even atheists and agnostics, and those of other religions.

As Jeremie read the pope's words they brought back memories from historical accounts he had studied of the deep and painful divisions in Christianity that began during the Protestant reformation. The Protestant movement through Luther embraced the belief of redemption through grace versus the Catholic Church stance of redemption through works.

During his homily at Mass in Rome, the pope emphasized the importance of "doing good" as a principle that unites all humanity. The pope referenced Mark 9:38-41 as his Scripture basis explaining how the disciples were upset because someone outside of their group of disciples was using the name of Jesus to cast out demons and doing good for people, according to Vatican radio.

Jeremie recognized the article was written some time ago.

He began to read through several other articles he had and was more concerned about, because of the relevance to where they were currently, and they mostly involved the head of the CCC, the Black Pope.

The pope, who had also been so openly enthusiastic with the idea of the Council of the Court of Coexistence, and merging of the world's religions, publicly came out against the Messianic Jews and radical ecumenical right-wing Christians as creating division in a world already torn by strife and despair.

The pope said that, "Yes, we Catholics should worship Jesus, but every religion has its own purpose in God's plan and to be intolerant of others was a sin. He urged all Catholics to stand against the bigots now trying to control others through their beliefs."

"All Catholics are asked to join in a special day of fasting and praying of the rosary to bring enlightenment to the world beset by pain and suffering," he said.

The Messianic Jewish and Christians were very outspoken against the CCC, saying that the merging of faiths promoted by the CCC amounted to no faith at all. Further, they were adamant that the chip system now being pushed worldwide was the mark of the beast spoken of in Revelation 13. They said the chip would lead to eternal destruction of all who accepted it, because they aligned themselves to the Antichrist world system instead of trusting in God.

They also were quick to point out that the mark of the beast and his name comes just after the mid-tribulation time in the Bible.

The Black Jesuit Pope had risen to mainline news since becoming leader of the CCC because everywhere he went miracles, were taking place seemingly just because of his presence. The news was carrying the story of the Black Pope stating that he was speaking directly as the voice of God. Two people who had died in Barcelona through an accident when a heater mal-functioned, were asphyxiated and declared dead. When they brought them in to him to perform their last rights, they began to breathe, and rose "from the dead." People began to say that the Black Pope was the greatest prophet that ever lived.

Because of the information he had been given, Jeremie was sure that the leader of the CCC, the Black Jesuit Pope, was the False Prophet written about in Revelations who would herald the Antichrist's rise to power.

Janice was pleased with how she had advanced in such a short time. So many people had wanted to hear directly from Ramel that she now had two full time people who would do her email and Facebook interactions.

The new age had truly begun for her, and there were many who had come to hear the words of Ramel spoken through her. Janice could not believe the number of people who would not do anything without getting a special reading from her.

Many famous people stood in awe when she would speak with Ramel's voice, and they would do and follow what he would say. It especially got their attention when, on occasion, she would levitate. When that would happen, she would be under total and complete control of Ramel, and the people would treat her as royalty.

She was so much better off than anyone else she knew, and she had at her disposal even a small plane to travel around the countryside. Now she was booked weeks in advance.

It was hard for her to understand why she was chosen by Ramel to be his spokesman, but she knew she enjoyed his great power over people and what she received was a living better than probably even the president. *Hell, everyone wants to hear something good from Ramel. If I tell them that they will have money and the things that they want, or that they will get laid, or whatever they are seeking, then I've got them, then they are mine and will eat out of my hand. When I find that hook, then I will find what will make them spend their money,* she thought.

Ramel goes one step further than what her husband John used to say about the 1-900-numbers they used to have on television. He called them 1-900 dial-a-witch people. The psychics on television always have had a hook for gullible people wanting to have their ears tickled, and they made good money at the same time. *Suckers,* she thought. *What a bunch of suckers they are. Most people don't have the desire to think for themselves or to do anything that requires effort because they want everything handed to them. Hell, Ramel wants control of them in a different way than I want. I just reap the rewards through him. He reaps what he wants, which is to get those who would not bow otherwise, to bow for the old ones who are coming soon. Then every force in all creation, which is waiting in expectation for what is now coming, will be fulfilled.*

The new age believers have long known what was coming when the Age of Aquarius arrived, and it already started with the destruction of all those who would oppose the total peace that was about to come onto the world.

"Christians and Jews have a terrible revelation coming soon," Ramel said. "Everything that they have ever been taught will be destroyed in a very short time, and they will be destroyed as well."

Ramel had one message that became increasingly clear, and that was that the biggest hindrance to the coming peace was the Messianic Jewish and Christian communities.

Ramel wanted Janice to tell them that they are the gods of their own destiny and that through themselves, they would be blessed and brought to a higher plane of life.

Janice, while meditating began to have visions away from her body. It was a form of astral projection, and she would see many things taking place even a long way away from her. When people would talk to her on the phone, she would often see them in a vision and know what was even hidden in their face. What she often saw would show her what she needed to know about them, and Ramel spoke to them through her, and they would get the word that they wanted to hear.

"When I tell them what they want to hear, they eat right out of my hands, and anything I want from them is mine," she laughed out loud in the husky voice of Ramel.

The thing that startled Janice the most about Ramel and the voice coming out of her was that it began totally taking over her. Even sexually when she would make love now, she would be the aggressor, and she would have a stronger and stronger role in what would take place. She had become almost sexually violent with her partner, and so much so, that he was beginning to act almost afraid to have sex because he no longer knew what to expect.

The thought of how she had become sexually almost deviate in her desires was an area that she didn't understand. She always enjoyed sex, but she had been submissive, except on rare occasions, and had enjoyed letting the man she was with lead in the making of love.

"Tonight's meeting, where is it anyway?" She mumbled softly. Then she remembered that she was to meet with some of the senators from Washington. They have so few answers on how to fix the country they want to hear from Ramel, hoping for an answer from the spirit world. Even the senators want to hear from the god Ramel on how to lead the country.

"Tickle their ears." That's what Everia told her before she died. She told Janice many things, like how to listen carefully to what the person was saying. If they want a reading, they will eat out of your hands, and will accept what you say if you find that thing that they are looking for. Then tell them that what they are wanting is right before them and they will be putty in your hands."*Almost like Democrats,*" she thought and laughed.

Everia told her that many times, she did not have anything explicit to tell the person, but generally, it is a progressive thing that you can focus on to give them what they are looking for. If you ask a person about money, for instance, ask them if they've been seeking a financial blessing and that you see a financial blessing coming to them in the very near future. People always accept that, and they always want to know about their love life. If you leave it loose, they will fill in all the details for you and do all the work. People are so gullible that they will actually give you the answer if you give them even the simplest of leading questions.

That's how it started, and now Janice knew all the tricks, and with Ramel, the people had another hook in them.

Ramel would teach today that anyone who would speak against any area of government should be treated as the anarchist that they are.

There is to be a one-world government and a one-world church where all belief systems would be equally tolerated, and anyone who would not allow others to have the peace of their own belief system would be a hindrance and would keep the world from the peace and prosperity that the old ones want it to have. The old ones will not be pleased when they come if the world is not in unity, and any who will not come into alignment must be dealt with.

Janice stood at the podium, cleared her voice, and began to speak in the voice and authority of Ramel; "Death must come to all who will not come into oneness with all others throughout the world!!"

CHAPTER SIXTEEN

Mid-Tribulation– War against Christians Events in the time of Revelation 12

Ann struggled with her thoughts and what had been taking place over the last two months. Sue, who had been a faithful lover and friend, was beginning to become a constant source of irritation for her now. Sue had started being a problem after Ann had dated Ken, the loser, for a short time. At that time, they had agreed that they would stay with each other, and she and Sue seemed to have everything worked out. Instead, it was only on the surface that things were okay. Sue had become so jealous the last two months that even when she didn't say it, Ann could feel a rising resentment with Sue whether Ann talked to a man or a woman. Either way, it brought out an anger that Ann could not understand.

Ann still didn't consider herself to be gay, but rather bi-sexual would be a better way to say it. She would still prefer to be with a man and not a woman, but Sue seemed to have made up her mind that they were going to stay together the rest of their lives. That was not what Ann chose to do.

A major problem seemed to be looming before them. Talk about the old adage not sleeping with the hired help; this really exemplified it. Not only was she going to have to face the pain of telling Sue that they did not want the same things, but she was going to have to go through the humiliation of having people know that the two of them were much closer than just friends. For some reason, she really felt that Sue would not let their relationship die a quiet death, and Ann did not want that relationship known in the work place.

It seemed that so much had gone so bad again. Everywhere she looked, and every news story that came in seemed to bring more death and destruction with it. Ann wasn't sure, but it seemed that there were more people than ever that were so distraught with the government and their lack of being able to control in any way the problems that besieged the country.

The food supply, at least in the southern United States was at least enough to survive, and she was very thankful for what they had. The famine that had been in Southern California and throughout parts of the Eastern Seaboard had seemingly been solved by food drops from helicopters and that helped many survive even in the parts of Los Angelis that was so hard hit by the tidal wave and earthquakes.

The latest reports she had seen stated that, in all, worldwide, at least three quarters of a billion people died in the last three years.

Ann could not help but think how self-centered she was. The deaths and disasters were unprecedented in history, and her biggest problem right now was one of a jealous lover, and not even a man lover at that. A short time ago, she would have been reviled at the very thought of touching another woman, but now she was only concerned not with touching a woman, but rather of breaking off a long-standing relationship. How much she had changed, and if she was honest with herself, it probably was not for the best.

Ann began to wonder about Patty, her daughter. She had not been able to talk to her, or her ex husband since the people disappeared. Ann hoped she was okay, but she had never been able to get through to her ex. Ann missed her so much. *A thought crossed Ann's mind of what would Patty say if she knew that Ann had been sleeping with, and been intimate with, another woman. Not a very good role model for her, that's for sure,* she thought as she let the pain of her heart creep across her face.

Probably everything that Ann thought that was good about herself had changed in a short time. She hadn't thought about it too much, but she really had changed in so many ways. Not only just with Sue, but also in the small ways of how she no longer loved her work or how she was no longer appalled by the constant stories of death that would come in to the newsroom each day.

Even the reports of people who chose to be euthanized no longer bothered her. It bothered her at first when it was made known that people, who were for the most part healthy, made the decision to opt out of life.

What was it now? she thought to herself. *Fifteen years, maybe twenty years ago that there was a creep of a doctor in Michigan, that because of a loophole in the law, would meet people in Michigan and supply them with everything that they needed to kill themselves. Now, it's become just an everyday occurrence, even here in Florida. The doctor ought to be satisfied now, he liked seeing people die so much, he's probably got the biggest do-it-yourself shop in town. Creep....*

Jerry knocked on the door, and told her, "Hey Ann, A report just came in that Mark asked me to let you know about, so we can run it in tomorrow's edition. He said it needs to be our lead because of its importance to all of us."

"Thanks Jerry, I'll take a look at it."

"Jerry, how's Sandy doing? I haven't seen you two together in so long that I was wondering about her."

"She's fine," said Jerry. "We haven't been out in so long that I sometimes wonder the same thing. Hey, Ann, I'm heading down for a coffee, would you like a cup?"

"You bet," said Ann. "You know I can always drink another cup. Thanks, Jerry."

"Okay, I'll be right back," said Jerry. "Maybe if you have some time we can talk some, I really could use a big sister talk right now."

"Sure, I need someone to talk with right now too. Thanks for offering the coffee Jerry."

Jerry walked out towards the break room, and Ann began to wonder about the unusual request. *Jerry is generally not one to talk about problems, especially to me. It must be serious,* she thought.

Jerry had been so faithful to Ann since she started at the paper. Many people were much opposed to her when she was first offered the job as editor of the paper, but Jerry never seemed to have a bad word about her or anyone else for that matter. She was very lucky to have him working with her. He was always a smiling face in the crowd and a hard worker who was never late or making excuses but just always managed to get the job done.

Ann opened her computer, and started to read the report Mark wanted her to review.

The report was through the Whitehouse Spokesman regarding what had been discussed for several months now. It was one of the first acts of the New World Order.

The Whitehouse spokesman began; "At 9:30 this morning the President of the United States signed into law that everyone living within the United States will be required to receive a RFID chip on their hand, or in their forehead, to be able to buy or sell anything. This is being done because the most important thing is to make sure everyone has what they need. This is one of the first mandates put in place by the New World Government, and agreed to by the President. The Congress has shown they are in full agreement, and voted their approval."

The spokesman continued, "The president understands that a number of people have already received the chip since they were made available. The chips will be free to everyone who does not already have one. There will be medical personal available at most open grocery stores, gas stations, and medical clinics who will be able to do the implant. The new 5G technologies that are already in place in most metropolitan areas will allow the technologies to work much better, and faster, even in areas with limited power sources. If the power is out in an area, or if they have limited Wi-Fi, then battery operated scanners, and even phone scanners can be used for transactions."

The Whitehouse spokesman said; "It is important for survival for all of us during this current crisis, and the RFID's have proven that we can fairly, and equitably, take care of all of our people in this unprecedented time of distress. Anyone who does not have their chip yet can get them at the approved sites the same day. Every transaction will go through the secured government system, to better control distribution so everyone can be equally, and equitably treated until normalcy returns, and the current emergency is over."

The spokesman continued: "Similar laws are being implemented, or are in process, worldwide and the UN General Secretary is urging all countries to consider similar measures as rapidly as possible. Additionally, the New World Government has declared they are immediately going to push to implement the RFID system worldwide, as rapidly as possible to stabilize the failing world economic system."

Ann and Sue both got the chip a few months ago. For the most part they were very pleased because it worked the way they were told it would. It was much simpler even, than a debit card because they would simply run the food through the scanner, and then you put your hand under the reader, and it automatically pays from your personal account.

Ann's mind began to drift again to the problem of Sue. She didn't want to hurt Sue, but she knew that she had to change the way things were, she could no longer continue her relationship with Sue. Although she was sure that everyone knew about the two of them, she still was not very comfortable with admitting to the people at work, and having them knowing that she was living with another woman. Worse yet, the entire office would know that they were lovers.

As Ann sat thinking, Sue broke into the office short of breath. "Ann, come quick! We've got big trouble!" Sue ran out of the doorway, and Ann trying to act at least somewhat professional, walked calmly from behind her desk to the door. Sue was already well down the hall, and running toward the conference room. She looked back at Ann and shouted, "COME ON! Ann hurry. Quick!"

Ann ran after her, and when she came into the conference room she saw four of the office staff looking incredibly at the news channel with the civil defense blasts blaring from the speakers. "What's the matter?" asked Ann as she began to read the message going across the screen.

"Ann, another underwater earthquake, but this time it is just off the coast of Mexico, directly across from us. They are saying that we may get hit with a giant tsunami in the next twenty to thirty minutes."

"Are they sure?" asked Ann? "Are they sure? How big is it anyway?"

"There's no way of telling," said Jerry. "The reports that we got after the wave hit LA, was that, on the surface they can't really tell, that all the energy of the wave is directed equally across the depth, but the full height of the wave won't be known until it gets into the shallows. As shallow as the gulf is, it could be huge. The news service said that preliminary reports are that it is an earthquake of over 8.5 and the wave could be extremely big if there was a big shift in the under water crust. It's kind of like jumping into the bathtub, if you jump in fast, you splash the water out. It depends on how much displacement that there is. If the earthquake just shook under water, we may not get anything, but if it instead shifted the sea bed twenty feet, you have a tremendous amount of energy released.

A sudden panic filled Jerry's face. Sandy! Oh my God, Sandy. I have to call her right now. I've got to warn her to get out of the house!"

"Jerry, call Sandy first and make sure she gets somewhere safe, and then get to the print room as fast as you can. Get everyone up here, do it now! We've got over twenty people here. Let's make sure that they are all up here before this thing hits. Sue, Janice, and Peg, begin calling everyone's family to let them know to get to high ground as best they can. We can't really do anything to help them any more than that. Everyone who is not getting the others from downstairs is to be on the phones. We've got maybe twenty minutes, and we need to use that time to warn as many as possible. Quickly! We don't have much time! Hurry! Let's Go!"

"Where can we go?" said Sue. "Is there anywhere that we can go that is safe?"

"Hell, Sue, we're almost a mile from shore and three stories up," said Ann. "I don't think that there's any way that the wave could reach us here, and if it's going to be here in twenty minutes, we probably can't get far enough away from the water in any direction to make any difference. The top floor is our best chance, and get on the side opposite the water. Even as low as we are to the water, I don't think that we can get any place that's safer. Get everyone in the print room out of there, and up to the top floor quickly! Move everyone to the conference room on the third floor, and see if we can shut down the power so we don't have a fire if the water reaches this far in. Hurry! Everyone; Get going!"

They immediately began calling the families of the staff, and everyone they knew. There was really no way that they would know if there would be a wave until it was too late, and all they could do was sound the warning to get to safety.

Jerry yelled out to Ann that he got through to Sandy and she was heading to the over pass at Highway 19 and would meet Jerry there after it was over.

As they were all scrambling to ready themselves, another; ALERT!!! ALERT!!! ALERT!!! moved across the screen. "An earthquake of Biblical proportions has struck the heartland of America. An earthquake exceeding 9.2 in the New Madrid fault line has opened up a miles-long chasm under the Mississippi River, and brought down buildings as far away as Chicago and Indianapolis."

Less than a mile away from the paper, a couple was fishing on the bank of the intercostal waterway. Dick and his wife Joanne, had been vacationing three years ago when the people disappeared.

A pleasantly plump couple, they were always the two cards to get everyone laughing and seemed to get the most from even the short side of life. When people would look at them, they could always tell that they were made for each other. Both were near the five-foot-five mark and seemed to carry identical smiles for everyone. Dick had a large robust nose that put Durante to shame, and Joanne's round face seemed the perfect match. Their smiles always brought them instant friends where ever they went.

The cottage they were staying in was a small two-bedroom they had rented from friends in Redington Beach. When the people disappeared, they could no longer get back home to Maine. The friends they rented the cottage from were among the ones who disappeared. Dick and Joanne were never approached by anyone to leave. When the banks shut down and they were left without any money, they had a very difficult, but not impossible time. They felt very fortunate that at least they weren't up in Maine during the winter without any heat, like some of their family who still lived there.

The government programs that Washington put into place for food distribution kept them from starving, and they had actually gotten to where they were enjoying their time together. They were away from the problems downtown, and because of the gas shortages and economy, few travelers made it to the beaches anymore. They were very fortunate indeed.

Joanne was the first to notice that the water was rushing away from the shore extremely fast. The water was dropping at what appeared to be a foot a minute, and in the three years that they lived there, they never saw that happen. Even when there was a real low tide, it never dropped that fast.

The cottage was across the street, and they heard several of the neighbors hollering for them and waving frantically.

Quickly winding the poles up and grabbing the bucket, they headed to the cottage to see what was going on. Jackie and Andy were standing at the edge of the property and motioning for them to come quickly and see what was happening. What they saw absolutely stunned them. It was as though the plug had been pulled on the whole ocean, and the water went out.

As they walked toward what used to be the shoreline and looked out, the water was too far away for them to even see clearly, just a slight line on the horizon. Everything was exposed to the air. The coral reef four hundred feet away from shore was visible, and in all the time they lived in the cottage, they had never seen it.

Joanne stood by Dick, and they watched as the water receded further from view.

"My God, what's happening?" said Joanne softly, almost in shock.

All Dick could respond with was a profound, "I don't know."

They stood on the white sand along with their friends from the cottage and watched the horizon in disbelief. Johnson, from two doors down, was the first to see it. "LOOK!" he said. "It's coming back!"

Too mesmerized to move, and with nowhere to run, Dick and Joanne stood on the beach, and within less than a minute, saw the wave reach over one hundred feet high above them. The last thing Dick said was, "Oh, my God, have mercy on us!"

Brenda was beginning her rounds after one of her constant battles with the administration for more supplies. The administrators wanted her to continue to operate with few supplies and in ways that had been outdated even before she became a nurse.

It had almost gotten to the point of not even being worth the hassle to continue with what she was trained to do. Government rules and regulations had created an almost-impossible situation for her to work in. She had few of the supplies needed for the care of the patients and had to spend much of her day filling out need requests that often would not be responded to for weeks. The constant red tape and hoops she had to go through had nothing to do with the care of the patients and everything to do with pleasing some pompous ass in Washington.

The hospital was rapidly falling into a state of disrepair, and the patients were suffering because of a lack of even the most basic of supplies.

She was excited when she located some unused supplies in a clinic that had been shut down some time ago. They were outdated, but most of it was usable, and they were certainly better than nothing. Even after what she had been through, she was proud that her focus still remained on the welfare of the patient.

Stepping into her office, Brenda found a memo from the hospital administrator regarding a meeting at 2:30 to discuss the direction the hospital was taking and that he wanted her to take part in it. Finally, she might be able to get the help she needed to cut through some of the blockage of supplies she was facing. She would really like the opportunity to see if she could effect and help implement the changes she wanted to see.

CODE 1 ALERT! CODE 1 ALERT! All supervisors report immediately to administration, all supervisors report immediately to administration! blasted the intercom.

Brenda heard that used before, *Maybe there's another riot. Something's wrong. Something is seriously wrong.* Brenda thought, as she ran toward the administration offices to find out what it was.

She arrived to find that most of the other supervisors and directors were already there. The hospital administrator was there and already speaking.

"We have a major crisis. We have just received a call telling us that a major earthquake off of Mexico has taken place, and they believe it may create a tidal wave like the one that hit LA last year. I don't need to tell any of you that we are only fourteen feet above sea level. If a tidal wave hits here, there is no way we can protect against it, and we do not have the time to move the patients to another hospital that is on higher ground. What we must do is to move all patients from the seaward side of the hospital and to the middle aisle, and move everyone from the ground floor to a higher floor away from the windows and doors. We have been informed that we probably have no more than ten to twenty minutes before this hits, if it does. Good luck all of you, let's get the patients moved NOW!"

Brenda turned and ran back towards the ER. Quickly, she went through her mental checklist of things she had to do to get the people to a higher elevation in the hospital. She knew that they had three or four patients that had been admitted within the last hour or so, who would need help getting upstairs, but for the most part it would be mostly staff needing to get upstairs. As Brenda reached the corner going into the ER, she was already barking orders to the staff.

"Everyone who can walk, get yourselves to the stairway and walk up to the higher floors!" she yelled. "I want all of the staff to move any bed-ridden patients into the elevators and move them into the hallways of the second floor or higher now! As soon as you have the patients unloaded come back down until we get all of the patients moved. We must move them all to higher ground, NOW!!"

Brenda was amazed at the efficiency of those that worked for her. She was proud of the nurses that she had chosen and trained. They were probably among the most efficient nurses in the entire hospital, and it showed.

Within ten minutes, the entire floor was evacuated, and Brenda began a quick walk through to be sure everything was secure and there were no stragglers.

The last thing Brenda heard was what sounded like the rumble of a large freight train approaching.

The last thing Brenda saw was the explosion of the wall coming toward her.....

As Jerry and the others reached the conference room, the warning sirens were wailing in the background.

"Ann, Sandy just called, and she made it to the 19 overpass. She'll meet me there when this is over," said Jerry when he saw Ann approaching.

"Thanks for letting me know," said Ann. "I'm glad you got through okay. She'll be okay, she's pretty resourceful, and she has to be tough being married to you for so long."

"Thanks, Ann, I needed that." He smiled.

"Is everyone here?" Ann yelled out.

"No," said Pat from personnel. "Fritz and Hank Alexander are on the other side of the building, watching for the wave, and they will alert us when and if it comes. They are going to try to get some shots of the wave coming in for tomorrow's paper if they can".

"Damn it! Don't they know that the waves travel at several hundred miles an hour under water? The waves came in at nearly a hundred miles an hour when they hit LA. They may not have time to get out of there. I want everyone accounted for when this is over!" said Ann.

"I'll get them!" yelled Jerry as he quickly left the room. He got to the doorway where Fritz and Hank were standing just in time to see a wall of water over forty feet high coming down East Bay Street, covering every-thing in its path. Jerry just yelled, "My God! Come quick. Get out of there!"

Fritz stood his ground snapping pictures, and Hank turned to Jerry with a look of knowing it was too late for him.

Everyone in the conference room was filled with fear as the sound approached them. It sounded to Ann like a freight train running out of control. There was nothing in any of her memories that even remotely sounded as loud.

The wave hit with such a force that the windows exploded from all sides of the building. The entire building wretched and groaned from the foundation and swayed violently with its death throes screaming out, and the entire west side of the building collapsed into the rushing water. Glass filled the air, and the water came rushing through. The entire building shuttered and threw them to the floor.

They were still in shock when the muddy receding water brought back a semi-trailer and crashed it into the offices below.

Within minutes, it was over. Half of the building was still standing. When they looked out across the parking lot, they could see the *Sun* was one of the few buildings left standing in the entire area.

Ann stood in shock. The beautiful oaks outside the building were gone, and as far as she could see, there was only total, and absolute, destruction.

Behind her, she heard Pat cry out first, "Ann! It's Sue! Come quick!"

Ann turned and saw two of the employees pulling a desk from off the top of Sue's broken body. Ann ran over, and Sue began to moan and cry out from the pain. Sue's arm was badly broken with the bone protruding through the skin, and she was bleeding profusely from deep cuts across her chest and stomach.

"Does anyone know first aid?" yelled a panicked Ann. "Hurry. Help me stop the bleeding!"

"Help me, Ann," Sue whispered, "Please help me."

They tried to stop the bleeding by compressing the wound. Sue was coughing up a lot of blood, and her breathing was labored. She had a heavy wheezy sound to her breathing, and Ann recognized it as "the death rattle."

Ann held Sue gently as her lifeblood slipped from her body, and she cradled her head until the breathing stopped. "I love you Sue. I love you. Please don't leave me alone. Please don't leave me alone," Ann whispered, oblivious to those around her. Through the wrenching pain and blurred eyes as Ann gently laid Sue back to the floor, she said, "You are the lucky one, sweetheart. You are the lucky one."

Janice was enjoying the recognition and perks of channeling the famous Ramel. She was surprised when Jon said that they were going back to Tampa for a meeting.

She had been going from meeting to meeting and on the road now for nearly six months. A return to Tampa was something she had been looking forward to.

When they arrived, she asked Jon to drive her past the old house. It looked as though it was vacant. When she saw it there was an instant hurt, and she decided she didn't want to go in. The thought of her daughter lingered too heavy on her mind, and she was torn inside when she saw the house. It was her dream home just a few short years ago. She wondered if her daughter ever came back, if maybe the police found her daughter and never contacted her.

It was harder for her to look at the house than she could have imagined it would be. Seeing the house made her remember how much her past life meant to her. She had Jon leave without getting out of the car. It was best to leave the past behind and move on with where her life was going.

Jon had gotten them the penthouse on the top floor of the Sheraton near the airport. It was a beautiful view from the top floor of the hotel, and she was enjoying it immensely. If only the snobs down the street from the old house could see her now, they would really flip their wigs.

In such a short time, she had become one of the most influential people in the country, with the senators and famous people everywhere wanting to hear from the famous Ramel. *What a bunch of suckers people are. There's one born every minute,* she thought.

She could have anything she wanted because of the tremendous power Ramel had over people. Everyone wanted to know the future, and Ramel knew the future they wanted was the one that tickled their insides so much. Everia was right, much of what she did was a show, and she learned to play the show to the max. She could have anything-anything.

She had really thought about getting rid of Jon, but instead, she talked him into some three-way sex. It surprised her when Jon agreed, and now, she was enjoying being serviced by two men at the same time. The power over them was exhilarating, and she knew how progressively and increasingly demanding she was becoming in her sexual needs, but it didn't matter.

Two men and she would tear them up. *Stupid, puny, wimpy, punks,* she thought in Ramels voice. She no longer knew if it was she who thought her thoughts or Ramel, but she was insatiable in her lust and no longer ever satisfied.

The phone rang, and she answered it. "Miss, the management wants to warn you against going outside, there is an alert out which is for a possible tidal wave that may be headed here. We want you to be sure to stay safe up in your room," the man said in a very formal British way.

"Thank you," she said. "We will stay here until you say its okay."

Janice slowly got out of bed and began to walk to the window to look toward the ocean. Jon and the other man were still sleeping in the bed. Janice stood naked at the window and called to them to come over to watch with her. Jon was the first to get up, and they could see that the bay had nearly dried up.

Then they saw it in the distance. Even from the top floor, they could see the wave was a massive dark wall of water moving across to Clearwater. It looked to them to be at least fifty feet tall and swallowed everything in its path. They watched as it moved toward the hotel at a neck breaking speed.

Several cars were on the 49th Street Bridge when the wave hit the bridge and enveloped them. They watched as the wave followed the causeway and destroyed everything in its path. By the time it reached the hotel, there was only a remnant of the wave left. It stopped just short of the hotel, leaving a pile of debris at the edge of the parking lot.

Jon and the man who was with them stood reeling from the horror at what they had just witnessed. Only a very few of the larger buildings remained standing, and they looked to be totally destroyed.

The three stood together at the window, but neither of the men felt Ramel's presence or saw him dancing with glee in the eyes of Janice.

CHAPTER SEVENTEEN

Israel in the Desert – Saints over comers Events in the time of Revelation 12

The praise and worship part of the service had been extremely joyous, and there was a beautiful peace over the congregation as their hearts were touched from the music and singing. Many of the townspeople had come to be with the people at the camp in anticipation of what was to take place today.

Summer harvest was drawing to a close, and already, some of the trees had begun to change. The harvest was a good one. It would be enough to feed the camp even if there were more arrivals during the winter.

So much growth had taken place in Spiritual Life over the summer. No longer was this only a place for those seeking to get away, but there was a growth here, spiritual and mental, and one of peace for all. They had grown so fast and in so many ways. Many of the housing needs they had because of the additional people were met with the empty buildings and cottages around the area.

They found enough musical instruments to make a "joyful noise onto the Lord," as Jim called it, and they were not lacking now with the number of people who knew how to play them. Joe was fantastic on the saxophone, and Chinney was doing extremely well with the piano. A new arrival, Samantha played the guitar. They had a wonderful time playing and singing, and all of them enjoyed the music.

Jim began the service with a prayer. He was very weak, but he told Chris and Chinney that he wanted to bring the message to the congregation.

Jim had been getting progressively weaker, so Chris found a microphone and a speaker they could run off batteries so Jim would not have to speak too loud to be heard.

A number of people came from town, and everyone at the camp was looking forward to a great day. Jim had always been the spiritual leader for the camp, and everyone in the camp looked to him for guidance. His failing health made it very difficult for him to be outside, and even the smallest exertion now was causing him severe breathing problems.

As he cleared his throat to begin to speak, a hushed sense of anticipation came over the room.

Jim began, "Brothers and sisters in Christ, I want to bring this message to you for two reasons. One is to reveal what God has shown me through his word for these last days, and the second is to have a formal ordination service to recognize by man what God has done in the lives of two of our brothers. Both have been doing the work of the ministry for some time, but I feel that now is the time to formally pass the mantel to them. "

"Chris has learned much in such a short time, and his love for God is unquestionable. He walks with the Holy Spirit in truth and integrity. Chinney, who came from the streets of Detroit, has been guided by God to be here. He has a love for God and a sensitivity to God's leading that few have. God has called both to be his ministers and to preach the Gospel. Chris will be ordained by me this day to fulfill in man's eyes what God has already done in his life. Chris is my choice for the one to replace me."

"Chinney is my choice for assistant pastor of the flock that God has brought together here. Chinney has been chosen to be an assistant not because of loving the Lord less but because he is younger in both age and in time with the Lord. Both are to be given the highest respect due their office and calling. The service for ordination will be after the word given me by God for these final days."

"Brothers and Sisters in the Lord, I have been given a word from the Lord to convey to you concerning the remaining time before the next taking away of the saints. As you know, the first rapture took place almost three and a half years ago. If we are worthy, we will be taken up as well sometime after the middle of this tribulation time. We will be taken up just before the wrath of God is poured out over the world. One of the things that will take place to trigger this will be when the Antichrist goes to Jerusalem and breaks the peace treaty with Israel. He will go into the rebuilt Temple of Solomon in Jerusalem, and blaspheme God by announcing that he is god. Shortly after he does that, God will begin the pouring out of his final wrath upon the earth.

"For those of you who have a Bible turn to Revelation 14:14. Please share it with the people on either side of you. We are still trying to find more Bibles so everyone has one."

"In Revelation, John, the Revelator, wrote down what he saw about much of what we are living in today. We are truly living in the end times, and we all are very aware of what is happening throughout the world through the limited news receive. We only have to look at current events to understand what is coming and how to best prepare for it."

"Today, we're going to look at Revelation 14:14 to 14:16 to better understand what will trigger the next taking away of the saints. I want all of you to realize that this next rapture of the multitudes will include the Jews. When the Antichrist desecrates the temple, the Jewish people will have their eyes opened and realize Jesus is the Messiah. The Bible tells us the Jewish people, at that time, will flee to the desert away from the Antichrist rule."

"We have heard on the radio that the rebuilt temple is ready, and is to be formally dedicated in the next few days. This is a prelude to what must happen for the eyes of the Jewish people to be opened, and for them to be part of the great harvest to come. Please turn to Revelation 14:14-16"

> [14] I looked, and there before me was a white cloud, and seated on to the cloud was one "like

> a son of man" with a crown of gold on his head and a sharp sickle in his hand. ¹⁵ Then another angel came out of the temple and called in a loud voice to him who was sitting on the cloud, "Take your sickle and reap, because the time to reap has come, for the harvest of the earth is ripe." ¹⁶ So he who was seated on the cloud swung his sickle over the earth, and the earth was harvested.
> Revelation 14:14-16 (NIV)

"What I want to share with you today is the time leading up to the harvest of the great multitude. With God's mercy, others may come that we may share God's word with those who might still turn to God. I propose we send everyone out two-by-two, and cover the entire area, searching for anyone we may help. We must work diligently for the people who may still come. How many we are talking about I don't know, but I do know if only one more comes to the Lord because of what we collectively do, then it will have been worth every effort we can possibly make."

"For what price can you put on the soul of even one person?" continued Jim.

"We must set this camp up and work diligently toward sharing the word of God everywhere there might be people we can reach. Let's all work together so that we can help them to know Jesus as Lord and Savior, and to know he is the only living God."

"We have a responsibility before God to spread his word to everyone we meet. We know about where we are in time, based on what has already taken place. The people who went into glory in the first rapture, prepared themselves through prayer, helping others, and loving the Lord."

"The Bible tells us that the Lord is quick to forgive, and for us to ask forgiveness, and it will be forgiven as long as we have a sincere heart. Seven years from the first rapture will be the coming of Jesus Christ in all of his glory. All of us, who go to be with him in the coming harvest of the earth, will be returning with him. We are born through his Spirit to be sons of the living God, and we will reign with him over all the earth, in the millennium."

"The wisest people of all were the ones who came to a saving knowledge of God, and were in the rapture. Blessed are they, for, right now, they are in glory and the presence of our Lord Jesus. This I would have you learn, and I desire to leave you most of all. Teach Jesus, his way, his life, his love, and seek him as your best friend, and you will see everything inside you come alive. Share that love for those who come, that they will have a chance to be with our Lord and Savior for all eternity."

Jim's voice began to weaken and fall to a softer pitch. He told the congregation that he would give the ordination services now for the two new pastors.

He got up from the chair he was in, and with a great deal of pain from his shortness of breath, he ordained them with the laying on of hands. When he had finished he presented them to the congregation and a celebration was soon to begin.

The last thing that he told them was that he was soon to go to be with the Lord. He was tired, and his body was full of pain. He had done what the Lord wanted him to do and had fulfilled what he had been called to do. He did not want anyone to grieve for him when he was gone, but rather rejoice for his joy of being with the Lord. "In all things give praise onto the Lord," he said. God had brought two to them who would guide them and teach them, and Jim told them that he would be waiting for them in heaven.

"Praise God for his great mercy and kindness for all he has done. Thank him for his Son Jesus always in everything you do," said Jim as he left to go to the bedroom.

The tsunami devastated the entire western coastline of Florida, and the Tampa Bay area seemed the hardest hit of all. Jeremie went into St. Petersburg from Lakeland to meet with some of the St. Petersburg leaders to survey the damage. The leaders wanted to set up food kitchens to feed the many people coming for help and needed additional supplies.

The leaders discussed expanding the camp in the center of the state near the small town of Avion so it would hold more people. They estimated they had room enough for as many as three hundred additional folding cots with the buildings they already had, and they could get enough supplies or scavenge enough to put up a few small buildings to house more if needed.

Jeremie and the leaders scheduled a drive to the destroyed areas of St. Petersburg to determine how they would best be able to help the survivors.

Even though Jeremie was briefed on the destruction, when he saw it, he wept openly. As they drove across the bridge from East Tampa into St. Petersburg, the debris pile from where the wave had ended was twenty feet high. Cars were piled one on top of the other and littered about were pieces of homes and buildings. As they drove near several destroyed cars, he saw some of the homeless, bent over with a hollow look on their faces, scavenging through the debris. There was no mistaking where the wave had stopped its advance.

God would soon begin to bring forth his final wrath on mankind in a complete and powerful way that would herald the end of time.

Jeremie was surprised at the speed by which the time seemed to have gone by. It was almost as though time itself had speeded up. The Scriptures say that near the end, God would speed up the time so the elect could survive, and he was sure that's where they were now.

So much to do in such a short time and so many depended on him for direction in what they were to do. God would speak to any who would seek him, and he would do that in many different ways. Sometimes, however, Jeremie felt as though many of the leaders who looked to him as a spiritual leader would choose to hear only what God was saying through him and not seek God for themselves.

The church they were heading to this morning was the first church he went to shortly after the rapture. It was the church where the pastor had the same size cloths and shoes as he did.

As they pulled into the church parking lot, Jeremie saw that what he had started by God's direction had become a living, breathing

thing. The church parking lot was full, not with cars but rather with people who had come to the church to receive help and to hear God's word.

Jeremie walked with the other leaders through the parking lot and several people recognized him and came to greet him. He was especially happy to see some of the people who were helping with the crowd in the parking lot, had been some of the first who came after the people disappeared in the first rapture.

After a short time talking with several of the congregation, the leaders moved Jeremie toward the building where many people were gathering to hear him speak.

When Jeremie walked into the building, the praise team had been playing for some time and was finishing the last of the worship songs. The senior rabbi led him to a chair near the back of the platform.

When the praise team finished singing the last worship song, the rabbi walked to the microphone, and as the song was nearing the end he introduced Jeremie. "He has been set aside by God as a witness to the people in the end times, and is one of the 144,000 spoken of in the book of Revelation. Pastor Jeremie is from the tribe of Asher," the rabbi said.

Jeremie thanked the rabbi and began with a prayer for the people and all believers throughout the world.

"My brothers and sisters in Christ Jesus, it is a privilege and honor to be with you today," said Jeremie as he began.

"I remember with awe that first day when the angel of the living God came to me and woke me to begin what God had set me aside to do since before the beginning of time. I give the one true living God praise because he called me to do his work for the final harvest. It is a blessing to me to again be among some of you that I have known so long," said Jeremie.

"I am going to talk to you today about where we are in history and where we are in the timing of Scripture, especially the books of Daniel and Revelation, and help you understand why we are going through the pain and struggles each of us has been experiencing. While the Lord is providing for all of us even now in the time of tribulation, we are still to go through much, and for many, it is even onto death. The persecution is taking place, and as you know and many are painfully aware, this persecution has, and is, and will be increasing because the very name of Jesus is an affront to a lost and dying world."

"Believers in these United States are under attack by Washington led-liberals. After the rapture, as we all know, conservatives, Christians, and Messianic Jews have been blamed for the resulting anarchy and ultimate devastation in many areas of the United States."

"I constantly pray that God gives strength to those who are being persecuted, for I know that the persecution is real and can cause many to fall. Only those who are totally sold out for God will be able to stand without falling from the test. It is not that God is not a loving God, but he is a fair and just God and will judge each of us by our actions. If you put your trust in God, and lean totally on him, you will stand in the midst of this time of tribulation and the persecution, and you will be saved from the coming wrath of God."

Jeremie continued; "How much easier it was for believers who found God and his salvation through Jesus before the first rapture, which was the rapture of the church. They were sold out to God and reborn through Jesus by accepting Jesus as their Lord and Savior. But now, my brothers and sisters, many of us will die for our beliefs. There is no in between. It is not easy, and to belong to God everything else has to come second, even to the point of death. In some places in the world it has become open warfare against us."

"The Jewish people have been blamed for the destruction of Syria and Iran," continued Jeremie. "Few leaders have taken the position or acknowledged that Israel had no other choice but to attack Iran because of their blatant continuation toward nuclear armament and vows to destroy Israel."

"Those of us who believe in and have acknowledged the saving grace of Jesus have been declaring that the reason the people had disappeared, was because God had taken out those who were saved, this is commonly referred to as the rapture of the church."

Jeremie continued. "We know that there will be a great harvest and taking away, which will come before the end of the seven year time of tribulation. This harvest will take place to take to heaven the Jewish people, and the people who have come to a saving knowledge since the first rapture. When we openly proclaim that the only way to not be left on earth when the final outpouring of God's wrath is poured upon the earth is to be born again in Jesus Christ. This does not sit well with many of the religions of the world. In fact, there are many religions and leaders in the world who are saying that the ones who disappeared from the world was because God had taken out all who were not going to become one in unity and harmony."

"Many religions have banded together against us under the banner of the Council of the Court of Coexistence, often referred to as the CCC, and Chrislam. By against us, I mean the Messianic Jewish community, and believers in Christ Jesus. They are telling their people that divisiveness comes through those who say that Christ Jesus is the only way to heaven. They are saying the world religions must stand together in this time of despair to promote world unity under a one-world order and a one-world church-the CCC, for the common good and survival of mankind."

"The pope recently said again that the Messianic Jews, and Christians are the most divisive and destructive elements in the world today. He went on to say that all Roman Catholics need to remain firm to the teachings of the Church, and remain under the blessings of the holy mother. They are to accept that the members of the CCC are co-laborers with them to bring harmony and peace back into the world."

"The pope went on to say that going into the future the world would be filled with Joy. The people would begin to learn of their own divinity and rule over their own destinies," Jeremie continued. "The pope has endorsed the Council of the Court of Coexistence as being truly what God intended. He stated that the CCC formed a bond between all nations and peoples to express the love of God in their own way and in peace, and he endorsed the oneness and unity of mankind entering a time of peaceful co-existence with God as the head."

"The pope nominated the former Jesuit Leader to be the first leader and his representative to the CCC, and has in effect joined the

Roman Catholic Church with Muslims, Buddhists, and every other religion."

"When the pope unexpectedly announced, by decree, that the Roman Catholic Church would be part of the CCC, he brought about an immediate outrage from many of the cardinals and leaders of the church that he was deliberately destroying the very foundation the church had been built upon. Angry accusations were shouted out, and one of the cardinals stood up and stated that the prophecies of the 266th pope being a heretic of the faith had now been fulfilled. Already, many of the leaders and even entire congregations have separated themselves from the church because of it."

"Some accounts stated that it seemed surreal, and it was almost as though the pope was fantasizing and danced as though he was deliberately stepping over the bodies of the people whose lives and beliefs he destroyed as he left the cathedral."

"Shortly after the announcement by decree, the pope attacked Christians by stating the part of the Gospel message that says 'that you must be born again,' and 'there is no other way to salvation but Jesus,' is taken out of context of what God had wanted," Jeremie continued.

"The pope very pointedly said the Catholic Church, was, and always has been, God's chosen church. The pope stated it is through consistent communion with God through the priests, who are trained to lead the people of the church, that one is saved."

"The pope continued by saying the problem with the Messianic Jews and Christians is that they read the Bible, and try to decipher what it says themselves. They actually think they hear God, but they are being deceived by Satan himself. What can the untrained man know of God but that he exists? The priests, through the guidance of the most holy church, will lead man to all things."

Jeremie continued, "The Catholic stance is that the priest hears from God through the direct guidance of the pope, and the pope is God's voice on earth."

"The pope further went on to say to pray the rosary and all will be right in the world. Mother Mary would intercede for all who would pray to her, and she would guide and enlighten them to the way God would have them go. They were, after all, the first church, and the church has been chosen by God to lead the people to him. The pope concluded by saying that the Council of the Court of Coexistence brings unity to the world in a time of crisis and we must love all our brothers in the world. We must respect them and their beliefs to create one world of peace."

Jeremie took a deep breath and paused briefly before continuing. "I have never preached against the Catholic believers of Christ, and many Catholics were part of the rapture. But I must tell you that the pope is wrong, and he is leading many to the very brink of hell. Gods speaks through his written word."

"There are many Catholics who know Jesus and many who were part of the rapture. Many do not though, and when they say, 'I went to church this week and so therefore I am saved,' is wrong, they are wrong. They must seek God for themselves. The word of God clearly states that there will be many who say, "Lord, Lord" who will not enter the kingdom of heaven. Jesus said, 'Then I will tell them plainly, 'I never knew you, Away from me, you evil doers!'"

"I want to warn you about Chrislam as well. It's a blending of religions of the world very similar too, and a part of the CCC. It has been a leader of the attacks on the Messianic Jewish community."

"We have been shown that Jesus is the Christ and is the Messiah the Jewish community has waited for. By our belief of a doctrine that does not allow for the multitude of other gods, the Messianic Jews and Christians are not accepted. To tell a Buddhist, Muslim, or anyone of any other world religion that Jesus is the only way to salvation, and that they have to be born again, creates divisions. It has in part led to the mass killings of Messianic, Jewish, and Christians in many parts of the world."

"In closing, you are the light of the world, and it is imperative you maintain and keep close to the people who will teach and guide you. We also have brought many Bibles for the feeding of your soul and food for the feeding of your body. Anyone who needs either, please join us, and keep in the local groups that will help you and support you in these final times," Jeremie concluded. He nodded to the musicians, and they began playing worship once again."

The Gone

Jeremie stepped down from the platform, and as the music played softly in the background, he asked if anyone wanted to receive Christ as their Savior to come forward. Eight people came to the Lord that day. Jeremie was amazed at how God has a way of bringing his people through even the hardships of life to his saving grace.

Jeremie left the sanctuary to meet with the leaders of the church in order to go over their needs.

Jeremie told them that the camp they had in the middle of the state was being expanded to accommodate more people. Everyone who needed to remain in St. Petersburg, and especially, the people who were called to preach and teach the gospel, every effort would be made to help provide them with what they needed to stay.

There were those who would be needed in both places, and shuttle vehicles would be made available for transportation back and forth. The word of God must go out to everyone, and the time was growing short. It was felt there was only a short time left, and much needed to be done.

The entire West Coast of Florida collapsed again into anarchy from the destruction caused by the tsunami. FEMA was nowhere to be seen. Ann heard someone say they no longer had the resources or manpower to handle another disaster. The ongoing nationwide crisis left too few resources, and the government leaders only seemed concerned for their own survival.

Ann walked to the condo and rummaged through her belongings in order to gather together what she needed to get away to the center of the state. She needed to escape what she saw as the end of all civilization as she knew it. When she reached the condo, she found it was heavily damaged and the garage wall was gone. The door was open, and it was clear someone had pried it open and broken into it. The power was not on, but from what she could see, it appeared they took most of the food and rummaged through drawers for whatever they could use. The tsunami took everything from her: Sue, work, and even Homer, her cat, was gone.

She found an old backpack of Sue's and filled it with a change of clothes and a few toiletries. She put on her tennis shoes and heavy socks for walking. She scrounged through the kitchen and found some chips, a can of tuna, and two cans of pork and beans near the back of the pantry. Ann had little more than the clothes on her back, but she was determined to get away from what she saw coming. She saw her pair of in-line skates and decided to take them as well. She was saddened as she walked toward the door, her entire life was in a backpack and a pair of skates.

Riots raged across the area. A cop who stopped her while she was walking told her that the riots were moving her way. He said she was in danger if she stayed out on the streets and that she must get inside somewhere, and lock the doors.

Ann decided that, instead, she would try to go to the center of the state to get away from the cities and people. Ann walked for several hours keeping as far as she could from any groups of people. She had grown accustomed to seeing the destruction of the neighborhoods from her condo to the office, but she had not been on this road for over two years now, and if she didn't see the street signs, she would not have known where she was. Everywhere she looked, she was appalled, and saddened. If this was what the rest of the United States was like, she knew they would never recover.

As she walked she came to a car that was left running near the gate where some soldiers were talking and unloading small boxes from a truck. She had never stolen anything before, but impulsively she climbed in it and sped away. One of the soldiers yelled and cursed at her, and she thought she heard gunfire behind her. Ann would go as far as the gas would take her. She didn't know what was ahead, but she would continue go towards the middle of the state. If she ended up dying there, so be it.

As Ann sped south on the I-275 bi-pass, she passed close to the church where Jeremie was speaking, but they would never meet.

Her mind drifted to her daughter and her ex-husband, and she wondered how they were. She thought of Sue and what she had meant to her. Sue, for all her faults, was the friend that she missed so much.

She had a strange feeling that she was going to her destiny and maybe her death, but she had really lost all hope and no longer cared. What was ahead for her, was ahead. *Caesura, caesura, whatever will be, will be, the futures not ours to see, caesura, caesura.* "As the old song sang in her head she remembered her mother singing it to her when she was a child.

She thought back to her mother and how she used to take her to Sunday school. Her mother always told her that when she would get to know God, he would be her best friend. She really needed a friend right now.

As Ann traveled into the center of the State, she began to realize that this stretch of road had not changed from what she remembered some six years ago when she had last traveled this way. She didn't like it then because she thought it was so desolate, but now the desolation gave her a sense of peace. There was no visible destruction she could see from the road. It didn't appear to her that it had changed at all. Looking across an empty field into the woods, she almost felt transported back to a better time, and she was beginning to look forward, for the first time in many months, to what lay ahead.

Maybe life will be good again, she thought. For the first time in what seemed an eternity, a small bright smile of hope came to her face.

Yostock was resting with several of the other rabbi a short distance away from the temple. They were reflecting on the events of the last few weeks. Such a great honor had been bestowed on them in this time of all times. To be part of the events taking place now was an honor they could have never known without Gods leading and help.

The celebration had been continuous since they brought the Ark of the Covenant into the Temple. It had taken several months longer than they thought it would, but now everything was prepared for the formal dedication of the Temple. Today would be a day that would go down in history. All was ready, and the beginning of the daily sacrifices to God would begin.

They were expecting the Messiah to soon enter the city and take his place in the Holy of Holies. The excitement and anticipation, of what they felt was imminent, was almost surreal.

Leaders from around the world, including hundreds of the Jewish leaders, were expected to be at the dedication. There were multiple journalists and news crews outside the gates. It would be broadcast world-wide for all to see.

They were told that the president of the New World Order and the leaders of the Council of the Court of Coexistence were coming as well. They were scheduled to visit the site of the CCC, between the Masque and the Temple after the dedication of the Temple was over. It was unknown if the New World Order leaders would visit the Masque afterwards as well, but the rabbi speculated it would take place. Yostock and the other rabbi with him were scheduled to return to the inner sanctuary of the Temple in an hour.

Three weeks ago, there was an assassination attempt on the New World Order President, and he was rushed to the hospital where he was declared dead. The world mourned for a short time, but on the third day the mourning turned to celebration when he arose from the dead.

He was the reason that the Middle-East peace agreement was signed, and the Temple could be rebuilt. He was considered the most powerful man in the world. Yostock was ecstatic to hear he was coming.

As they were reviewing the schedule for the day, a messenger came in and told them that the president and the leaders of the CCC arrived at the airport earlier than expected. Both of their planes landed, and it was not certain how long before they would be arriving at the Temple. The messenger told them it would be good if they went back into the inner courtyard early. He also said something that concerned Yostock. A very large contingency of UN soldiers started to arrive, and it appeared they were stationing themselves around not only the Temple Mount area, but also around the outer court area. The messenger said, a friend of his called him a short time before, and it appeared as though soldiers were amassing in several strategic areas throughout the city.

Yostock and the other rabbi quickly began preparing themselves to go into the inner court.

As they were getting ready, the messenger received another call telling him, the leaders had left the airport, and were heading directly to the Temple Mount. The newly elected New World Order President, the new CCC leader, who Yostock understood was the former Black Pope of the Jesuits, and the Roman Catholic Pope, along with a large delegation would be arriving within twenty minutes.

Yostock and the other rabbis walked to the entranceway to the Inner Court. Yostock had a very uneasy feeling as they were walking. He felt sick to his stomach, and he couldn't remember ever feeling such anxiety. They made a quick check to be sure everything was in order, and moved off to the side to wait for the arrival of the delegation.

The excitement for them continued to increase, and Yostock was beyond thankful he was part of it. The President of the world was coming to be part of the celebration of the dedication of the Temple of Solomon. The most incredible moment in history was about to take place.

Thousands were already gathered in the outer court, and many more were outside the Temple Mount waiting for the celebrations to begin. Within the few minutes that seemed to last forever, Yostock looked back over his life, and how everything seemed to be exploding to a grand finality of historical proportions. .

A few blocks away, the sirens announced the approaching cavalcade.

As the delegation arrived and walked into the outer court, they collectively moved to the side, and stood waiting for the president to walk in.

Yostock was surprised at the large number of security people who came in, pushing aside the people who were already standing there. The security team blocked off a path for the president and the pope to walk through.

The president walked in first. The Roman Catholic Pope and the Black Pope walked a few feet behind him through the gate. All three were given secured seating to allow them to watch the dedication.

Yostock was standing on the other side of the inner sanctuary with the other rabbi.

It was a proud moment for the rabbi when the President's delegation was set in place. Dedicatory prayers were read, and preparations were made to begin.

The perfect red heifer was brought in to be the first blood sacrifice for the sins of the Jewish people. As they brought the heifer forward, the President unexpectedly stood, and began to walk forward to the altar of sacrifice.

Everyone was in disbelief when he climbed up onto the altar.....

Yostock heard the President speak in a thundering voice, "I was the sacrifice! My blood was shed for the people! And I am back from the dead! Do not sacrifice animals for what my blood was spilled for!" He stood quietly looking across the people, and then yelled out, "I am god, and there is no other god like me! I am god, and you are to worship me. Do not put any animals in my place. There is none like me; I am the god you have waited for!"

Two of the rabbi started moving forward, and armed UN soldiers stepped between them.

The President continued, "I, your god, have determined you are to worship me in a way that is worthy of me. Open the veil, for that is where I am to be. My blood was shed for humanity, and I am to take the holy seat behind the veil!"

The Black Pope walked over next to the altar of sacrifice, and stood below the president. "All of you must bow before your god! He is the one who is the god over all the earth, and all the heavens. All of you must bow to the one who returned from the dead to lead us," the Black Pope declared.

Suddenly, shots rang out in the outer court. The people could be heard yelling, and screaming. Within seconds, machine-gun fire could be heard outside of the Temple walls.

Yostock felt a searing pain in his chest. Instinctively, his hand went to his chest as he fell backwards to the ground. As he lay on his back, he lifted his hand, and saw his hand was covered in blood......

CHAPTER EIGHTEEN

Mark of the Beast – Beast out of the Sea Events in the time of Revelation 13

The people gathered together to bury Jim. It was the end of October, and the ground was covered with a deep blanket of snow. A gentle, quiet snow was falling, and Chinney thought how beautiful it was as it gently drifted to the ground. Even with the snow-clogged roads making it difficult getting to the camp, nearly twenty people came from town. Everyone rejoiced and praised God the way Jim had asked them to in celebration of him going to be with the Lord.

Jim's health had deteriorated to the point that his breathing problems turned to pneumonia, and he died quietly in his sleep.

They kept the service outside short in consideration of the cold, and after a short time, they headed back into the log church for some time together. They rejoiced for his victory in death because they knew Jim was with the Lord, but they would miss his guidance and the vision he shared with everyone who had come to Spiritual Life. They had grown to some thirty people now at the camp, and the attendance at the church in town often was double that amount.

To save batteries, the camp radio was played only once a day. Everyone would gather around to hear the news because they knew from the news and current events that many of the Bible prophecies were coming to pass around the world. The camp members would compare the daily news reports to Scripture to better understand where they were in this time. When the Middle East war took place, and Damascus was made uninhabitable, Jim would often teach and show where it had been written in the prophecies of Isaiah Chapter 17 - that Iran and Syria would be devastated by Israel. The Scripture even was very clear about Damascus being laid waste.

When the world currencies were revalued and changed to being gold-backed and asset based, it was thought that it would stabilize world markets, but it seemed to have little long-lasting effect. In the Spiritual Life camp and the town nearby, there was no longer a monetary system. For the most part, everyone who had extra supplies shared them with those in need, much like the first century church.

From the Scripture they knew that the Antichrist would be identifiable. They heard brief reports that over seven thousand people died when the President of the New World Order went into the Temple in Israel. Riots broke out shortly after he arrived, and many of the Israelites fled into the desert. From the little information they had, they were convinced the New World Order President is the Antichrist. The radio said he was the one who appeared to die from wounds to his chest from an assassination attempt, and then came back to life. They felt that either the Black Pope, or the Roman Catholic Pope, must be the False Prophet, because they were with the president at the Temple. They were not sure which of them made the proclamation, to worship the president proclaiming he is the risen god. What they heard from the reports coming from the Middle East, many of the prophecies on the end times were being fulfilled.

Chinney knew from his studies that when a person takes the mark of the Beast they are accepting the Antichrist system and leadership. It is not just the chip or mark, but rather, the belief that the government system and the Antichrist would supply all of their needs. If one did not totally sell out to the system, you would be cast aside to be on your own.

Initially the chip was optional. They said it would stabilize the economic system, and assure everyone who took the mark would be able to have access to food and medicine. The camp heard on the radio that it was now mandatory, and it is considered a crime if you don't get one. Without the RFID chip no one is able to buy or sell anything. Everything needed for survival within the government system, could only be had with the chip.

So much was happening so fast, and so many would perish. The sun will increase in intensity, and total darkness will fall over the Antichrists kingdom, which is the new Roman Empire. The saints who are victorious over the Beast and his image and over the number of his name will be taken in the great harvest shown in Revelation 15:2. Following the harvest of those who are victorious, the wrath of God will be poured out upon mankind as described in Revelation 16. In the time of the seven bowls of God's wrath being poured out, the battle of Armageddon will be fought, and the most severe upheavals in nature of all of history, will take place. At the end of that time, the Bible says, that two hundred million men will be killed in one battle alone. That is the battle of Armageddon.

Chinney was placed as pastor of the church group in town. The town had nearly become a ghost town because of the people who left to go south, and those who had died. He had grown both physically and spiritually. He was six feet tall, and even though he was gangly now, he was going to be a stately man. The congregation in town really enjoyed his enthusiasm, and teaching, and Chinney looked forward to what the Lord was doing in his life.

There was a desire of the people of the congregation to study the events leading to the next rapture. They all looked forward to meeting Jesus in the air and the sound of the trumpet call.

Chinney recognized now that what took place the night of the rapture was the Holy Spirit moving across the land to gather the believers who had prepared their hearts, and had washed their robes clean. What he remembered most about what happened was that there was warm electricity in the air, and then the brilliant light, but he did not remember hearing a trumpet call.

The congregation all had similar stories to tell. Everyone remembered feeling a kind of gentle electricity in the air before the light, and they felt now that it was the Holy Spirit moving like a wave across the land.

They all looked forward with great expectation to what soon would take place. They based the expected time on the fact that the

Bible says that the tribulation time would last seven years. They knew the gathering of the multitudes would take place sometime after the Antichrist would mandate everyone receive the mark of the beast.

Shortly after the saints of the tribulation time are removed the seven bowls of God's wrath will be released upon the remaining inhabitants of the earth. Chinney could not imagine how terrible it will be for the people who remain on earth after the harvest.

Janice was feeling the strength of Ramel overwhelm her in a way that was nearly indescribable. Ramel began speaking, and his words brought the audience to their feet. She began to levitate from her chair as she spoke in his deep voice.

"Those who defy the old ones and do not purge themselves will be guilty of bringing many others to destruction as well. There are those who are left that will bring destruction on all of you if they are not dealt with. The Jews and Christians who will not accept the universal harmonic convergence of souls must be dealt with, and those who refuse to change must die to be reborn again to a form and a purpose that is not offensive to the old ones who are soon to come."

The audience was brought to their feet.

"Kill them! Kill them!" said Ramel. "Kill them that the world may enter into the final stages of the purification of the new age of mankind. All who would destroy the works and beliefs of others around them must themselves be destroyed to preserve the new coming of man!"

The crowd of several thousand went wild and stood applauding Ramel as he floated off the floor in the body of Janice.

"You have seen the son of the gods rise from death, and you know now that he is the one who is to lead the entire world in this time of need. He who has come back from death has come to lead the dying planet to life. Do not turn from him but worship him for he is your god and deserves to be worshipped. In the last three weeks, you heard of the one whom I speak, you heard he died, but he has risen, and I say to you, rejoice! I say to you again, REJOICE!, for you have seen his power rise, even from the grave."

"Murder is not wrong," he said. "To take a life to preserve others, that is what must take place. Those that would die now will be able to be rehabilitated when they return. Your reward will be one of great power and peace for humanity, and within your very being, you will find your god within. You will find that you have risen to your god state by what you do."

Tremendously powerful, overwhelming, incredible, were the responses of the audience. They were mesmerized by what Ramel was saying.

To actually rise up that way and to speak with such force and power to the people brought many to their knees, and they worshipped the god Ramel. Such great power! Many could see the wisdom. A fervor of agreement began to grow within the room. Many of the audience began to rise up in one voice against the Jews and Christians who would destroy the coming of the old ones and the ensuing peace to follow.

Ann had never been so miserable. She no longer had anywhere to go, and she knew that she would be in the middle of nowhere for the rest of her life unless something drastically changed. She found an abandoned small house at the end of a very long narrow dirt road. It was the kind of place that she never would have even walked into before. It looked to her no one had lived in it for some time, probably even before the people disappeared. It was not the condition of the house that bothered her so much, though; it was the lack of people and the total solitude.

She was not too far from the state-run vegetable fields, and she walked there every two days to glean what she could from the side of the fields. She was concerned the government workers would find her and send her to a camp so, she was constantly watching the sky for drones.

It wasn't a real balanced diet unless you liked tomatoes, squash, and oranges, but it was enough to survive. Her fitness training for the past few years had been a big help, and she would be all right with what she could glean. She decided she would try to find seeds for some other crops and plant them behind the small house she was staying in.

Her loneliness was a problem though, and she felt that before long she would have to find someone she could talk to in order to overcome an overwhelming desire to go back to the city and what would be certain disaster for her.

Ann sat by the bank of a small slow-moving river and watched the current take a leaf lazily down the other side toward wherever leaves went. The sun was fully up, *close to noon,* she thought, and for a change it was not too hot. It really was a very pleasant day. The weather had been a little cooler the past few weeks, and although she didn't have a calendar to mark off the days, she was sure that it was somewhere around mid-October or so.

The time she was alone gave her what she needed to sort out the thoughts that seemed to be so jumbled up in her mind. Since Sue died, and the paper was destroyed, the last remnants of all order and purpose in her life seemed to be gone. She wondered sometimes if life was at all worth living anymore, and although she kept putting it to the back of her mind, the thoughts of suicide were constantly with her. Ann could not bear the thought of going to one of the death clinics to have someone give her a shot, but she was at the point where that idea no longer reviled her.

Sue really was a good friend, and Ann had to admit that Sue was a tremendous lover. There never had been a man who had known how to treat her the way she needed to be treated, and who knew how she felt about her own sexuality like Sue did. How had she become so deviate anyway? She had never been with a woman before Sue, and now when she was alone, that was what she really had been thinking about most-was her time with Sue.

Ann missed her work, and she wondered if there even was a paper that survived in that part of the state. The government, through Mark, had taken the paper over, and by the time he finished editing the news, there was nothing left but false talk and hot air. But she still missed it. The paper was important to the government only because it was a distraction for the people. The paper and what was left of the Internet and television cable system had, for some time now become nothing more than another means of control the government used over the people.

She thought there had to be at least thirty or forty thousand people who lived in the area where the tsunami hit, and she wondered how many survived. *So many,* she thought, *And yet I am alive.*

The thought of so many dead, and that she was still alive reassured her that she was left for a reason; she just had to find out what that reason was. *Over one and a half billion people dead in such a short time. What was it? Three years, three and one-half years maybe, and how many people were never reported?* she thought.

Why would God let this happen anyway? Why? Who was it, she tried to remember who wrote the book, *or at least started the saying "God is dead" anyway? Whoever it was, there was a good chance God was dead now, along with his creation.*

The dilapidated house was okay, and for the most part, she had gotten familiar enough with it to tolerate it. The dirty curtains bothered her enough that she washed them in the creek and used them to cover the old kitchen table.

Ann had to laugh at herself because she realized that everything had to be taken in its own context. The cottage was better now because she washed the curtains, and what made terrible curtains made a reasonably good table cloth. *Talk about finding that little ray of light in the worst of everything, this was it,* she thought. It made her realize how maybe things weren't as bad as she was thinking, and it made her laugh.

She was so lonely though, and she didn't know where to turn. She had no transportation, and the truth was she really didn't know where she was anyway. The middle of Florida is a no man's land, and she didn't even know where the nearest town was, much less where she could find someone she could trust.

She looked around the house and other than the tablecloth, it was a hot, musty dump in anybody's way of thinking, and the feeling of hopelessness came rushing back with a vengeance.

Jeremie was leaving a short meeting he had with the group leaders. The meeting was held because of the rising anti-Semitism against the Jews and the Messianic Jews in particular. There had been a rising resentment for some time against anyone proclaiming Jesus as Lord, and it seemed especially true against the Messianic Jewish segment of Christianity.

Satan is a liar and the father of all lies. Many fall to that power because they have chosen to. A friend of Jeremie's often said the people and ministries fall because of PMS, which he described as-power, money, and sex.

You cannot have both God and Satan. If you are a lover of money, power or of anything else which you would not give up for God, then that very thing which rules you sends you to your destruction.

The rapture of the great multitudes would soon take place. They could sense that God had speeded up time for their sake. Most of those who are now within the body of the believers would escape death through being taken up into heaven.

Jeremie knew he would be left for only a short time, and soon after, the saints would follow.

God would have all come into salvation, but many would decide not to. Jeremie was called to speak the word in truth, but he could not decide for them, for any of them. Most would no longer listen, but there would be some that do, and there is not a price that can be put on a soul for eternity.

A great upheaval of nature would take place in the next few weeks. It would follow the rapture of the saints who are victorious over the beast and his system. Many now though, have hardened their hearts to the point that there now would be very few more that would come.

The Gone

The Antichrist broke the treaty made with Israel by desecrating the Temple, and declaring himself god, thus fulfilling scripture. About six years had gone by since the rapture of the church.

The wedding feast of the saints would take place shortly before the battle of Armageddon and the seven bowls of God's wrath are poured out on the earth. Jeremie had much to do before the timing of the much-awaited rapture of the multitudes was reached. He did not know the exact time that the next rapture would happen, but, he did know that it would be soon.

He would be gone before the rapture of the multitudes because the Word of God shows the 144,000 will be with Lord just before the final harvest of the tribulation saints. He could not be harmed because of the seal of God upon him. The seal said to the spirit world he belonged to Jesus, and it declared him to be off limits to all of Satan's hoards.

Jeremie stood in the now empty Synagogue, and looked about for the last time. It seemed sad in a way that he had done the work he was to do for the people and now he would leave them alone. The Synagogue that had teamed with life stood so quiet, and so empty. He could hear the sound of distant sirens and felt the pangs of sorrow for those who had hardened their hearts. They were not all bad people and God still loved them, but Jeremie knew the seven bowls of God's wrath was soon to be poured out upon them.

Even now they are stubbornly locked into everyone else's ideas for their eternity. *So sad,* thought Jeremie, *the kingdom of heaven is so near to them, they just needed to seek it, but each person had to find his own salvation, everyone has a free will and no one else can do it for them.*

Jeremie walked along the long aisle, and by habit picked up some paper that had been left on the floor. The people here will soon be rejoicing in heaven for the salvation that they believe in. What will take place soon after, is that the wrath of God will fall upon the people that are left on earth. There will be many horrors that will take place, and the first will be the sun scorching the people across the land that are already ravaged by famine, disease, and a broken economy.

So many lost, so many lost, he thought, and he openly wept for those who hardened their hearts, for they were many.

Sam was in one of those moods that was hard for him to break out of. A burly man of five-foot-ten in height, but "built like a damn tank," is what his sergeant used to say. The tattoo he was so proud of that he got from the famous Lou's Tattoos in sixty-eight just said "PROPERTY of U.S.M.C."

He was mad at everything, mad at not having work for so long. "Damn fags. Damn country. Damn Jewish Christian bigots," he said just under his breath. He was so restless he felt like his insides itched all over and that he was going to explode if he didn't have something change or some kind of relief in his life. He felt like a prisoner since he lost his job a few years ago, and it was finally coming to an end.

He would end it tonight and take as many as he could with him. "I ain't takin it no more, I ain't takin' it no more," he said out loud as he packed the shells into his browning shotgun.

Sam was angry by the constant lack of everything and having to do without. No job, no wife, and he was sick all the time. Government regulations and shortages kept him from getting the meds he needed to keep himself calmed down.

Sam muttered to himself. "I can't work, I can't do nothin,' and it's not my fault. I didn't do nothin,' and I can't take it anymore!"

When he finished loading his shotgun, he calmly put it under his coat and left through the front door. All that kept going through his mind was, *Damn Washington fag Jews.*

Sam never was considered to be a bad person, and the next day, those who knew him could not be convinced that he was the same Sam that they knew.

Sam walked down to the synagogue on First and Palmetto and entered through the main door. The meeting for local leaders was about twenty minutes away from starting. Many of the leaders were there, and talking at the front of the sanctuary.

The Gone

Sam walked through the open front doors and down the main isle. He pulled the shotgun from under his coat, and began shooting. *BAM! BAM!* It seemed an eternity before the reality of what was happening erupted, and people began to scream and run for the doors. *BAM! BAM!* Again, and again, *BAM! BAM!*

In all, seven people died before Sam ended his own life.

CHAPTER NINETEEN

Beast out of the Earth - Mark of the Beast Events in the time of Revelation 13

Jeremie was told by John, one of his staff, that over fifty people had been burned alive in an old church in Savannah Georgia where they had been meeting. He was grieved in his spirit and asked John to gather the staff for a quick meeting so he could let them clearly know what was coming.

John quickly gathered the staff together, and they entered the conference room for the meeting.

Jeremie entered a short time later, and motioned for everyone to bow their head, and he prayed a quick prayer before starting.

Then he began…..

"From the Scriptures, we know that when the Antichrist went into the newly rebuilt Temple of Solomon and seven thousand people in Jerusalem were killed. The stage was set for the time of God's wrath to be poured out upon the earth."

Jeremie continued, "As we know, most people have already made their choice. Now, all the world governments under the New World Order are in the process of mandating that everyone must have a government approved identification chip implanted in their hand or forehead. This chip is referred to as the 'Mark of the Beast' in Revelation 13. The people are being told that by getting the chip they will no longer have to carry cash, and it will allow the world to move to a cashless society. The governments worldwide, under the New

World Order, are assuring everyone that with the newly developed technologies no one can access anything of theirs, and everyone in their family will be protected. What the new technologies do is give each person's individual finances the same level of protection they would have if they owned Crypto Currencies. We know from the Bible, however, that what happens when people accept the chip is they have put their trust totally in the beast system, and deny God as their Creator and giver of life."

"What is being fought is far beyond the things that are seen in the natural. The battles that are being fought are in the spirit realm, and even the persecution many are going through, needs to take place because it is written, and every word that is written-will be fulfilled."

"The eyes of the Jewish people were opened when the Antichrist went into the Temple of Solomon, and desecrated it, by saying he is god. At that time most of the Jewish people in Israel fled Israel into the desert where God is protecting them. Seven thousand Jewish people were killed that day, and the eyes of all of the Jewish peoples have been opened. Elsewhere, there are still some people whose hearts have not been totally hardened against the word of the Lord, and will not take the mark of the beast."

One thing many do not realize, and that is that throughout the world there are many people of Jewish descent who are not even aware of their heritage and I believe that their eyes will be opened as well. They may not even know why, but they will be seeking answers to what is stirring in their spirit. I believe they will run away from the Antichrist system and we need to be ready to lead them into the kingdom.

Jeremie paused and took a sip of water before continuing, "I know there is a growing expectation among you that the taking away will soon take place. I am excited, and blessed to see that many of our people have been going into the streets and sharing the Gospel with a great boldness to anyone who will listen. All of us are driven, at least in part, knowing that the time is short. I know that right now Gods grand finale is coming to pass, and I am so thankful that I am part of the most incredible hour of mankind, in all of history."

"We know that very few people outside of the tribes of Israel will accept and follow Jesus because their hearts have been hardened. In fact, the Bible says that they will curse God for what they feel should not be brought upon them. By the end of the tribulation time *one-half* of the seven billion people on the earth that were alive when the people were raptured will have died. The word says that Death rides the Pale Horse, and Hell follows close behind him. Those who die now, who take the mark, and who have not accepted Jesus as Lord and Savior, will go to hell for all eternity, for the two ride together."

"I know this is a much shorter time than I usually speak, but I have to be on the road shortly. Let me conclude this meeting by saying that as much as it hurts us to hear that our friends and brothers in Christ are being killed and persecuted for the sake of the Gospel, we are assured we will all be meeting them soon. May we all meet again at the gathering and taking up of the multitudes."

"I must be leaving, please bring my car up."

As Jeremie was about to step into the car, one of the leaders came running from the church office to let him know of an attack on six churches in the Miami area. The body count appeared to be extremely high.

'Thank you for letting me know. Please tell the local leaders to come together to come up with a plan to see what security measures can be taken in the local churches. I will try to send Gerald Smith, our security supervisor to the meeting, he may be able to give some good insights on what we can do to help," said Jeremie.

Now it has begun he thought. *Now it has fully begun. Many more will die before it ends. Dear Father may you give all your children strength in these times.*

Jeremie knew that many of the new believers could be the first to fall when the killing begins in earnest. The camp they established in the center of the state was already running at full capacity, but with the expansion being built, the number of people would be doubled. He knew now that wouldn't be enough, and they needed more housing. He would direct the leaders to add temporary tents as soon as possible.

THE GONE

Jeremie knew he would be taken up into heaven very soon. The saints and the Jewish people he had been training would do well. God had put a tremendous hunger in them, and he was confident they would continue the work of the ministry until it was the time for them to be taken to heaven in the great harvest of the earth.

"Thank you Lord for the many blessings, and the love, grace, and mercy you have shown us all," he prayed.

Chinney had just given one of the most powerful sermons that Chris had ever heard. God had done so much in both of them in such a short time, and he was now seeing the fruit of what God had done in Chinney. He preached for nearly one-and-one-half hours on the love of Christ for all humanity, and how God would have none perish, but that all would come to his saving knowledge and accept the free gift of eternal salvation.

The entire congregation gathered daily to listen to the twelve o'clock news. It seemed to many of them that, in many ways, every news update was scripture being fulfilled. Seeing the events come to pass as written in scripture over two thousand years ago brought an apprehensive excitement among the group that they all could feel.

Many of them, especially during praise and worship, felt the Spirit of the Lord come over them in glory, and they would dance before the Lord just as David had. They had such a happiness knowing that their Lord and Savior would soon be calling them with a loud shout from the archangel and the trumpet of God.

Several of the men from town decided to pool together the last of their gas and fill gas cans they could tie them to the side of a motorcycle. They made nearly one hundred signs that would help direct people to the town, and they decided they would put the signs up within a fifty-mile radius. The signs would help lead the remnant of people who might still come. The signs had directions to the town, and let them know they had food and shelter. There were very few people left in Upper Michigan, but Chris thought the signs could help guide people to where they were.

Chinney had never been as happy as he had been the last few months. Even with all the difficulties and hurts, it seemed as though he had a joy inside that he couldn't explain. It wasn't that everything was better because he still had problems, but it just seemed as though because of the peace of God, he was taking everything better. He knew he would be gone soon with the others and would be with Jesus.

The joy he felt was what his mama had talked about when she tried to get him to go to church. He was sure that he was saved because of his mama's prayers for his salvation. He looked forward to seeing mama soon. She would be so proud of him and how he had turned out. "Thank you mama," he said just under his breath.

Janice was lying with Jon and three other men. She had become insatiable in her lust, and several times now, Jon left only to come back again. When she thought with the mind of Janice, which was seldom now, she knew she had lost all control to Ramel. He came out nearly all the time now, and he was always in control.

"MORE! MORE!" he would bellow, and everyone near him would hurry to satisfy.

One night Janice came to the forefront, and she looked around at the men who were with her. One man was indulging her, and two other men were satisfying themselves while they waited. She looked at herself in the mirror and saw that she was unrecognizable, even to herself. She no longer had control over what was taking place in her life, but Ramel controlled all. Her life was lost..... She was lost. Janice knew that what she had tried to find, playing in the spirit world, would destroy her in ways she could not even imagine.

As Ramel again called out, Janice silently cried out inside her spirit because of the death she felt inside, while man after man abused her flesh.

She had great power through Ramel, and in two days, she was to meet with the Black Pope, the leader of the CCC, in Washington. Ramel had talked of what was coming, and that a purging of the people who would not believe was to take place. Many would die, and Jews and Christians from all over the world were to die for their insolence. Many already had died, and many more must die to purify the race for the coming of the old ones. Janice, through Ramel, was to be the leader of the CCC in the Eastern seaboard area of the United States.

Janice knew that Ramel would not hesitate to kill, and she also knew that Ramel had taken over her totally and was so strong that she had no way to stop him anymore.

She now knew what no one else did, that Ramel lived in her, and that he was evil beyond anything she could have ever imagined. She was an observer in her own body, and what she saw was that what was inside her was from the devil himself.

She had sold herself to the only one she thought would listen, and she sold her soul too cheap.

CHAPTER TWENTY

GONE
Angel proclaiming FEAR GOD over all the earth - 144,000 in Heaven
Events in the time of Revelations 14

Ann looked across the small shack she had lived in for the last few months. She decided she would leave at first light. The idea of staying longer was just not an option. It had been good for her here, she had been able to relax somewhat and get away from seeing the constant suffering and heartache of so many lives.

She felt fortunate that she had found this place and that it was so far away from other people. Now, however, she found that the very thing she needed to be away from before was what she now needed most.

She would get through this terrible time. She was strong, and she again knew that she could face whatever was ahead. She knew that being so strong willed, and having such a strong personality, she had kept many good men at a distance from her. They were intimidated by her strength.

Sue's death had affected her much more than she ever imagined that it could. She had lived her life to the fullest in everything she did, and until the death and destruction of everything she ever valued.

She often thought about the paper and the people who survived the wave, and she wondered if they were still alive. *Did Jerry find*

Sandy? Are they still alive? And the others, all the others.... So many had died in such a short time, she thought. She would deal with only the living now. She felt that she was ready to go forward with her life wherever that would take her. Ann felt a strength that had come back inside her, the strength to forge ahead no matter what the cost.

Ann needed to be with other people. She would embark today to the places where she thought that she might meet that one person who would make life worthwhile again. She decided to head to the Keys-that is if there were any Keys left to head to. She knew that the wave that hit Tampa and St. Petersburg could have easily destroyed much of the Keys as well.

By the time she got a little closer to them, she would know.

The "Keys" and especially Key West always held a special place for Ann. She had gone there several times, and she and Sue planned on going there together when things were better. She enjoyed the water and the snorkeling, and the wide beaches. Ann had a real desire to just get naked, run in the sand, and jump in the warm surf of the Florida summertime. It was beginning to get really warm now. *Almost too hot for this time of year,* she thought. She hoped the clear blue water would be as she remembered it from before, it was always so beautiful.

If she could, she would go as far as Key West, she would begin her new life there, and she would take the time to look for the "flash of green" she had read about but never saw. There was an article in an old *Readers Digest* that she read years ago. The article told about the very rare atmospheric phenomenon that could be seen as a brilliant green light just as the sun set. She so wanted to see the flash of green, not because of any tangible reason she could think of, but she felt that it would put something back into her life. One of her ex-husbands parting comments to her was, "I hope, Ann, that you find your flash of green." Ann would look for that, and look for enough good pieces from her past to put her life together again.

She finished packing her backpack. She filled an old jar with water from the well pump, and fit it into an old purse she could hang from her shoulder. She was still in very good shape, and she had spent much of the time she had alone working her frustrations out on her body. She was looking forward to using her skates again. She felt so happy that she had thought to bring her skates with her.

There were no paved roads where she was, but she knew she would find the pavement three miles away, at the end of the dirt road.

Ann stepped through the door and glanced back across the now-familiar house and the old table. Looking at the kitchen table, she had to admit that even the tablecloth she was so happy with really didn't help the place. It still was a dump, but at least for a while, it was her dump.

The sun was up just enough to begin casting its rays across the field in front of the house, and Ann could see it would be a beautiful day. There was just a hint of mist rising from the heat striking the damp grass, and the birds had begun their morning calls through the stillness. Ann let the old screen door slam shut, and the morning, although cool, was comfortable.

Ann pulled the backpack higher onto her shoulders to put it in a position where it wouldn't bite into her skin as much, and started down the road to her future. She tried to remember the date, but she couldn't. She was pretty sure that it was still February, and she thought it was near the end of the month, but she didn't know what day. Those things used to bother her, but now, she could see the foolishness of it all.

She remembered that she was so much of a stickler about never being late, and that she was so sure that other people were always ready to judge her for her shortcomings.

Ann had been walking nearly two hours before she finally reached the pavement. When she saw the asphalt going out before her, she was so excited that she ran up to it and sat down on it to put her skates on.

Immediately she jumped up! She laughed at how quickly she had forgotten about the daylight heat on the Florida roads.

"HOT BUTT! HOT BUTT!" she yelled out loud. "Watch out Keys. Here I come!"

She almost felt like a kid, so free for the first time in several years. Why she would even think that she had no idea, but she was excited and happy inside, and she would enjoy that happiness for the joy that it was.

She was so excited about skating that she barely noticed the warm electricity that seemed to be such a part of the air. It was gentle, but firm, an almost sensual soft gentleness that totally surrounded and enveloped her. Ann sat to the side of the road and finished putting her skates on. She pulled her backpack higher on her shoulders, and stood up to skate.

It was a glorious moment of freedom! Like a ballerina, she turned and twirled on the tips of her skates. She was excited to know that what she learned before had not left her. She grinned for the first time in what she was sure was several months.

The light was so brilliant, and so blinding, that she nearly fell over from the suddenness of it. Ann stopped, and she looked around for any kind of an answer but the one she feared. Tears welled up in her eyes, and a slight whimper came from her lips. From deep inside her, a sharp pain of grief welled up, and she nearly doubled over from her spirit crying out, for that which was lost to her.

"Oh, my God! It's happened again! Oh, my God! Please have mercy on me!"

Ann cried.... but she was not heard.

Jon Pierce walked from the hotel lobby back toward the room. Janice had gotten way out of hand, and he had decided to leave her. It was just not his bag to be with her after she had three or four other men. She really hurt him, and she had become the most reviled thing that he had ever seen. He got back to the room, and she was still in bed.

Ramel was fascinating to listen to, but Jon was sure that there really wasn't anything of Janice left. *If this is from the gods of the old ones, then I don't want to be part of it,* he thought. How had it gotten so far from the ideals they had started with? He left the paper to tour with her, and he believed in Ramel and felt privileged to be with Janice during these times.

He had so wanted to be part of what was soon to become the new age of man and become a living, breathing part of what was taking place in the changing world. What he saw instead was nothing more than the same greed and lust that there always was. Even as important as he felt when he would be seen with Janice, he could not stand the hurt of what was taking place.

The men that seemed attracted to Janice were almost all bi-sexual, and she had gotten so far from the wonders of the coming changes Ramel spoke of. Jon would leave as soon as possible, it was time.

What had happened to her anyway? When he had first met Janice, she was so eager for those things that were new to her. She was so alone after her husband had died and her daughter disappeared. Their friendship, he knew now, developed only from that loneliness.

Everia took Janice under her wing to teach her the things of the spirit world, and Jon had been there to support her all the way. He guessed that he never had really loved her, but it did hurt him when she used him. The time had come for him to leave, and he knew it.

Things seemed so much simpler when they first met. They would talk and have fun learning together some of the secrets that had been hidden from the world for so long. He still believed that the future world was upon them, but now, that future looked bleak. If that future was to be ruled by the brothers and father of Ramel, it looked bleak indeed. He had been as wrapped up with Ramel, as everyone else had been, and when they were on stage, it was glorious to see the power and the wisdom come forth from Ramel through Janice, and when she would levitate, it was incredibly powerful to witness.

What others did not see, and what he did see, was that the world would never satisfy Ramel no matter what form it took.

Jon walked to the balcony and looked out over the city below. *What city is it today anyway,* he thought. *Phoenix, or is this Dallas? I don't even know anymore.* All he knew was that it was west of the Mississippi and the sun was just breaking through the clouds. A sweet gentle breeze saturated the air, and gentle warmth moved across him.

When electric feeling and the flash of light came, Jon heard a single large groan from Ramel, and then silence.
It has come again, he thought. *It comes again.*

Spiritual Life camp was silent. A gentle breeze picked up slightly and stirred the camp with its whisper. Here and there could be seen the remnants of the people who were there minutes before. Bible passages and scripture were written on the walls and in every area across the camp. A gentle fire was still burning in the wood stove. Vegetables were cut, and the meat for stew was on the counter. An eerie quiet filled the halls.

Far away, cold and haggard from fighting the deep snow, and nearly imperceptible still, came a single lone figure. Perhaps he was drawn by the signs that had been left along the highways; perhaps he was following only instinct, he walked forward.

Stu was sick and in a lot of pain. He wasn't sure what he had, but he thought it might be AIDS. The sores in his mouth had made it so difficult to swallow that for the past few weeks he had mostly been eating only soft food.

His body ached from the constant pain, but he got some relief with Tylenol, and when he could get an occasional Oxycodone, he felt really good. There was no way he could get treatment in the only hospital still open in Ft. Wayne, and he wasn't sure if they were even open any more. Besides, if the tests proved that he had AIDS, they could not help him anyway because of the shortage of long-term treatment drugs.

The only thing that they would be allowed to do for him was to administer euthanasia. Stu thought about that for a long time, and if he got much worse, that would be what he would do. There wasn't really much pleasure in his life any more except for sex, and he found a never-ending supply of sex when he wanted it, even now.

Homosexuals were everywhere around him, and it seemed as though there were more than ever before. He found many places to go where they would meet, and throughout his time with them, he had developed many friends. He didn't know their names, but he saw them often, and theirs was a mutual knowing that they shared.

Stu sometimes had sex with as many as ten men a day, and he still never seemed to get enough. He found it strange that he would be so excited about it, especially when he would see someone new, who he hadn't seen before, and yet at the same time, he hated himself because he was there. It seemed that sex now was the only thing in his life that mattered, and the best days for him were the ones where he would meet two or three men at the same time. He smiled at the thought of the last time that happened.

Stu was in Pastor Jim's old house, which was the old church rectory. It had long since been abandoned, and now, like so many of the harsh winters in Indiana, the wind blew sharply through the broken windows in the living room.

The snow had drifted to a height of over two feet below the living room window, and ran across the floor to near the dining room. What Stu was hoping to find was a good pair of socks. The house had been picked over many times, and most things of any value had been taken long ago, but he hoped that maybe he would find something he could use.

Stu's mind raced back to the church and how he had nearly gotten physically away from homosexuality. If his wife would have been a little more accommodating, he would not have had gone to the movie house at all. He had to admit that he remembered that he was very happy then. He actually felt as though that was the only time that he had any purpose in his life, or at least he thought he did. *What a joke that was, me……… in church. Probably kept me from getting AIDS for a long time*, he thought, *but what the hell. It doesn't really matter now does it?*

He tried on occasion to remember who might have given him AIDS, but he had no idea. Really, if it wasn't for the sores in his mouth, he didn't feel too bad, and those sores would feel better when he would take a half dozen aspirin and just let them dissolve directly on them.

As he emptied the drawers from the dresser of what few things that were left, he finally found a pair of the socks that he was looking for. The socks would really help him today.

The socks made him smile, and he knew that this was going to be his lucky day. Stu sat at the edge of the bed and put the socks on first and then put his old pair on over the top of them to help keep out the cold.

There was a party house down the street, and although it was still pretty early maybe there would be someone there. It really wasn't a house but rather a large old building. It didn't have any heat in it, but there were some old barrels there, and they usually were filled with wood and kept burning by the guys who lived in there and in the nearby abandoned boarding houses. He was bundled warm anyway, and if it was cold, he would go to a couple of guys he knew that were always ready for a good time.

Two days ago, when Stu was with two men, he did not sense the warm electricity filling the air and flowing over him. When the flash of light came, he thought he had imagined it, and he shook his head and rubbed on his eyes. Neither one of the other two with him felt it either.

Stu walked from the bedroom to the dining room and across the buckling, and cracked wooden floor to the kitchen. The back door had been left open for some time, and the snow swirled in on the floor and around the door, looking almost like an alabaster sculpture. When Stu stepped on the snow, it crunched from the severe cold and made the irritating heavy noise only rubber against cold snow makes. Stu looked around one last time for anything that could help him.

On the way out, he stepped over one of the very things that he helped put together for the church.

On the floor, partly covered by a dusting of snow, was a water-stained Sunday service bulletin from six years before. It was a bulletin that Pastor Jim prepared, and Stu printed and handed out before the service began.

The sermon for that week was based on the shortest sentence in the Bible and........

This Weeks Sermon

Brought to you by:

<u>Pastor James Franklin</u>

Based on this week's Scripture:

John 11:35

(And)

Jesus wept.

NOTES FROM THE AUTHOR

Over comers of the Beast system in Heaven - Jewish and Christians
Events in the time of Revelation 15

The first part of the seven-year tribulation period is but a shadow of what will follow. The comprehension of what will take place when the Seven Bowls of God's Wrath is loosed upon the earth is nearly beyond description. The plagues released at that time will be more than we can even vaguely understand, and the world has never experienced anything even remotely like it in all of history.

You do not have to go through the tribulation period and Gods wrath if you right now accept Jesus as your Lord and Savior, and make a commitment to follow him. Jesus is real and alive, and he awaits right now for those who would ask him to be their Lord and Savior. There is no cost, it is freely given. - God's free gift of grace. What you need to do is ask for forgiveness of your sins…. And ask Jesus to come into your heart. Many of you who wait, will wait too long, and the pain of what will happen will be beyond anything this author can comprehend.

There is no sin that you have done that will not be forgiven you. Jesus died for your sins, and his love is greater than any sin. No matter what you may have done in your life, anything that is in your life right now, it will be washed away forever by the blood of Jesus. You will be set free from all the sins of your past, if you ask the Lord to forgive you and commit your life to him.

If you feel guilt - uneasiness inside you right now - that is the Holy Spirit of God tugging on your heart.

There is no reason for you to have to go through what is described in this book. If you wait, you will have to go through much of the tribulation time as described in this book, and you must realize that with Death rides Hell.

Those of you who do not feel as though you have done anything bad enough to deserve eternal hell, the Bible very clearly reads that "**all** have sinned and come short of the glory of God," and "the wages of sin is death and "the gift of God is eternal life through Jesus our Lord." Even a good person must be born again. You must ask Jesus into your heart, and when he comes in, you will be reborn.

If any of you have turned your back on Jesus and fallen away, he is waiting right now to forgive you. Return and re-dedicate your life before it is too late. Jesus loves you, and awaits you to ask for forgiveness.

If you are down and out there is one who cares, one who wants to be your friend, and his name is Jesus. When you accept that personal friendship from him you will never again be alone. Jesus said, *"I am the Way and the Truth and the Life; no one comes to the Father except by Me."* Now is the time of your salvation.... Now is the day of the Lord.

The Bible also reads "whosoever calls upon the name of the Lord shall be saved. And you like all of us, are a whosoever right? Of course you are, all of us are.

I'm going to say a quick prayer for you. "Lord I ask you to bless this reader and their family with long and healthy lives. Jesus make yourself real to them, and do a quick work in their heart. Lord, if this reader has not received you into their heart I pray they will do so now."

If you, the reader, would like to receive Jesus into your heart say this with your heart and with your lips out loud:

> Dear Lord Jesus come into my heart.
>
> I ask your forgiveness for all my sins.
>
> Wash me and cleanse me, and set me free.

> I ask to be born again by being filled with your Holy Spirit.
>
> Lord, I give you my life, I dedicate my life to you.
>
> Lord, I thank you that I am saved.
>
> I believe you have risen from the dead and are coming back for me.
>
> Thank you Jesus, for saving me.

Give me a passion for the lost, a hunger for the things of God, and a holy boldness to preach the Gospel of Jesus Christ. I'm saved, I'm forgiven, and I'm on my way to heaven because I have Jesus in my heart.

As a minister of the Gospel of Jesus Christ I tell you today that your sins are forgiven. Always remember to run to God, and not run from God because he has a great plan for your life.

You have taken the first step of your most incredible journey, and each step from this time on, though at times may be difficult, will be the best of your life, and you will never be alone.

Go to a Bible believing church near you and buy a Bible, the New International Version, or the Amplified version are easy to read and are written in the new style English. The King James Version is written in old English and for some people it is a little harder to understand. The most important thing though, is to take the time and read the Bible for yourself.

Don't take my word or the word of anyone else on what is written; take the time to find out yourself. **Don't leave your eternity to someone else. Read the Word yourself.**

For all who have accepted Jesus as your Lord and Savior I look forward to meeting you, and walking with you on the streets of pure gold.

MAY GODS BLESSINGS BE UPON YOU AND YOUR FAMILY!

James L. Larson

JAMES L. LARSON

Rev. James Larson is the founder and President/CEO of Life Link Missions, Inc., a Not-for-Profit Humanitarian 501-c-3 corporation.

Life Link Missions (herein LLM) has developed a comprehensive plan to create jobs to bring the world's most advanced education and medical distribution systems to Christian schools in developing nations. The objective of LLM is help others improve their lives by creating jobs and opportunities under a Christian-based humanitarian platform, teaching the poor to become more self-sufficient, and investing time and resources to advance education of the next generation to better prepare them for the challenges the future holds.

Since being incorporated in 1995 LLM has sent medicine, food and people into third world countries. Following the earthquake in Haiti in 2010 Life Link Missions worked with a partner organization, America's Heart, to deliver over $200 million in first response medical equipment and humanitarian supplies to help with the rebuilding efforts. In the years prior to the earthquake we sent people and medicines into Haiti, Jamaica, and the Caribbean. We have worked with several agencies to provide medicines and equipment. We have been very successful in dealing with the problems encountered in these countries.

We are associated with several international networks of churches. Life Link Missions is not a denomination but we work as an association corporation to denominational churches. Life Link Missions is not in competition but rather serves churches as an enhancement to their purpose and focus. We work within the networks of denominational churches and provide the technologies and materials to help them increase the educational depth of their classes using the world's most advanced blended educational programming platform. Life Link Missions distributes food and relief supplies, through the regional local associated churches to enable them to help the needy, while expanding their church membership. The reason for using regional local churches for our delivery system is because they are typically a stable force within the communities, as well as being the primary educational system in many countries.

www.ingramcontent.com/pod-product-compliance
Lightning Source LLC
LaVergne TN
LVHW021654060526
838200LV00050B/2345